Readers love *Music Box*
by JOHN C. HOUSER

"I found *Music Box* by John C. Houser to be profoundly gritty, realistic and compelling to read."

—Joyfully Jay

"*Music Box* is a beautifully told story about love, forgiveness and the strength to be oneself... If you are craving a story with a lot of depth as well as romance, *Music Box* is definitely the book for you."

—Top 2 Bottom Reviews

"Along with a gentle, believable romance, Mr. Houser asks hard questions about... what people both inside and outside the school environment can do to stop practices that are harmful both to individuals and the community."

—The Romance Reviews

"The writing style of this author was outstanding, the characters were developed very well and the emotion portrayed by the author for each character was strong and endearing"

—Crystal's Many Reviewers

By JOHN C. HOUSER

The Door Behind Us
Valentine Shower

DIY FAMILY
Music Box
Billy Goat Stats

Published By DREAMSPINNER PRESS
http://www.dreamspinnerpress.com

BILLY GOAT STATS

JOHN C. HOUSER

DREAMSPINNER
PRESS

Published by
DREAMSPINNER PRESS

5032 Capital Circle SW, Suite 2, PMB# 279, Tallahassee, FL 32305-7886 USA
http://www.dreamspinnerpress.com/

Billy Goat Stats
© 2015 John C. Houser.

Cover Art
© 2015 Reese Dante.
http://www.reesedante.com
Cover content is for illustrative purposes only and any person depicted on the cover is a model.

ISBN: 978-1-63216-936-5
Digital ISBN: 978-1-63216-937-2
Library of Congress Control Number: 2015904654
First Edition May 2015

Printed in the United States of America
∞
This paper meets the requirements of
ANSI/NISO Z39.48-1992 (Permanence of Paper).

For all the gay boys who thought they couldn't be athletes—
and all the athletes who thought they couldn't be gay.

CHAPTER 1

Stats

Girls I'm pretty sure wanted to kiss me: 5
Girls I've kissed: 3
Boys I've kissed: 1

If Dad ever finds this, I'm dead—like broken spine, belly slit, and guts slithering out all over the floor dead.

THE E-MAIL waiting for Billy when he got home from basketball camp didn't come as a complete surprise. But that didn't mean Billy didn't want to throw himself onto his bed and beat the pillow into a cloud of feathers. All summer, as he sweated through the shooting drills, passing drills, and endless debates on the merits of zone vs. man-on-man defense, he'd depended on texts and e-mails from Jonah to keep his loneliness and confusion at bay. Nearly everything he knew about himself and his place in the world was changing, and Jonah understood. He'd been through some rough stuff in the last year too.

The easy part had been graduating from high school. He'd looked forward to that, even though it meant leaving old friends behind and, hopefully, making new ones at Hoosier State. But the kiss he'd shared with Jonah last year had, in an instant, blown his self-image to kingdom come. He was still fitting the pieces back together. But if he didn't quite recognize the eighteen-year-old staring him in the face as he shaved every morning, he was clear on one thing. He wanted to do it again. Maybe not run out of the room like a frightened rabbit this time.

Only now it wasn't going to happen because Jonah had cut him loose before they'd even had a chance to try. Billy got that their differing circumstances would make a physical relationship a challenge. Jonah was finishing his last year in high school in Glen Falls before heading off to music school, and Billy was leaving for Hoosier State on a basketball scholarship. But he'd thought they had a connection.

It was particularly galling that Jonah broke the news via e-mail. Didn't Billy at least deserve the courtesy of a face-to-face dismissal? He could have met Billy at the bus or the café across from Martin Luther King High that had been their favorite hangout last year. Instead, Jonah had to send him a fucking e-mail. Billy couldn't fault Jonah's logic or his poetic language: their lives had thrust them into wildly different trajectories, and the energy it would take to push them into close orbit was beyond their reach. He hoped they could stay friends. He would come to see Billy's games when he could. Billy knew it wouldn't be the same.

After banging around his room over the weekend, supposedly packing for college but mostly just shifting shit from one pile to another on his bed, his mom had finally come up to survey the mess. She glanced at the bed and then waited until he had to look her in the eye.

"It didn't take you five minutes to pack for camp."

"College is four years, Mom."

"It's not like you can't buy anything once you get there. Or call us if you need something sent." She was asking, in characteristically oblique fashion, what the hell was bothering him. But it wasn't like he could tell her. The only person who knew he was bi-curious, or whatever, was Jonah. Now who was he going to tell about this stuff?

His mom meant well, but she was a former cheerleader who'd married a high school basketball star when she got pregnant—her attitudes were more Sarah Palin than Barbara Boxer. And his dad would shit a cow if he knew his son was... if he knew his son liked to look at other guys. Whatever else he'd been, Jonah had become his safety valve, the guy he could talk to about anything.

"I don't know what I'm doing." His mom would know he wasn't talking about the piles of towels and underwear on the bed.

"Give me a hint?" she said. "We talking about going to Hoosier State? Life in general? Basketball?"

Billy reflexively checked to see that his dad wasn't standing in the doorway or something.

"He's in the garage. You can tell me, you know, if it's not what you want."

Billy collapsed onto the bed. "It's not the basketball."

"You worried about the coursework? Forgive me, kid, but I can't see you homesick."

His mom liked to call him kid when she was trying for wise parent mode. He'd better come up with something plausible, or this conversation was going to shit fast. Only he wasn't really used to having to hide stuff from his mom.

"I feel like I'm living somebody else's life."

His mom's eyes narrowed. "It doesn't seem like such a bad life to me. Most kids have to pay for their college—or their families do."

"I didn't say it was bad. I get that I'm lucky."

"So let's get this stuff packed, huh?" She pointed. "Hand me those towels. They can go into the big suitcase."

Billy covertly let out a sigh of relief that she wasn't pursuing the issue. They'd have to talk sometime, but he'd rather it was after he was out of the house. At least with the scholarship, he'd still have someplace to live when they found out.

THE LOCKER room was not unlike the ones he'd seen in high school, if a bit newer. The same yeasty mixture of ripe sweat, feet, and athlete's foot powder wafted from ventilation slits pressed into metal locker doors. The same wood-topped benches were bolted to the floor between rows of metal lockers. The lockers were bigger. That was nice. Billy followed the coach to his office, careful to keep his eyes from the crotches of the young men who laughed, snapped towels, and paraded shamelessly from the showers. He met them with a loose-limbed saunter of his own.

"I understand congratulations are due, and not just on your state win. Digger tells me you got MVP at your last game. What was it, 62 points and 18 rebounds?"

Digger, Billy gathered, was Assistant Coach Paulson. They'd met briefly at orientation. "Yes, sir. But the other team's point guard was injured. I'd never have made so many—"

"Hold it right there, young man. There are always circumstances. Great players know how to take advantage of them."

"I'm really not that great—"

"A little humility can go a long way, Billy. You don't actually want to convince people you don't deserve your successes, do you? Tell 'em you're something special, and they'll more than likely believe you. Muhammad Ali taught us that."

"But he *was* a great boxer, wasn't he?"

"Sure, sure."

Coach Rocker showed Billy into his office and waved him to a chair.

"So how's your dorm? Getting settled in?"

"It's fine." Billy didn't know if it was because he'd won a basketball scholarship, but he'd been given a room in a suite with two other athletes in Brookhouse, a dorm that was only a short walk from the Athletic Center and Basketball Coliseum. The truth was, he'd rather have been nearer the quad with its green lawns and shaded walks, but he wasn't going to complain.

"Meet your roommates yet?"

"One of them. Jason Pritchard? He's a catcher, I think, from Ann Arbor. On a baseball scholarship. The other is Mike Brooks."

"Oh yes, promising shooting guard." The coach seemed distracted, his eyes flicking back and forth between Billy and the small TV mounted on the wall of his office as if he wanted to catch the scores. "I'm sure you'll get along." Coach Rocker's eyes returned to meet his. "Tulane Sampson is over there too. Nice guy. You have a lot in common. You should look him up."

Billy knew who Tulane Sampson was. Everyone knew Tully Sam. He was Hoosier State's star center. Last year he'd led the league in scoring at twenty-seven per game. He was also a black kid from New Orleans, and more significantly, a senior. What in hell did Coach Rocker think the guy would have in common with Billy, a freshman and small-town Midwestern white boy who might have played point guard in high school but who would be lucky to get off the bench at Hoosier State?

"Well, thanks for stopping by, Billy. We'll look forward to seeing you at practice."

Billy rose, wondering why he'd been summoned to speak to the coach only to be dismissed so soon. Maybe the coach made a point of welcoming all the scholarship students.

"You be sure and introduce yourself to Tully—421 Brookhouse. Nice guy."

Okay, this was just weird. Billy made his way out past the rows of lockers. Maybe it was because Billy had played in Jazz Ensemble in high school with Jonah. New Orleans was known for its jazz heritage. But Coach Rocker didn't seem the type to pay much attention to extracurricular activities that didn't involve tossing balls around. He wished he could call Jonah to ask him what he thought, but their friendship was on hiatus, and Jonah would be in class at Martin Luther King High School, three hours' drive and a world away.

Billy's father didn't know about Jonah, or more precisely, what Jonah meant to Billy. It had taken a lot of explanation and even more persistence to explain to Billy's father why he'd wanted to accept the scholarship at Hoosier State instead of the one at Michigan. His father had been certain Billy was deliberately trying to hurt him when he had refused the scholarship to his alma mater. Ironically, it was the truth that had been most persuasive. Billy had told his parents that he wanted to be closer to Glen Falls. If he'd led them to believe he wanted to be closer to home, instead of closer to Jonah, what was the harm in that?

Heading past the looming football stadium on his way to the library, he passed into the older, greener part of campus. The term hadn't even started, but he had reading to do. Keeping his scholarship meant keeping up his grades, and he was determined that his degree would be fairly earned, not the result of laxness or special treatment applied to athletes. His pride, and Jonah's regard, depended on that. It was stupid, but he still cared what Jonah thought of him, even after the guy had dumped him.

BROOKHOUSE WAS a reinforced concrete structure with vertical slit windows that, from the outside, looked as though the architect had recycled blueprints for a jail. Fortunately, the inside was friendlier, or at least more comfortable, and featured modern amenities such as air-conditioning and wall-to-wall carpeting.

After returning from the library, Billy stopped in the men's bathroom to pee and wash his hands before dinner. Dropping his pack on a dry patch next to one of the eight sinks that filled a kind of lobby, he stepped into the stinky side, which contained a row of urinals and steel toilet stalls. Beyond a gray-and-pink tiled wall, the clean side contained individual shower stalls with tiny curtained spaces outside just large enough for a bench where you could dress. The shower stalls were only three-quarter height, so you could still hear your neighbors, but Billy was grateful for the measure of privacy they afforded.

When Billy returned to the sinks, a tall, well-muscled black guy in tight workout shorts and a muscle-T held his open pack with one hand, the other deep in the interior. A rush of adrenaline set Billy's heart pounding.

"Hey, what are you doing? Leave that alone!"

The long muscles of the guy's back twitched, and he dropped the pack onto the counter, but he turned to face Billy nonchalantly. "No need to get your panties in a wad, man. I was just checking to see who'd left his pack in the gents'."

"Yeah, well, that's mine." Had they met at orientation? The guy looked familiar, but Billy couldn't place him.

The guy looked him up and down with open interest. "I haven't seen you before. You new?"

Billy, still keyed up for a fight, had trouble getting the words out. "Just got in last night."

"Then you're 'bout as fresh as a crocus in snow. I'm Tully. You got a name, newbie?"

Tully Sam. Oh. My. God. He'd failed to recognize him without his uniform. He'd practically just accused the basketball team's star center of being a thief. This probably wasn't the introduction Coach Rocker had had in mind.

"Billy Preston. I'm here on a basketball scholarship, so I guess we'll be seeing each other around. I can't believe I'm gonna be on the same team as you. I've been a fan since forever." Billy held out his hand and tried not to cringe when he noticed that it still trembled from the adrenaline rush.

Tully glanced at Billy's hand, something like surprise flickering on his face, before he flashed the trademark grin that had appeared regularly in sports blogs and magazines the last couple of years.

"Well, Billy Preston, pleased to meet you too."

Billy had never thought of his hands as small. They were, in fact, bigger than average, long fingered and well-suited for palming a basketball. But the massive brown hand that enveloped his own could make a basketball look like it had come from the softball bin.

"Wow, you've got the biggest...." Billy stopped, flustered, sure it wasn't cool to comment on another guy's body so soon after they'd met.

Tully's grin widened, and he thrust out a hip. "Honey, I sure hope that was my *hand* you was gonna compliment, 'cus we jus' don't know each other *that* well."

Billy's face heated. "Uh, sorry." He lowered his eyes. To his mortification, he realized that he still clutched Tully's hand in his own. He snatched his hand back.

Tully's grin faded, and once again an expression passed over Tully's face so fast that Billy wasn't wholly certain he'd even seen it. Disappointment?

Billy reached for his pack. "It's great to meet you, Tully. I'm sure we'll see each other around. At basketball practice, I mean. Or here, in the dorm. Since we both live here. Anyway, see you." He rushed out of the bathroom, certain suicide was the only answer. Pity the windows didn't open.

Tully's laughter, deep and musical, followed him down the hall to his suite.

"HEY, BILLY," Jason Pritchard, one of Billy's new roommates, called from the orange-and-blue striped couch that had already been in the suite when Billy arrived the evening before. Jason's bare legs were hooked over the back of the couch, so his floppy blond mop brushed the carpet.

"Hey, Jason. What's up?"

"You going over for dinner?"

"I guess. Seems a little early."

"Sure. Just planning my evening. Brooks is eating at the Student Center. You want to walk over when you're ready?"

It was weirdly disturbing talking to Jason's upside-down mouth, so Billy tried fixing his gaze where Jason's head should have been. Unfortunately, that had him staring at the crotch of Jason's loose white athletic shorts. The head of Jason's dick was clearly visible where gravity pressed it against the thin fabric of his shorts.

"Nuh." It wasn't quite a word that escaped Billy's mouth. *Get your head out of the gutter!* He dragged his eyes from Jason's anatomy. "Sure."

What was wrong with him? He hadn't been obsessed with guys' bodies before. Ten years of after-school basketball had cured him of any tendency to stare. But then Jonah had started getting hassled at school for being gay—even though he hadn't actually come out yet— and Jonah's father had died, and Billy had been the one to bring over Jonah's schoolwork while Jonah "took a break." And then they'd kissed, and all the feelings Billy had repressed came roiling back to the surface. Now all he saw were body parts. Big parts, little parts, muscular parts, crisply defined parts, like the bare ridges of Jason's abdomen where his T-shirt had slid down. Crap. He was doing it again.

"You okay, dude?"

"Fine. Just worried about my grades, I guess."

"Grades?" Jason's tone was incredulous. "Classes haven't even started yet. You're not some kind of *neurotic*, are you?"

"Listen, I gotta unpack. I don't even know where my toothbrush is."

"Right. Let me know when you're ready to find some grub."

THE FIRST practice of the year went pretty well, all things considered. Billy didn't particularly distinguish himself, but he did well enough in the passing and shooting drills. More importantly, he began to get a sense of the key players on the team. Tully Sam's presence was huge, his constant deep laughter seeming to exert an almost gravitational force over the players around him, each orbiting him in some complicated way.

Mike Brooks, the freshman shooting guard who supposedly shared Billy's suite—although Billy hadn't actually met him yet—turned out to be a quiet guy with a buzz cut and a Zen-like ability to stop time while he was shooting. He'd be in the midst of a shouting, sweaty tangle of players and rise up in slow motion to shoot a perfect arc as though he were alone in the gym. Billy asked him about it as they lined up for another drill, their hands on their knees.

"How the hell do you do that—just freeze everything while you shoot?" he panted. "You got some kind of superpower?"

Mike glanced over and grunted. "Don't know what you're talking about."

Billy hesitated, unsure whether Mike was playing with him. He gave Mike his best grin. "Come on, you've got great focus. It's like there's nobody else on the court."

Mike shrugged. "No superpower. Brothers."

Their turn came up before Billy could ask him to elaborate.

Of course, a major focus of Billy's attention was the team's starting point guard, Jamal White, a muscular guy rumored to have grown up in South Side Chicago. Billy had to be gunning for Jamal's position, if he was to have a successful career at Hoosier State. As point guard, Jamal was ringmaster to the circus. And it didn't take more than a few minutes of watching the on-court interaction between Jamal and Tully for Billy to realize the team had a problem.

At the end of practice, Billy watched from the bench as a squad of seniors finished a practice game, giving him a chance to give the point guard his undivided attention. While Jamal clearly knew his job—he was everywhere, calling to the other players, encouraging them, and directing plays—it was as if Tully Sam was invisible to him. Given their magnetism, other players were alternately drawn into Tully's or

Jamal's sphere of influence, but never all of them at once. The result was a kind of bipolar madness.

In one particularly egregious play, Jamal ignored an obvious pass to Tully and instead sent the ball in a hard flat arc toward the squad's obviously unprepared small forward. The forward, a guy improbably named Otutu Sullivan, reflexively batted the ball to Tully, whose opportunity had already passed, causing the squad to lose the point. Billy glanced at Coach Rocker to see if he'd noticed, and found the man's attention on him. Billy raised his eyebrows, and Rocker turned away, a frown etched on his face.

After the game, Billy returned from showering to dress at his locker, his mood pensive. What did the coach expect of him? Was the obvious problem between Jamal and Tully the reason for the coach's near order that Billy introduce himself to Tully? If so, Billy had already fucked that up. But it didn't make sense. Surely the coach didn't expect a mere freshman to play some role in fixing the problem?

In high school, basketball had elicited mixed feelings from Billy. On the one hand, it was the sport into which his dad had pushed him without stopping to find out if Billy was interested. At first, Billy had accepted basketball as the price for his dad's attention and reveled in it. But eventually his dad's ambition on behalf of his son, his driveway drills and endless postgame analysis, had turned his attention into a burden—and their home into a pressure vessel. On the other hand, there were moments on the court where Billy forgot his dad was watching, forgot that every missed shot or unexploited opportunity would be dissected until Billy wanted to scream at his dad to just leave it alone, and Billy lost himself in the exquisite stretch of long muscles, the slap of the ball against his palm, and the joy of knowing where the guys on his team would be before they did.

Billy knew he would never be a star. He didn't have the drive or the overwhelming need to be the center of attention that motivated many top players. Maybe it was his dad's disappointment at his lack of drive that had put them so much in conflict. What Billy loved was being part of a team, a thread in a mobile web of players that stretched across the court, quivering with every feint, pass, or shot. The best games were not the ones in which he scored the most points, but the ones in which he had the most assists—when the team connected and moved down the court with the fluid precision of a flock of starlings.

The only person to whom Billy had ever voiced these thoughts was Jonah, in the e-mails and texts they'd exchanged in the summer before he left for college, while he'd attended basketball camp and Jonah had stayed home at the Music Box to catch up on his school work so he could graduate with the rest of his class.

Billy was frustrated that their physical relationship was on hold, but he was also relieved, since any hint that he was gay could screw up his athletic career. His feelings about their friendship were less complicated: he missed their conversation. After Jonah's start of term e-mail, they'd mostly shifted to the banter and superficiality of text messages instead of exchanging the longer e-mails that had been Billy's electronic confessional.

Now that school was ratcheting up again for both of them, he wondered if Jonah would ever resume the long messages that had sustained Billy through eight weeks of shooting drills, passing drills, down-court drills, up-court drills, and intramural competition at basketball camp. The camp had been his dad's idea, one Billy had initially embraced simply because his dad wouldn't be there. But that had been before his relationship with Jonah had heated, and the summertime escape had turned into exile with a group of deluded kids who all seemed certain they'd be the one guy in a million who'd graduate from a successful college career to a coveted slot in the NBA. Billy missed his high school team. He'd known those guys for years—some since kindergarten—and enjoyed a rapport with them he never matched at camp.

Billy leaned over to tie his shoes, jeans on, but not yet zipped, his earphones already blasting a playlist of jazz standards he'd learned to love hearing Jonah play them on the piano. A slap on the back startled him into verticality.

"Wha'?"

Mike peered at him quizzically. "What the heck are you listening to, man?"

Caught off guard, unprepared to explain his relationship with Jonah, Billy stuttered. "Uh… just some old-school stuff a friend of mine sent me. He's kind of a music jock."

"Okeydokey. Whatever you say, Grandpa. You want to get something to eat?"

Grandpa? "Yeah, sure. If you don't mind Jason joining us. I said I'd meet him at Porter Commons."

"Of course. More the merrier. Hey, Liam, Tyler!" Mike yelled to a couple of other guys who were on their way out. "Grandpa and I are getting something to eat. Wanna come?"

Liam and Tyler had other plans, but just like that, the damage was done. Grandpa it was, and would be, for the foreseeable future.

CHAPTER 2

Stats

Girls I'm pretty sure wanted to kiss me: 5 12
Girls I've kissed: 3
Boys I've kissed: 1

If Dad ever finds this, I'm dead—like broken spine, belly slit, and guts slithering out all over the floor dead.

Boys who've dumped me: 1
Boys I would kneel on the floor and worship as a basketball god: 1
Stupid nicknames: 2
Public boners: 1

To: JONAHWIN784@GMAIL.COM
From: trumpeter0923@gmail.com
Subject: Nickname
Date: September 12, 2013

Jonah,

You said you still wanted to be friends, so I'm sending you e-mail. If you were fucking letting me down gently, just tell me, and I won't bother you again.

I am so screwed. Mike, one of my roommates and a shooting guard on the team, heard me listening to those MP3s you gave me. I guess he thought they sounded old, like something his grandfather would have listened to. Anyway, he started calling me Grandpa, and it stuck. I don't mind a nickname. The guys used to call me Billy Goat at MLK, but *Grandpa*?

Anyway, how are things at the Music Box? Is Mr. G still seeing Davoud? I like to think they'll stay together, but it's hard to tell with people. Maybe one of them will get bored or something.

Classes started last week, right? You're a senior. Booyah! Antony and Justin are gone. And you're cool now, since you're playing with Mr. G and the Rascals, even if it's not exactly a rock band. Nobody will fuck with you this year.

Mike and I are going over to the Rec Center to shoot some hoops. I should really head for the library, but since classes just started, I figure I can slack off for a few hours.

Just tell me, okay, if I should give it up.

Billy

JONAH CRIED with relief when he got Billy's e-mail asking if he was serious about staying friends. In the week following his Dear John letter, he'd started high school as a senior, realized he'd made a terrible mistake, and wrote his first piano concerto. The mistake and the concerto were connected. Since he'd sent Billy the stupid e-mail telling him to go off and find someone else, Jonah had realized his connection to Billy wasn't gravitational. It did not decrease in strength with distance. He missed Billy's calls, his texts throughout the day, and even his awkward e-mails. They'd been friends first and foremost, their boyfriend status unrealized potential. Maybe if they'd fucked or something, he would have been able to let go, but all they'd done so far was kiss. Once. In his eagerness to avoid the pain of separation, Jonah had cut off the connection he needed most. Unfortunately what was done was done, and all that remained was for him to minimize the pain.

None of this stopped Jonah from fantasizing about Billy when he jerked off every night: Billy's amber eyes bright behind their screen of straight brown hair, his long fingers gripping Jonah's butt while they kissed. Jonah's tears might have been from relief, but a part of him hated the way his feelings had risen so close to the surface ever since his dad had died, ready to seep from the corners of his eyes at the slightest insult or injury. He blurted out as much to Davoud that afternoon after school, when Davoud found him slumped at the piano in the back room of the Music Box.

Davoud slid onto the bench next to him and put an arm around his shoulders. "It's good you feel so strongly. You can use that, you know, as an artist."

Jonah leaned into Davoud. "But I feel stupid crying all the time."

Davoud's gaze seemed to explore the cluttered room, taking in the instruments mounted on the walls, the coiled cables, microphones, and amplifiers waiting for the next open mic night or The Rascals and Mr. G rehearsal.

"I think if you can figure out how to let a little of your emotion out every time you play, let it sound in your music, you won't need to cry so often."

Jonah still felt kind of broken. But Davoud's words comforted him. Maybe he could make some use of his ups and downs. That was the idea, anyway, when he started work on the concerto.

AT THE Rec Center, Billy and Mike found a free basket and fell into an informal game of one-on-one. After Mike made one particularly aggravating point by simply straightening up and shooting a perfect swisher from well beyond the three point line, Billy motioned for a time-out.

"Too much for you, Grandpa?"

"Fuck you," Billy replied without heat. "Hey, what's the deal with Tully and Jamal? They on the outs or something?"

Mike's grin faded to a more guarded expression, and he took a free shot at the basket. The ball bounced off the rim and rolled off the court to one side. "Crap." His shoulders slumped. "How the heck would I know? I'm just a newbie here, like you. I know Coach better do something or we sure as heck won't make it to the playoffs."

"So I wasn't imagining it."

"Heck no. Jamal barely looked at Tully all day. Maybe we could ask one of the older guys. I bet Otter knows. He's pretty tight with Jamal."

Billy jogged over to get the ball and dribbled back to the free throw line. Instead of taking a shot, he passed the ball back to Mike. "Otter?"

Mike lobbed it back. "Go ahead. You afraid you'll embarrass yourself?"

Billy took a couple of breaths to center himself and then sent the ball into the air. The ball glanced off the back of the rim, but it went in. "Ha! Otter?" he repeated.

"That's what I call Otutu Sullivan. You know how he's got that kind of slicked-back thing going on with his hair?"

Mike was apparently one of those guys who couldn't leave well enough alone and had to come up with his own name for every guy on the team. On the other hand, Otutu's sleek head did make him look kind of like an otter.

"Does he know you call him that?"

"Nah, I haven't said two words to him yet."

"You know I'm gonna call him that by mistake now, and he'll probably think I'm some kind of asshole."

Mike ran down the ball and curved around to drop it into the hoop in a perfect layup. "Better you than me."

"Thanks a lot, douchebag." Billy rebounded and ran the ball out to the three point line before starting in for the basket again. Mike was all over him, splayed hands blocking and swiping at the ball. Billy faked right and spun left, ducking under Mike's outstretched arm to break free. He leapt up at the basket to tip the ball over the rim.

"Where's Tully when you need him?" Mike muttered as he rebounded.

A melodious laugh wafted from the sidelines. Billy glanced over to see Tully lounging on the bench that rested against the wall of the practice court, long legs spread wide, elbows resting on the top of the backrest. When the hell had he come in?

"You gonna let Grandpa outrun you, Whirlpool?"

Mike spun toward the bench. "Holy mackerel." Billy wasn't sure if it was Tully's unexpected appearance or the nickname that had startled Mike.

Tully laughed again. The deep sound seemed to resonate in Billy's gut.

"I'll have you know I'm up four points on him," Mike said.

"Only 'cause you're taller. He's running you 'round like a pig in a mud hole."

"Wait, Grandpa?" said Billy, wondering how Tully had already heard about his new nickname. "And where did Whirlpool come from?"

"You ain't heard? They call him Whirlpool 'cause he's so calm when he shoots."

Whirlpool, huh? Mike hadn't mentioned his own nickname. Billy thought about it for a second and laughed. "I bet it was the spinning eyes. Like a hypnotist's—they suck you in and paralyze you while he shoots."

"My eyes do not spin, thank you very much, Grandpa."

As they bantered, he and Mike blasted the ball back and forth, the ball hitting their palms with meaty slaps.

"Got to head back to the dorm," said Tully, stretching languidly. "Y'all gonna keep at it for a while?"

Billy wasn't entirely sure, but he thought maybe there was an invitation of sorts there. He glanced at Mike. "Nah. Probably time we headed back."

Mike smirked. "You know you'll never catch me, *Grandpa*."

Billy couldn't let that pass. With his back to the basket, he stepped over to the free throw line. "Toss it here, *Whirlpool*."

Mike chucked the ball, eyebrows rising.

Billy lined himself up carefully with the basket at the far end of the court and then lobbed the ball backward over his head. After a few tense seconds, he heard a satisfying swish.

Mike's mouth fell open.

Billy smirked. "Get the ball, bitch."

Tully's deep laughter accompanied them all the way back to the dorm.

To: TRUMPETER0923@GMAIL.COM
From: jonahwin784@gmail.com
Subject: Grandpa Billy Goat
Date: September 13, 2013

Billy,

I meant it when I said I want us to be friends. I just thought it only fair that you be free to see someone else if you want. Please keep writing. Tell me about the team and everything. I'm no fucking prize, but I can listen, right?

I don't know how you can talk about Davoud and Mr. G like that. Of course they're still together. They LOVE EACH OTHER. Davoud says they're going to get married someday, even if he has to kidnap Mr. G and drag him to a state where it's legal. I'm going to play for them at the ceremony, maybe "The Way You Look Tonight" or "Bewitched, Bothered and Bewildered." Okay, so I reread that last part and I sound like a fucking girl, but please don't joke about Davoud and Mr. G. It's stupid, but I can't think about them breaking up.

Sorry about the nickname.

Shit. I can't lie. I don't know which name is funnier. Grandpa! That's hilarious, except it makes me Grandpa's ex or something. That's a little creepy, so I think I'll stick with Billy Goat. Maybe you should tell the team about it. I'm sure they would take it right up, LOL.

Everyone's fine at the Music Box except Rascal, who can't decide whether to start touring again or quit the quartet. I think he kind of wants to tour, except he feels guilty about leaving me and Mom while he tours. I think he should quit if he really loves her, but I might be biased about that. What would the Rascals and Mr. G be without the original Rascal?

Rascal and Paul are helping me write a new piece for bass fiddle for Davoud's birthday. We're going to spring it on him next Friday when The Rascals and Mr. G play in the music store again. Rascal wants to make Davoud sight-read it on stage, but I don't think that's fair, given that it's supposed to be his birthday present, so I'm going to put my foot down and tell Rascal to give him a break. Then if Davoud wants to play it right away, it's his get out. Are brothers always so competitive? I wouldn't know, because I don't have any. When Amir comes over and the three of them do their jam session thing, it's like tossing scraps in a box of wolf pups.

Speaking of the music store, Davoud says it's doing better since we opened the café and performance space. He says he might even be able to pay himself a salary this year. I hate it when he jokes like that! I don't like to think about the Music Box in trouble since it's home now.

Jonah

JONAH'S CONCERTO resulted from a passing comment of Rascal's that Ravel's Bolero was all about sex. Rascal's place in Jonah's life was a little hard to define. He was Jonah's composing partner and a founding member of The Rascals and Mr. G, their on-again, off-again music group. Rascal was also sweet on his mother, something Jonah couldn't quite comprehend, although he couldn't question the results. Since they'd started dating, his mother's brittle cool had warmed significantly.

Rascal was also Davoud's brother. Davoud ran Avakian Music and managed the Music Box, the Avakian family's nickname for the old converted hotel that housed both the business and their family apartments. The Music Box had been Jonah's home since last year. Davoud and his partner, Paul Gaston—Mr. G to his music students—were Jonah's adopted fathers. Not officially, of course. Jonah had never spoken to them about it, but he had thought of the couple that way pretty much since his real dad had committed suicide last year and the Avakian clan—Paul included—had taken him in.

In addition to being a cofounder of the Rascals and Mr. G, Rascal was a concert violinist. Professional musicians were a dime-a-dozen in the Avakian family. Even the matriarch of the family, Aida Avakian, was a retired opera singer. Davoud, in fact, was the only one of his generation not to perform professionally, and that was only because he'd stayed home to take care of the Music Box. He was a talented double bass player, and routinely jammed with his brothers as well as The Rascals and Mr. G.

The spark of connection in Jonah's brain from music to sex to Billy that resulted from Rascal's passing comment threatened to rewire the whole fizzy pudding in Jonah's head. It wasn't like he'd never connected sex with music before. Music was full of references to love, sex, and longing. It was just that Jonah hadn't previously connected the complicated kind of music he and Rascal wrote together with his feelings for Billy. But that connection, once made, lit up his mind with the satisfaction of a geometry proof.

After school the next day, he jogged home to the Music Box and straight to the back room containing the Steinway grand piano where he had practice rights. With his fingers resting lightly on the keys, ideas began to flow almost immediately, elements of jazz, popular song, and classical structure effervescing in a Wiccan brew both sating and not a little embarrassing. Determined to grow something lasting from this new inspiration, Jonah decided he would work on the piece however long it took to make it worthy of the boy who'd inspired it.

What would Davoud and Paul think of the result? For all the progressivism inherent in their gay union, the pair were pretty traditional in their values. Neither was inclined to PDAs, for instance. Would they recognize the passion that animated his fingers as he caressed the Steinway's ivory? For that matter, what would Billy think? The question was moot. He and Billy might be friends, but their chance to be anything else had passed. Billy would never hear the concerto.

OVER THE following weeks, basketball practice continued in much the same vein, with Tully and Jamal competing for the attention of the team, and the players bouncing between them. Coach Rocker was inexplicably silent about the problem, to the point where it became the elephant in the room. If a player hinted at the divide or questioned Jamal's leadership, Rocker backed Jamal, as the team's best ball handler and point guard. But at the same time, he rode Jamal mercilessly, questioning each missed pass or botched play, frustration straining his voice as he yelled from the sidelines.

Billy often found the coach's eyes on him. But the man said little beyond the occasional word of encouragement. Billy's primary contact with the coaching staff was with Assistant Coach "Digger" Paulson. Digger ran the drills that took up much of their practice. A tall blond man from Minnesota, Digger was possibly even less inclined toward chat than Rocker. But Digger had one characteristic Rocker did not: a wicked sense of humor.

On a Thursday in the third week of the term, Billy was retrieving his books from his locker on the way to a study session at the library when he heard a locker door slam. Loud voices and muffled snickering followed from the row where Jamal, Tully, and most of the other seniors had lockers. He grabbed his duffle bag and sauntered over to see what was going on. Jamal, stark naked, only a towel in his hands, faced a group of his teammates, including Otter Sullivan, Jackson Flack, Tyler Martin, Malik Brown, and Tully Sam. Jamal had his back to Billy, but he was clearly steamed, judging from his aggressive stance and the tension in his powerful shoulders. Tully, on the other hand, had his usual grin fixed in place.

From behind, Billy couldn't help admiring the dimpled muscular curve of Jamal's buttocks. With Jamal's legs spread wide, Billy caught a glimpse of the dark ball sac tucked forward of his taint. Glad to be fully dressed in loose jeans and a long T-shirt, Billy looked up to catch a knowing smirk from Tully and felt himself blush.

"Who took my bag?" said Jamal, still facing his teammates. "Come on, fuckers. Where's my shit?"

"What you on about, Jamal? You missin' something?" said Tully languidly.

"My clothes, fucktard. What'd you do with 'em?"

"Oh my, some nasty person stole his clothing. Why that's positively *diabolical*." Tully drew out the last word until it formed a complete sentence of its own. He turned his back to Jamal and addressed his teammates. "Fess up. Who stole the poor man's clothes?"

Tully's question met a wave of wide-eyed shrugs that would have done a choir of altar boys proud.

Tully turned back and gave Jamal a slow look from toes to scalp. "Sorry, pal. Maybe somebody can lend you some shorts. You might find mine a tad small, but Grandpa, there, looks like he could fill yours nicely."

Jamal spun around, his generous dick flopping against one thigh. Billy wouldn't be thanking Tully for bringing him into the joke.

"What the fuck are you looking at, *faggot*?"

Billy felt the heat coming off his face in waves. "Nothing! On my way to the library. Good luck finding your thing—*things*."

Backing away faster than a priest from a freeballer's meet, Billy nearly ran over Digger, who'd come up behind him. A logo duffle, of the type Billy had seen most of the senior squad carrying, dangled from Digger's fingers. "Somebody lose something, boys? Found this in my office." Digger lifted the bag into sight, his left eye closing in a deliberate wink.

Billy fled into the crisp September light, Jamal's angry curses and Tully's booming laughter rumbling behind.

"I OUTTA hang up my trainers and retire to some village in Siberia where they've never heard of basketball."

When he stopped laughing, Jason patted Billy on the shoulder. "Actually, I hear basketball's popular in Russia, at least if you've got a taste for pasty white skin."

"That's disgusting," said Mike, wincing. He stretched out his legs to put his feet on the old door set on milk crates that they used for a coffee table in their suite. "I wish I'd been there to see Jamal's face."

"He was not amused," said Billy. "And now he probably thinks I'm some kind of pervert." He dropped onto the other side of the worn couch.

"Well, aren't we all?" said Jason. "I mean, who isn't curious about his mates' tackle?"

Billy had no idea what to say to that. Jason wasn't gay, if the feminine giggles and rhythmic noises coming from his room on Friday nights were any indication. The guy was as regular in his habits as a nun. Well, maybe not a nun. But he seemed blessed with a limitless chorus of young women happy to help clear his pipes.

"Billy wouldn't be the first to pop a boner in the locker room," Jason added thoughtfully.

"Jesus! Would you give it a rest? I did not pop a boner. It was just a slip of the tongue. I don't know why I tell you these things."

"So we can give you the shit you deserve, homey," said Jason. "Right, Whirlpool?"

"Shut up, *bat boy*."

Jason launched himself onto the couch and climbed Mike's chest like it was a telephone pole. "You trying to insult me? Lame, dude."

"Ugh, get offa me, you mental case!" Mike thrust Jason off onto the floor. "All jokes aside, Coach Rocker better do something to fix the team or something's gonna pop. Jamal's about ready to punch the next guy who gets in his business."

Billy was pretty sure Mike was right. It would be all too easy to end up in Jamal's sights. He'd better keep his head down and not give the guy any excuse. What in hell was Jamal's problem anyway? Tully certainly wasn't to everyone's taste, but apart from laughing a little too loud and a little too often, he'd done nothing to deserve Jamal's enmity that Billy'd ever seen.

And why did Coach Rocker keep looking at him like he expected Billy to do something?

ON A Friday night, four weeks into the term, Jason rested head-down on the couch, as usual.

"Come on, dude. You gotta come with," he said. "You can't study on Friday night. If anyone sees you at the library, you'll get a rep for sure."

Billy risked a glance at his roommate. Jason had, for once, put on jeans before draping himself over the furniture. It didn't help much; his flat, bare belly was almost as distracting as the fully covered but plainly visible bulge above it.

Mike laughed from his perch on the arm of the cracked vinyl recliner they'd carted from a secondhand store over the weekend. "Come off it, Jas, you can't be an athlete and a nerd at the same time. It's a law of nature. Not unless you take up fencing."

Jason waggled his legs over the back of the couch. "They look like bugs in those masks."

"Aliens," said Mike. "You're not taking up fencing, are you, Grandpa?"

Billy looked up from the armchair where he'd been trying to read. "Uh, no."

"It's settled, then. You're coming with us."

Billy sighed. There was no contesting the nerd logic. He knew they'd harass him until he agreed. "Whatever."

"Right, so put on something chicks will dig, and ¡*Vamos*!"

Billy dropped his American Lit book onto the floor, then stretched to his full height to touch the ceiling with his hands. *Huh.* Could he be having another growth spurt? If so, it couldn't hurt. He was going to need all the advantages he could muster to make it off the bench.

Mike poked him in the side. "You with us, Stretch?"

Billy dropped his arms with a grunt. "Where we going?"

"There's this club on the avenue that gets a lot of older chicks." Jason's upside-down grin made for a strangely toothy frown. "We could find us some cougar."

"Ick."

"Gross," Billy and Mike protested simultaneously.

"You guys pick, then."

Billy looked at Mike.

Mike shrugged. "Beats me. I'm a beer and pizza guy. Clubs...."

"Think on it while I change." Billy turned toward his room.

"Wait!" Jason righted himself, his bare feet slapping the floor. "You gotta help me pick a shirt."

Billy rolled his eyes. The guy could wear a loincloth and bearskin vest, and some girl would follow him home. He followed Jason into his room.

Jason pointed at a couple of shirts he'd laid out on the bed. "I want something that says sophisticated man about town."

The shirts consisted of a striped polo, a shiny rayon button-down, and a black T with the words "Kiss me quick" written in red lipstick on the front.

"Here." Billy handed Jason the T. "Go with your strength."

Jason frowned. "You sure about this? It's not too much?"

"Never."

On their way down the corridor to the stairs, they passed the suite Tully Sam shared with Otter and Tyler.

"These guys will know where to go. Let's ask," said Jason. He banged on the half-open door and stuck his head inside. "Tully, we're going out. What d'ya think? Where should we go for some action?"

Jason thrust his slim hips a few times suggestively, the effect lost on the suite's inhabitants—the view was blocked by the door—but not on Billy. He closed his eyes. When he opened them, he found Mike watching, his expression unreadable. Before Billy could say anything, Jason backed away from the door and it was flung wide revealing Tully Sam in full regalia: skintight red jeans, a wide white belt worn loose on his hips, a black-and-white flower-pattern button-down shirt open to his belly button, and a necklace of colored beads.

"I hear you gentlemen are lookin' for a little action. Your guide to the underworld has arrived."

"Holy Moley!" Mike breathed to Billy.

Billy wondered if he was in for one of those experiences you're supposed to acquire in college so you can tell stories about it later. Or whether this was going to be the kind of experience best forgotten.

THE BUILDING to which Tully Sam led them occupied most of a grungy block in the commercial district. Grinning mysteriously and following instructions he read from a text message, he passed a set of boarded-up and chained front doors, then glanced around briefly before leading them into an alley. Halfway down, a set of steps led to a raised loading dock next to a garbage dumpster. A large set of articulated metal doors were chained shut, but somebody had painted a crude symbol resembling a dancer with his arms raised above his head in bright red paint next to a standard-sized door to one side.

Tully pointed. "Tomorrow, that will be painted over. Next week, the party will be somewhere else."

"You sure about this?" asked Mike. "We're not going to wake up in that dumpster tomorrow morning with our wallets gone?"

Tully laughed. "Trust your guide, man. I know the guys who set this up. They got security and shit to protect your lily white ass."

Mike nodded, but Billy could see he wasn't wholly reassured. Neither was Billy, but he wasn't about to admit it.

They crowded onto the narrow platform, and Tully hammered a fist on the door. *Boom, boom*, pause, *boom, boom*, pause, *boom*. As if in answer, a heavy bass beat thrummed through the metal.

The door swung partway open, and a beefy guy in a T-shirt labeled Security peered out. "Hey, Tully." Tully started forward, but the guy raised a hand. "Hold up. You vouch for these guys?"

"Yeah, sure. They're okay. Meet Grandpa, Whirlpool, and Hanging Fruit. Guys, this is Fist."

Jason's eyes bulged. "The fuck, Tully!"

"No names here, man." Tully grinned. "And you always upside-down."

"But—"

Billy lost it, bursting into laughter.

"Suck it up, man," Mike joined in. "You have been *tagged*."

"It's on you," said Fist to Tully, stepping out of the way.

They crowded through the door. Exposed beams, thick plank wood floors, and an iron track for an overhead crane suspended from the ceiling revealed the building's history as a warehouse. A string of dim Christmas lights lit a makeshift bar, but the rave's organizers had suspended a modern array of LED lights above the dance floor that flashed in time with the pounding house music. A skinny, hoodie-clad DJ presided over a raised platform at one side of the floor, his face hidden in shadow. On the dance floor, a writhing mass of young men and women strutted, ground together, and waved their arms in time with the music.

"I want a drink," yelled Tully, pointing at the bar. "Seein' as y'all are virgins, first round's on me."

"I don't drink," Mike shouted.

Tully cupped his ear. "I can't hear you." He winked, swaying his hips as he headed for the bar.

Jason punched Mike on the arm. "Suck it up, *virgin*."

Mike punched him back. "Fuck you, *fruitcake*."

"No fighting," yelled Fist, from behind. "Or I toss you both in the dumpster."

Fist might have been a few inches shorter than Billy, but he probably had thirty pounds of muscle on him. Billy didn't doubt he could make good on his threat. He squeezed in between his friends.

"Come on, children." He grabbed them each by the back of the neck and dragged them through the crowd in Tully's wake until they reached the bar: an old door resting on a bunch of aluminum beer barrels.

"Just like home," Jason mouthed. The makeshift table was covered with sixteen-ounce red plastic cups. A chubby white dude with a curly goatee took cash in exchange for foamy beers.

Tully handed over a sheaf of bills and started handing cups back to Jason. Jason passed the first to Mike. Mike reluctantly accepted the cup and sipped, grimacing. Billy got the next. He tasted the beer, glad it wasn't his first. This wouldn't be a good night to lose his head. The beer was sour and smelled sharply of yeast. Jason kept the last cup, closing his eyes in ecstasy as he took a long swallow.

Tully turned back from the bar, his already half-empty cup raised high. "That's the ticket. Drink up, boys," he yelled. "It's time. To. Get. Down." He already moved his long body in sinuous gyrations in time with the music. Tully finished his beer in one long pour down his open gullet. When it was gone, he tossed the cup into a garbage can that had been strapped to a bare steel pillar. Jason followed suit and disposed of his cup as well. Hands free, he raised his arms and began shaking his shoulders like a belly dancer. The two of them wound their way to the dance floor.

"Crazy!" Mike shook his head. He sipped his beer again, grimaced, and tossed the full cup into the garbage can. "Don't tell Jas."

Billy shrugged and mimed zipping his mouth closed. "You wanna dance?"

Mike nodded.

Billy grinned and gulped another mouthful of beer before tossing his cup after Mike's. They pushed through the crowd toward the spot where Tully's dark features and day-glow grin bounced and dipped above the crowd.

On the dance floor, Billy saw that many dancers seemed happy to bump and grind with anyone who caught their fancy, regardless of gender. At first, he and Mike faced each other, but after a moment Mike locked gazes with a curly-haired brunette in a skintight green leotard and focused on her. Billy soloed for a while, content to work up a sweat moving his body to the gut-shaking beat. Eventually he glimpsed Tully's head above the crowd again, and he moved in the tall center's direction, fascinated by the spectacle. A coterie of both genders surrounded Tully: slender young men in T-shirts and tight jeans and women in spandex or filmy outfits that barely covered their sleek bodies. Tully shamelessly humped both male and female rumps like a dog in heat, sweat flying from his chin and running down his neck into the open V of his shirt. His shameless sensuality and androgyny felt both exciting and dangerous, and Billy soon found his own gyrations increasingly mirroring Tully's. Tully caught sight of Billy at the periphery of his group and grinned. Tully drew Billy in until they faced each other, his movements matching Billy's, and Billy lost track of the rest of the group.

On the basketball court, Tully had a way of zooming in on you, his eyes telegraphing what he was going to do before he did it. It was one of the things that made him a great player, because he could get you to do what he wanted without an overt signal that might be picked up by the opposing team. On the dance floor, Tully was equally expressive, and so when the music changed, Billy knew what Tully was going to do before he did it. He could have prevented it by moving away, but he didn't. Instead, he let Tully spin him around and pull him close until Tully's crotch pressed Billy's backside, and they moved in unison, grinding together with Tully's cock sliding along the crease of Billy's ass. Deliciously sleazy and dangerous at the same time, the sensation made Billy's dick harden until dancing became uncomfortable and he pulled away. As Tully's arms fell away, Billy found Mike's eyes on him, and he spun away in shame.

FOR BILLY.

It was dumb. Jonah should have known the words on the cover sheet of the concerto would encourage questions he didn't want to answer, but he hadn't been thinking about his adopted fathers when he scrawled the dedication.

Davoud and Paul knew he and Billy were friends. But Jonah had been careful to keep Billy's secret. As far as Davoud and Paul knew,

Billy was straight. When Jonah handed out the music, he caught Paul's raised-eyebrows flash at Davoud and Davoud's answering look. Neither had said anything during the rehearsal, but afterward Paul stopped him at the elevator.

"Hold up there, partner. You got a second?"

"Uh, I've got homework?"

Paul laughed. "Come on, you're not in trouble or anything. I just want to chat."

"Okay."

Paul stabbed the button for the floor where he and Davoud shared an apartment. They waited in silence while the old elevator ground upward. When it creaked to a halt, Paul slid the cage open and put a hand on Jonah's neck. "Come on. Davoud's working in his office, so we'll have some privacy."

Privacy? Somehow Jonah wasn't exactly reassured. "What's this about? I do have an algebra assignment."

Paul smiled and guided him firmly into the apartment, removing his hand only when they reached the overstuffed velvet sofa that Davoud refused, despite Paul's pleading, to consider replacing.

"Sit. You want something to drink? We've got some soda, I think."

"I'm okay."

"Well." Paul sank into the sofa next to Jonah. It was not actually possible to sit *on* the old thing. Persons who tried to perch on the edge tended to lose their balance and end up lying on their backs. "So how is Billy? He getting on okay at Hoosier State?"

"He's good. I mean, as far as I know."

Paul gave up and sank backward onto the cushion, but the tension in his body gave away his interest in the conversation. "It can be pretty overwhelming living away from home for the first time. Lots of new experiences, new friends."

"He e-mailed me after he… he went to some party with Tully Sam." When the skin wrinkled over the bridge of Paul's nose, Jonah added, "You know, State's star center. Basketball?"

"Oh, right."

Jonah was pretty certain Paul had never heard of Tully Sam.

"It's great you're staying in touch. That doesn't always happen after high school. People tend to go their different ways."

"I know that. But Billy and I will always be friends."

Paul let some frustration show at that. He attempted to lean forward, giving up when the sofa refused to release its pillowy grip. "I'm going to be honest with you, Jonah."

Jonah was surprised Paul had lasted this long. He wasn't known for his patience—or his diplomacy.

"I'm worried that you've developed some feelings for Billy that—that aren't likely to be reciprocated."

Jonah knew he never should've let his dads see the concerto. Davoud probably wasn't really working in his office. The two of them had probably agreed Paul should ask Jonah about Billy through some kind of eye-to-eye text messaging superpower that only couples have.

"It's not like that."

"I'm just concerned that Billy will meet a girl and—"

"I *said* it's not like that."

"I know, but I've had some experience with straight men and it never—"

Billy would just have to forgive Jonah. It's not like Paul or Davoud were going to hold Billy's sexual preference against him. "Billy isn't straight. I know he's attracted to me."

"Okay, well, that's—" Paul cleared his throat. "That's good, but he's in the closet, right? That can be pretty uncomfortable for the other guy, when someone can't or won't—"

"It's not like we're having sex or anything. How could we, with him there and me here?"

Paul's face colored. "I… okay. I just don't want to see you hurt."

Jonah's eyes started to burn, and he focused on his hands, which he was surprised to find clenched in his lap. "I know."

"Does Billy know how you feel about him?"

It was Jonah's turn to color. "Do we really gotta talk about this?"

Jonah could see Paul really wanted to say yes, but he sighed and squared his shoulders instead. "No. Not now, we don't. I'll respect your privacy." He paused. "But I really hope you're talking to someone. You know what can happen when people don't talk."

God, did he really have to bring that up? Given the history of their kooky little made-up family, it was like the nuclear missile of persuasive tactics. "I promise, okay? I'll tell you if things go bad."

Paul nodded. "Okay." He extracted himself from the sofa. "It's my turn to make dinner. You're welcome to stick around."

Jonah pressed his palms to his eyes. It really wasn't fair when your favorite teacher pulled shit like falling in love with a man you really liked and started acting like he cared about you and all. How were you supposed to give him any shit?

"No, I really do gotta do my algebra."

CHAPTER 3

Stats

Girls I'm pretty sure wanted to kiss me: 5 ~~12~~ 10,012
Girls I've kissed: 3
Boys I've kissed: 1

If Dad ever finds this, I'm dead—like broken spine, belly slit, and guts slithering out all over the floor dead.

Boys who've dumped me: 1
Boys I would kneel on the floor and worship as a basketball god: 1
Stupid nicknames: 2
Public boners: 1
Teammates I'd like to knock some sense into: 2
Different kinds of underwear worn by guys on my floor: 5

"HEY, GRANDPA, Rocker wants to see you in his office."

Six weeks into the term, and Billy's new epithet was well established. Even the coaching staff had begun to use it. Digger Paulson caught Billy as he arrived in the locker room to get ready for practice and followed him to his locker.

"What's up?" Billy asked, as he dumped his pack onto the bench.

Digger shrugged and placed a size twelve on the polished wood. "Beats me. Maybe Jamal has decided to throw in the towel."

"You don't really think…?"

Digger snorted. "Not in a hundred years."

"Then what?"

"He didn't say anything to me. You get anyone pregnant lately?"

Billy glanced at Digger's face. The man's habitual half smile didn't appear to hide any serious intent. Billy spun the combo on his locker and threw his pack inside.

"Not unless you can do it long distance." The words were out before Billy could fully consider their effect.

Digger smiled knowingly. "Got a girlfriend back at home?"

Shit. He'd sworn to himself that he would never lie about Jonah. Now he was going to have to measure every word. "Nah, we're just friends."

Digger looked at him out of the corner of his eyes. "She dump you? Happens all the time. People leave for college. Get accepted by different schools…."

Billy feigned indifference. "It's not like that." What was with the inquisition, anyway?

Digger examined him for a couple of seconds before turning to go. "If you say so. See you on the court."

"Right." What had spurred Digger's interest? They'd never talked about personal stuff before. Maybe the guy knew more than he was letting on.

Billy trotted to Rocker's office and tapped on the door before poking his head inside.

"You wanted to see me?"

Rocker glanced up from a stack of papers on his desk. "Have a seat, Preston."

Billy dropped into the chair in front of Rocker's desk and looked around the office. Signed photographs from sports figures decorated the walls. A shelf of dusty trophies ranged along a shelf on the back wall. Rocker signed the sheet in front of him and looked up.

"How's it going? You getting settled in? Classes okay?"

Billy shrugged. "Okay, I guess." Surely Rocker didn't really want to hear about his progress in Economics 101.

Rocker tapped his pen on the desk. "Roommates okay?"

"Sure, Jason's a good guy—for a baseball player. And Whirlpool—Mike's great."

"Good. Say, you ever hang out with Sampson? He's on the same floor, right?"

Crap! Had the coach heard something about the rave? "A bunch of us eat together sometimes. Tully comes along when he's not busy."

Rocker's brow furrowed. "But you get along with him, right?"

Okay, so it's not about the rave. Billy found himself unwilling to meet Rocker's gaze. He didn't want to go where the coach headed. Jamal might be hard to understand, but he didn't deserve to be shunted aside because he and Tully Sam were having a spat. Somebody ought to talk some sense to Jamal before he lost his starting role in the squad. It was Rocker's job. Billy couldn't understand why Rocker hadn't already told Jamal to suck it up or hit the bench. All that aside, there was no way Billy was ready to take Jamal's place on the squad. If he started with the big boys and didn't do well—a distinct possibility—he'd scuttle his career before it started.

"He's okay, I guess." It was time to find out what was really going on with Rocker. Billy searched for the right word. Rocker's response would tell Billy some of what he needed to know. "A little *flighty.*"

Rocker seemed reluctant to meet Billy's gaze. He scanned the papers in front of him as though they might contain a suitable script for his response. His face gave nothing away, but his answer was a long time coming. Finally, he shoved the stack of papers to one side and folded his hands on the desk.

"And is that a problem for you, if Tully is a little *flighty?*"

Whether Rocker intended it or not, the contempt with which he pronounced the word revealed his attitude for the first time in the conversation. Rocker thought Tully was a fag, and he didn't like it. But he followed a politically correct line in dealing with his star player. Or more likely, he knew a talent like Tully was rare, and he'd probably never get another chance to work with one. Either way, Rocker had come to the conclusion that Jamal couldn't or wouldn't adapt to the situation, maybe because he himself sympathized with Jamal. But Rocker was prepared to sacrifice his senior point guard to get Tully a player he could work with. Whatever the reason, Rocker's mendacity stunned Billy, and he wanted nothing more than to escape the presence of the man whose coaching record had been one of Billy's arguments for coming to Hoosier State.

First he had to answer Rocker's question without communicating any discomfort with Tully, and at the same time, without signaling acceptance of Rocker's prejudice or his willingness to sacrifice Jamal.

"You know what, Coach? I get along with Jamal pretty well." It wasn't true. He'd hardly spoken to the guy, but Rocker wouldn't know that. "Maybe I could talk to him, you know, about Tully?"

Coach Rocker's frown suggested he was less than excited at the prospect, but Billy soldiered on anyway as if he was too taken with the idea to notice Rocker's reaction.

"Jamal will come around if he knows what's at stake. I'm sure of it. He's better than I am right now. The team needs him."

Coach Rocker stood suddenly and plucked his windbreaker from the back of his chair. "Okay, Billy. You talk to Jamal if you think it will help. Thanks for stopping by. See you in practice."

Billy was never so relieved to be dismissed.

PRACTICE WAS a disaster. Mike couldn't have gotten the ball through the hoop if it had had propellers and a remote control. Billy was pretty sure he knew why. After they'd returned to the dorm early Saturday morning, Mike had gone to bed without saying anything about what he'd seen at the club, but Billy knew it bothered him. Billy might have said something to him—what exactly, he had no idea—but he and Tully had been occupied preventing a sloppy drunk and very sick Jason from drowning in the toilet. By the time Jason was done hurling and they'd gotten him to bed, Mike was locked in his room with the light off.

Malik and Jackson were puffy-eyed and irritable—likely hungover—and got into a shoving match when Malik elbowed Jackson in the gut driving for a rebound. Digger shoved them apart with an oath instead of his usual crack about lovers' spats.

Then things got worse. Digger benched Billy and the other freshmen between drills to lecture them about zone defense. While they listened, a scuffle broke out among a squad of seniors running drills at the other end of the court. When the yelling started, Billy looked over to see Coach Rocker straight-arming Jamal with a meaty hand in the middle of his chest. Otter and Tyler restrained Tully Sam.

"What the hell, Jamal?" demanded Tully. "What was that for?"

Jamal sputtered, his face dark. "Motherfucking ho!"

"He's got the wrong guy for that scene," Jackson cracked.

"Why you gotta—" Jamal spat.

Billy stood to get a better view.

"You got a question about zone defense, Preston?" asked Digger.

"Huh?" Billy sat down again, but Digger took a backseat to the drama at the far end of the court.

Tully yanked an arm free to rub his face. "The fuck you expect, asshole?" he yelled. "Pass the damn ball now and then, and I wouldn't have to resort to extreme measures."

"What the heck did he do?" whispered Mike.

"Faggot mooned him," Malik cackled. "He fucking mooned him."

"That's enough!" Rocker's glare shifted between the miscreants. "Jamal, get out of here. You're done for the day. Tully, in my office, now!"

"Right," said Digger. "All of you. On the court. Set up for passing drill."

"This place is out of control," Mike muttered, as they filed into position.

WHEN THE concerto was done, Jonah tried unsuccessfully to imagine a time when Billy might hear it. Even though they'd exchanged e-mails now and then since his big mistake, there was a layer of reserve in Billy's communications that hadn't been there before. Jonah knew he'd hurt and offended Billy.

On Monday morning, he trotted down the corridor of MLK High thinking he had to find a way to repair things with Billy. Slipping into history class as the bell rang, he threaded through a couple of chatting students and slid into a seat in the back.

Mr. Albertson rose to his feet and cleared his throat. "Good morning. I hope you all had a good weekend and enjoyed reading chapter four." Albertson probably wasn't that old, but he looked as though he'd been installed along with the ancient chalkboard and graffiti-scarred desk. His blue slacks bagged at the knee, and his tweed jacket sagged at the pockets. Jonah would have rather taken the AP European History course from Mr. G—Paul at home in the Music Box—but Paul had said it was probably best Jonah limit his classes with him to music now that they lived together. Jonah wasn't entirely sure why.

A wave of rolled eyes turned the classroom into a garden of pinwheels at Albertson's comment. Albertson always made some hopeful comment about their assigned reading after the weekend, as though he secretly dreamed of the day a student would announce she'd been so fascinated she'd read the text in one sitting. Albertson adored history. Jonah gave him credit for that. He was pretty certain the old guy had been a total geek in school. Maybe he'd even been bullied like Jonah. He felt he ought to like the man more, but he wasn't Mr. G with his ironic tone and barbed comments that never failed to entertain. Nevertheless, he caught the man's eye and pasted on a smile. *Go geeks!* Albertson paused as if confused, actually spinning completely around, as if there might be another teacher present, or more likely, a rude comment scrawled on the chalkboard.

Jonah sighed. *Sorry, Mr. Albertson. Didn't mean to throw you off.*

Albertson shook his head and reached for a stack of photocopies on his desk. "Today, as you may recall, we start work on our collaborative history projects. Each of you will work with a partner to create a website containing pictures and text pertaining to a topic of your choice—selected, of course, from the list in your handouts."

When the handouts reached him, Jonah took one and passed the stack to the girl behind him. In addition to details about the assignment, the handout included a computer lab sign-up form and partner assignments. Albertson had paired Jonah with a sleek dark-haired guy from the back row named Tony Morretti. They'd never talked, but Jonah had seen Tony's name posted in swim meet results. Why did God always torment him with the handsome ones?

"Please find your partner and take a seat next to him or her."

Jonah grabbed his pack and looked around. Tony stood next to his desk in the back of the room. The girl next to him abandoned her desk for one in the next row, so Jonah snagged the free spot.

"Hi, I'm Jonah. I guess we're in this together."

Tony smiled warmly and held Jonah's gaze. "Guess we are."

OMG! Jonah had never before had the experience of meeting another guy and knowing instantly he was gay. Maybe Billy had recalibrated his gaydar or something. Knowing Tony was gay made him curious and uncomfortable at the same time, sort of like discovering someone's secret pornography stash. He shifted his gaze to the handout.

"Uh." He cleared his throat. "I guess we choose a topic."

Jonah felt rather than saw Tony's disappointment.

Tony shifted in his seat. "I asked Mr. Albertson if we could work together."

"You did?" Jonah glanced up, unable to keep the surprise from his voice.

Tony's smile broadened. "I figured we have something in common."

He's hitting on me. Never in a thousand years would it occur to Jonah that *he* might be the one to meet someone while he and Billy were separated. He always pictured Billy surrounded by cheerleaders and hangers-on after a game. Some guy would compliment him on the win, and then they'd retire to Billy's room to exchange workout tips and tongue. *What to say to Tony?* The crowded classroom was the last place to talk about being gay.

The heat of Tony's smile warmed Jonah's face. He hastily looked down to scan the list of topics. "What do you think about The Economic Causes of World War I?"

"I think you and I should meet after school to discuss the terms of our partnership."

Oh. My. God.

JONAH AGREED to meet Tony at the Glen Falls Café after school. He thought about inviting him to the Music Box, but rejected the idea as dangerous. The café was neutral ground. Nothing much could happen there. The café was crowded with students when Jonah arrived. He snagged a vinyl-topped stool at the counter.

"What can I do you for?" The waitress who ambled over had dark, almost black skin and a riot of kinky dark hair held off her face by a brightly colored headband. He wondered if she was a student at the college. She looked exotic, but she sounded more like Brooklyn. Actually Brooklyn *was* exotic in Glen Falls.

"I don't know. I'm waiting for somebody."

She sighed dramatically, apparently unconcerned about the customers that crowded every table. "Aren't we all?"

"Maybe unsweetened ice tea."

She made a point of looking him up and down. "Counting calories? Not like ya need to."

"No, Billy says sugar isn't...."

"And who's Billy?"

Jonah wasn't sure he wanted to explain who Billy was. Tony's arrival saved him from trying.

Tony hopped onto the stool next to Jonah. "Hey."

"Hey."

"This the guy who don't like sweet? I'm Kalisha, by the way."

Tony's eyes narrowed for an instant as he took in the waitress, but then he grinned and made a point of checking out Jonah. "Nah, I like sweet just fine. Nice to meet you, Kalisha."

"Huh." Kalisha cocked her head and stared at Tony out of one eye like a bird. "You want something, Mr. I-like-sweet-just-fine."

Jonah felt like he'd stepped onto a movie set without a script.

"Just a Coke for me," said Tony.

"One unsweet and one Coke," said Kalisha, moving toward the soft drink fountain.

"She's fun." Tony jerked his head at the waitress. "She a friend of yours?"

"No, just met her."

"She thinks you're cute."

"Me?" said Jonah, still a bit bewildered by the whole conversation.

Tony nodded. "She's got good taste."

Jonah gulped, wishing he had that ice tea. "We're supposed to be talking about our history project."

Tony rolled his eyes. "Right, that's why *I'm* here."

Pretending this wasn't happening wasn't working for Jonah. Fortunately Kalisha dropped off their drinks before Jonah had to say something. "One unsweet for cutie pie and one Coke for Mr. Sweet."

Tony grinned at her. "Thanks, Kalisha."

Kalisha winked. "Good luck," she added, already heading for a waving patron.

"See."

"See what?"

"She called you cutie pie."

"She probably calls everyone that, like some people call everyone dear."

Tony snorted. "Whatever you say."

Jonah took a breath. "I have a friend."

"Good for you. I got a couple myself."

"You know what I mean."

For the first time, Tony's good humor faltered. "Billy."

Jonah's surprise had to have shown.

Tony took a sip of his Coke and spun on his stool. "Billy says sugar isn't...."

"You heard that."

Tony stopped spinning with his stool facing Jonah. "I'm kinda surprised, actually. You're talking Billy Preston, right? I knew you guys were friends, but I didn't think he leaned that way."

Jonah glanced around to see if anyone was listening. "You can't tell anyone."

Tony sighed. "Mr. Unsweet's secret is safe with me."

"Thanks."

"So I thought Preston was up at Hoosier State. How's that working for y'all?"

"I'm not sure I should—"

Tony's smile this time was both less bright and more real. "Give me a break, Jonah. Can't we at least be friends? It's not like I got so many guys to talk to about... you know."

Jonah relaxed a little. "I guess that would be okay."

"Whew! Glad we got that out of the way." Tony picked up a menu. "You want to get something to eat? Or is Billy against eating too?"

Jonah repressed a snarky reply. He could deal with Tony's disappointment. "Some fries would be good." He couldn't resist adding, "They're Billy's favorite."

Tony rolled his eyes. "Give me a break."

"HEY, WHIRLPOOL, wait up," Billy called out, chasing Mike through the double doors of the gym.

"What's up, *Gramps*?"

Billy fell into step. "Where are you going?"

"Library."

"Listen, we've got to talk."

"Do we?"

"Come on, Mike. We were just blowing off steam. It didn't mean anything."

Mike stopped in the middle of the concrete walkway. "I know what I saw."

"What was that?"

"You liked it."

Billy glanced around the grass-bordered walk. "Can we not do this here?"

"You wanted to talk, so talk."

"Fuck." Billy looked around again. It was a sunny day, and there were students all over the place. Some guys were playing a game of ultimate Frisbee on the grass in front of the gym. A girl slumped on a bench, facedown in a book Billy recognized as his Economics 101 textbook. A group of baseball players from Jason's team rambled in their direction.

"Can we go somewhere more private?"

Mike gave in. "Whatever. Liam's got a study carrel in Tucker Library he told me I could use. He'll be in class now."

They walked to the library in silence, Billy glad of the chance to figure out what to say. He didn't want to lie, but Mike's attitude so far wasn't exactly encouraging. If Mike asked him directly if he liked guys, he would have to tell the truth. If Mike told anyone, he could kiss his basketball career good-bye. Even if most of the guys didn't care, some would, and he didn't have the star power to deal with Coach

Rocker. He'd lose the scholarship and have to drop out. The idea made him sick to his stomach.

At least he'd get to see more of Jonah.

Mike led him to the third floor mezzanine. A set of private carrels lined the balcony overlooking the circulation desk. He pulled a key from his pocket, unlocked the flimsy door, and ushered Billy into the tiny space.

"Jesus, this isn't designed for a basketball player, much less two of them."

Mike squeezed in next to him. "You wanted private."

"What do you have to do to get one of these?"

"Lead the conference in rebounds two years running."

"Oh."

"You were going to tell me that I didn't see what I saw. You had a hard-on, dude. So did Tully, for that matter."

"You would too, if somebody were grinding you that way."

Mike grimaced. "I would never let Tully do that to me. You not only let him, you encouraged him."

"We were dancing."

Mike stared at him, raising his eyebrows.

"Okay, fine." Billy gave up. "You want the truth? Tully is hot, and he made me feel hot."

"At least you're being honest now." Mike closed his eyes and sighed. "We are so screwed."

"What do you mean?"

"You want to know what pissed me off about that night? You encouraging him."

"Who?"

"Tully, you moron. Tully! If he keeps pressing Jamal's buttons, the team is so screwed. I want to win."

This was not quite where Billy had seen Mike taking the conversation, but he went with it. "Rocker thinks Tully's gay. He practically offered me Jamal's position if I can get along with Tully better than Jamal does."

Mike tilted his head to stare down at the circulation desk on the floor below. Billy followed his gaze to a bored-looking group of students getting an orientation tour gathered around a gray-haired librarian. He'd taken his the previous week.

Mike spoke without shifting his attention. "Yeah, well, forgive me for saying so, but you're not ready to start, and you know it."

It was true, but it still stung to hear Mike say it. "What about Jamal? It's okay with you, what he's doing?"

"Don't put words in my mouth. Jamal's being a jerk, and so are you and Tully. I don't give a fuck what you guys do in bed, but last night—"

"All we did was dance."

"I thought you were gonna start dogging right there."

Billy glanced at Mike's face. He didn't seem the type to even know what *that* term meant. He only knew it because he'd run into a website dedicated to the pursuit online once when he was looking for something to jerk off to. It was a few years ago, before he'd met Jonah, and he'd been so embarrassed by the videos on the site, he'd hastily closed the browser window and deleted the history so his parents wouldn't know he'd ever been there.

"So it's okay if I'm bi or whatever, but not if anyone knows about it?"

"I didn't say that. There's a difference between coming out and rutting in public."

By this time Billy was mad, and he had to escape the cramped space to stretch his legs. "Move, I gotta get out of this closet."

Mike slid out of the carrel and leaned down, a half smile stretching his cheeks. "I can't believe you just said that."

Billy was too angry to respond to the humor in Mike's voice.

"We weren't doing anything a dozen straight couples weren't doing."

Mike's eyes narrowed. "You're not saying you're—"

"Tully and me?" Billy slid out and stood up. "I hardly know the guy. But what if I did?"

"Just do us all a favor and stay the heck away from him. He doesn't need encouragement." Mike locked the door and stalked off, leaving Billy rubbing his cramped knees. He watched until he saw Mike stride across the floor below and out through the security gates.

BILLY AND Mike didn't talk for three solid days after the conversation in Tucker Library. Mike kept to his room, and Billy didn't push.

Instead, he wrote e-mail after e-mail to Jonah, pouring out his frustration about what was happening with the team, not even waiting for the replies. When he mentioned his promise to talk to Jamal, Jonah's eventual reply caught him off guard.

"What the fuck did you do that for?" Jonah wrote. "Talking to bullies never helps. If Rocker wants you to start, then you say 'Yes, sir!' and do it. You're better than you think you are. Mike's an idiot if he doesn't see that."

Billy hadn't been thinking of Jamal as a bully. Jamal was pretty quiet off court, so it was hard to get to know him. But every time Billy had spoken to him, apart from the incident in the locker room when he'd been pretty mad, Jamal had been friendly in a gruff kind of way. Tully was the one who made everyone uncomfortable, the one who dug at people's insecurities. Jonah got points for loyalty, but his judgment when it came to the team was suspect. Billy had to question whether Jonah was right about Jamal.

Jonah's doubts withstanding, Billy decided to fulfill his commitment to talk to Jamal. He knew instinctively it would have to be a private conversation if it was going to do any good at all. He'd get nowhere in public, or in the company of other team members. But he'd need help to make it happen. That gave him an excuse to reestablish relations with Mike. He caught up with him in the dining hall, when Mike was reading by himself. Billy pulled up a chair without asking.

"How's it going, roomie?"

Mike's nose stayed firmly planted in his book. Billy leaned over to read the upside-down title from the top of the page.

"Get your coffee-breath out of my face."

"What are you reading?"

"Robert A. Heinlein."

"What's it about?"

"Science fiction."

"I need your help."

Mike didn't answer, but he hadn't turned a page for a while, so Billy figured he was listening.

"I need to talk to Jamal, but he may not want to hear what I have to say, so I need help setting it up."

Mike closed his book. "What makes you think you won't make things worse?"

"How could they get worse? The season starts soon, and Jamal and Tully aren't working together. We're screwed if we don't do anything."

Mike looked at him. "You think people haven't already tried?"

"If so, it hasn't helped."

Mike shook his head. "What do you want from me?"

"I want to catch him somewhere private where he can't run away."

Mike's eyes flew open. "I'm not helping you corner him on the can."

"Jesus! I'm not—"

"Where, then?"

"We need to ask someone who knows him."

Mike thought for a moment. "Otter."

"Do you think he'll help us?"

Mike rubbed his chin, reflectively. "Otter's his best friend on the team, but he wants to win. And Jamal's screwing himself as much as anyone."

"You know him better than I do. Will you ask him?"

"I've got class." Mike shoved his book into his pack.

"Will you ask him?"

"I'll think about it."

BILLY FELT silly hauling the giant sack of dirty laundry across campus, but if the plan worked, he'd come out with clean clothes and a clean conscience. Johnson House, the dorm where Jamal and Otter roomed, was an older six-story brick building with sash windows. The feature that made it popular was the patio on the roof that students could reserve for parties and other events. Billy's destination, however, was the basement, not the roof. He yanked open the double doors and hauled his bag to the stairwell. Otter leaned casually against the door, his sleek head a full inch over the top of the frame.

"He's there."

"Thanks, man. I really appreciate your help. Wish me luck."

Otter shook his head and moved aside. "You're gonna need it."

Billy pulled open the door and trotted down the stairs to the basement. Opening the door at the bottom, a billow of moist air warmed his face. He peered into a small brick-walled space with pipes hanging from the ceiling. Four commercial-grade washing machines nestled under barred windows tucked under the ceiling. Dim sunlight filtered through weed-filled window wells. A pair of gas dryers lined each side wall. A scarred wooden table sat in the center of the room. Jamal leaned over a washing machine, pouring liquid detergent into the bottle cap. He turned, eyes widening in surprise.

"Grandpa? I thought you lived in Brookhouse. What're you doing over here?"

Billy was surprised Jamal even knew his nickname. "Everyone wanted to do laundry at once." He held up the giant sack. "I waited too long. Got nothing clean left." It was true Brookhouse's laundry room was busy on Sunday, but his sack contained laundry borrowed from a bunch of guys on his floor. The sack in which he collected his dirty clothes hadn't contained enough to justify the expedition to another laundry room.

Jamal grunted and pointed at a pair of washers. "Well, those ones are free. Hope you brought a comic book or something, 'cause you gonna be here for a while judging from the size of that bag. Watch your head on the pipes. This place ain't built for tall."

"Thanks." Billy hoisted the sack on the table and dumped it out. He started sorting like colors. "Looks like you're just getting started."

Jamal shrugged and set the dials on his washer. "Digger bored you to death with his theories on zone defense yet?"

Good. Billy didn't even have to bring up basketball. "Nah. He says we got a good chance at the division title this season."

Jamal sat down at the table. "He's always sayin' that. May *be* it's true this time."

"What do you think?" Billy asked.

Jamal examined him warily. "What do *you* think?"

Billy stopped sorting and met Jamal's look. "I think you and Tully gotta decide you're on the same team."

Jamal stared back coolly.

"I know you want to win." Billy started sorting again. "I know he does."

"I don't give a shit what that fruitcake wants." Jamal's tone was bitter.

"He pushes your buttons. You gonna let that get in the way of a championship?"

Jamal stood, nearly bashing his head on an overhead pipe. "What the fuck you know about it?" He eyed the laundry machine containing his clothes like he wanted to leave, but he sat again instead. Billy's plan was working.

Billy let him rest while he finished sorting, then carried a pile to a washer and dumped it in. "Maybe he pushes mine too."

"You see what the crazy bastard did to me at practice?"

"He's got a point, you know. He's the center. You can't just ignore him."

"That don't give him the right to... to—he's always fucking shaking something at me. How am I supposed to react to that? It's... disgusting."

The laundry room was hot, and Billy began to sweat. Jamal, however, wasn't reacting with the heat Billy had expected. He barely voiced the word disgusting, like it wasn't his first choice, only what he thought Billy expected of him. Billy had expected a conversation with a homophobe. He'd prepared arguments, thought about what he might say. But there was something else, something off about Jamal's reaction. Billy struggled out of the sweatshirt he'd thrown on for the walk over, feeling air on his belly as his T-shirt rode up. When he could see again, he found Jamal staring. Jamal looked away quickly and thumbed the textbook on the table in front of him.

Was Jamal blushing? It was hard to tell with a black guy, but the skin at the tips of his ears seemed to be brighter than normal. *Whoa.* It didn't seem possible, but it occurred to Billy that there could be another explanation for Jamal's discomfort with Tully. If so, he was going to have to tread even lighter than he'd thought.

"He's over-the-top, isn't he? Flamboyant. Have you seen him dance?"

"Humps like a fucking ho. Yeah, I seen it. He's got no shame."

Billy decided to move the conversation to a safer topic. "You grew up in Chicago, right? What was that like? I've only been there a couple of times, but it seemed like a cool city."

Jamal was silent for a while, pushing the textbook around in front of him with sharp jabs like he was trying to bring it into focus. "I got out."

"What do you mean? Were there like gangs and stuff?"

"You are one nosey motherfucker, you know that?"

"Sorry. Jonah says I'm too stupid to know when to shut up."

"Who the fuck is Jonah?"

"He's my… friend." *Holy shit!* He'd almost called Jonah his boyfriend. What the fuck was wrong with him? "Back home. We hung out in high school."

Jamal's eyes narrowed like he'd caught the hesitation at the word friend. He gestured at the pile of clothes on the table. "You always do laundry for the guys on your floor?"

"What? No, I just waited too—"

Jamal poked one of Billy's piles. "You wear size 32 briefs *and* size 36 boxers?"

"No, mine are the—" *Whoops.* Billy's face heated. The conversation was definitely not going as planned. Setting aside the lie about running out of clothes, he didn't want to be talking with Jamal about underwear.

"Uh… some of my roommates' must have gotten mixed in."

Jamal shoulders began to shake. "Right." He broke into a grin. "Pretty soon you'll be telling me you're working your way through school as a laundress." He chuckled, a full diaphragm sound, deep as Tully's boom, but warmer. "You really a piece of work, man."

Billy dropped his forehead on the table and started laughing, more from relief than for the humor of it.

"Who sent you, anyway? Liam? Otter? Not Coach Rocker. That ass would never think something so… so…." Jamal stopped, seemingly at a loss for words.

"Idiotic." Billy supplied the word. "It was pretty stupid to think you wouldn't…. It's just that everybody wants to win, and you and Tully…."

"Gotta work together. I *know*. You shoulda heard Coach rip me a new one yesterday after practice. I think the only person he's madder at right now is Tully." He grimaced. "He don't like Tully."

"Can you do it?"

Jamal got up to check one of his machines, which had stopped spinning. He pulled the clothes out and stuffed them into a dryer, patting his pockets afterward.

"Motherfuckin'…."

Billy jumped up to lend him a quarter and knocked his forehead on one of the overhead pipes. The ringing blow had him staggering dizzily.

Suddenly Jamal's arm was around his shoulders. "I told ya to watch those pipes. Sit down before you hit your head again." He guided Billy into a chair. Fuddled as much by the warm weight of Jamal's arm as by his throbbing forehead, Billy was sorry when Jamal's arm fell away. Jamal peered into his eyes. "You with me, Grandpa? I need to call for help?"

"Fuck, that hurt."

Jamal seemed to relax a little. He chuckled again, the same warm rumble he'd produced before. "Now when you report back, you can tell 'em you took one for the team."

"They're gonna think you punched me." Billy started to laugh but stopped when it made his head throb. "Ouch."

The buzzer on one of Billy's washers went off, indicating that his load was done. He started to get up, but Jamal put a hand on his shoulder and held him down. "Sit still. I'll get it."

Jamal snagged an empty laundry basket and began removing the clothes from the washer. Billy watched, admiring the high tight globes of Jamal's ass, his cock chubbing at the sight. Jamal carried the basket over to the dryer next to his own and stopped suddenly.

"Shit, I forgot. I left the rest of my quarters up—"

"I got plenty." Billy retrieved a handful from his pocket and dumped them on the table.

"I'll pay you back."

"No worries."

Jamal slid quarters in his dryer and Billy's. "You want I throw another load into that washer? We don't wanna disappoint your customers, do we?"

"I got it." Billy jumped up, just missing the same pipe.

"Fuck, Grandpa, you *tryin'* to hurt yourself?"

Jamal watched this time as Billy loaded the washer. "I chose Hoosier State to play with Tully."

The bald statement caught Billy by surprise. He spun around to look at Jamal. Jamal leaned back in his chair, his expression bland, but Billy could see the tension in his broad shoulders.

"It was good at first. We weren't friends, but we was—were *teammates*. Then we started winning and the press started sniffing around him like a pack of dogs and he's got the bone. Maybe it was the pressure, or maybe he just likes the attention, but that's when he started getting wild. Now he—it's like he's from another planet and I don't know what the fuck he's gonna do next."

"For what it's worth, I don't think he means to—"

"You're shittin' me. He loves to get my goat."

"More than he loves to win?"

"Fuck do I know? You saw what he did to me."

"Come on, man. It's not like you ain't been messing with him. Pretending you don't see him. How do you think that feels? Especially for somebody who thrives on attention, right? Exactly what you won't give him."

Jamal didn't say anything, but Billy could see wheels turning. Maybe he'd gotten through. He returned to the table and put his feet up on a chair.

When Jamal spoke again, the quiet, almost plaintive, quality of the request hit Billy harder than yelling would have. "We talk about something other than Tully fucking Sam?"

BILLY HAD to be homesick, judging from the deluge of e-mails flooding Jonah's inbox. Jonah answered as many as he could, but it was hard to keep his replies light when he wanted to ask whether Billy had a gaping hole in his chest too. Billy texted him as well, but those brief exchanges were easier to keep to lighthearted banter. The e-mails threatened to overwhelm, because Billy seemed to pour out his thoughts and feelings without a filter. Jonah couldn't process his own feelings fast enough to respond in kind. His head felt clogged with molasses. Only at the piano did his head clear and his hands clearly express what his words could not.

In the afternoon Jonah often rehearsed with the Rascals—or whichever Avakians were in town. Davoud even persuaded him to let Aida give him music lessons. By the end of the day, he was beat, but he treasured the minutes he spent each night before bed reading Billy's account of his day, even if he couldn't always respond. Always, he hungered to see Billy, and he often imagined what it would be like to kiss him again.

In the weeks following their pairing in history class, he and Tony met at the computer lab or the café to work on their history project. One afternoon he found himself spilling out his frustration to Tony in their usual booth.

"I miss him so much. I thought if we stopped seeing each other, he would, you know, move on or something, and then I would have to get over him. But he keeps sending me these e-mails and... and I've got to find a way to see him. It's not fair! Why did he have to be a year older than me? If we were the same age, we would still be in Jazz Ensemble together and I could hang out with him...." Too late, Jonah realized what he was saying and who he was saying it to.

"Instead of hanging out with me. Yeah, I get that." Tony slammed his laptop shut and started to shove papers into his pack.

"Wait, Tony. I didn't mean it that way. I *like* hanging out with you. I just—"

"Yeah, well, maybe I'm not liking it so much anymore."

Jonah rested a hand on Tony's laptop to keep him from putting it away. "I'm sorry. Please, Tony, I don't want you to go."

Tony slumped back onto the red vinyl bench, staring at Jonah. "Maybe this friendship idea wasn't such a good idea."

Jonah withdrew his hand.

Tony looked away.

"I'm sorry. I can't."

"Yeah, you said that."

"Last year before I came out, I was getting hassled by these seniors. Billy was the only guy who would talk to me. He made me feel... almost normal."

"So you feel, what? Grateful?"

"It's more than that."

Tony looked away. "I heard Antony's parents are getting divorced."

"You know about Antony?"

"It was all over the school after you kicked his ass in the boy's room."

"I didn't kick his ass, he slipped and fell."

Tony laughed. "Sure he did. That's why Mr. Paulson had to drag you off him."

"I'm not proud of that."

"Maybe you should be. The asshole deserved it. You weren't the only one, you know."

That caught Jonah's attention. He tried to catch Tony's gaze, but Tony seemed to be more interested in watching Kalisha wipe down the counter.

"I don't—"

Tony's eyes came back to meet Jonah's. "You think it's easy being the only gay on the swim team? Some guys still act like I'm gonna jump them in the shower or something, even though—" He waved his arms. "—they *know* me. I've been on the team for *years*. And then there are the guys who whisper stuff when the coach isn't around or put stupid shit in my locker."

"You never said—"

"You never asked, either."

"Shit! You always seem so confident. Like you've got it together. It didn't occur to me."

Tony thumped his chest ironically. "That's me, armor-plated."

"I'll listen. I mean, if you want to—"

"Thanks, but no thanks."

"What do you want, then?"

Tony stared at him, his face twitching. Jonah became aware that Tony's leg was pressed up against his own under the table. His dick swelled in response. *Oh.* He moved his leg away.

"I can't, Tony. Billy and I…."

Tony resumed gathering his stuff. "I gotta go."

Jonah stayed in the booth for a while after Tony had gone, staring at his laptop but seeing Tony's and Billy's faces in a never-ending loop. He had to see Billy. He had to know if Billy felt the same way he did.

CHAPTER 4

Stats

~~Girls I'm pretty sure wanted to kiss me. 5 12 10,012~~
Girls I've kissed: 3
Boys I've kissed: 1

If Dad ever finds this, I'm dead—like broken spine, belly slit, and guts slithering out all over the floor dead.

Boys who've dumped me: 1
Boys I would kneel on the floor and worship as a basketball god: 1
Stupid nicknames: 2
Public boners: 1
Teammates I'd like to knock some sense into: 2
Different kinds of underwear worn by guys on my floor: 5
Basketball players on the down-low: 1

STATE'S FIRST game of the season was part of an exhibition tournament scheduled for a Saturday in early October, and if the excitement of playing his first college basketball game wasn't enough for Billy, there was also Jonah's visit to anticipate. They would see each other for the first time since he'd left for basketball camp.

"Would you quit that!" Mike batted Billy's leg irritably. "You always this nervous before a game?"

Mike was still cool toward Billy, but he'd followed Billy onto the bus for the ride to Ball Hoosier State and slumped down into the aisle seat next to him as though they'd always ridden together.

"No. Yes. I mean, things were different in high school. My dad could be a real jerk if we lost, but I didn't—"

"Don't strain yourself, Grandpa. I didn't realize it was a hard question."

Mike slid down and jammed his knees against the seat-back ahead of him. "There was this guy I knew in high school who hurled before every game, regular as clockwork. It was weird because he was fine as soon as he lost his lunch."

"Thanks, that's a big help, making me think about vomit."

Mike glanced over, concern evident on his face. "You're not really going to throw up, are you?" Then he ruined the effect by adding, "Give me some warning, would you?"

"No, I'm not gonna puke, jerk. I just wanna win."

Mike looked away. "Not much chance of that."

"Tully's been better lately, and Jamal knows what he's gotta do."

"Yeah?" Mike gazed out at the passing countryside, which consisted mainly of flat fields and corrugated farm buildings. "Wait until you see what happens if we start winning again."

"What do you mean?"

"How do you think Tully's going to react when the press are shoving mics into his face after every game? When he needs to blow off steam? What's that going to look like?"

"It's not fair, you know. Guys do stupid stuff all the time. Just because Tully's not particular who he dances with, there's something wrong with him?"

"I didn't say that. But Jamal's going to lose his shit if Tully pulls anything and—"

The rare swear word from Mike caught Billy's attention.

"Jamal's not who you think he is."

Maybe it was the vehemence in Billy's voice, but Mike turned his head to look Billy in the face. "You're a funny one to defend him."

Billy couldn't help glancing around the bus to see if anyone was listening, but most of their teammates were either sleeping or talking quietly to friends. After his laundry date with Jamal, Billy had been reluctant to report the specifics of their conversation. Even though Jamal had sussed out his plan and presumably expected Billy to report back to his friends, Billy felt like talking would be a betrayal. So he'd told Otter and his roommates only that he was sure Jamal would do the right thing. When Jason asked about the swollen lump on his forehead, Billy had explained about hitting his head on a low-hanging pipe. If anyone had questioned that, they'd not done so to his face.

"He's not a homophobe, if that's what you were expecting."

Mike turned away, his mouth tight.

"Have you heard him call anyone a faggot?"

"He called Tully a ho. Whatever."

"You've given me more shit about dancing with Tully than—"

"Would you give it a rest? I told you, I just want the team to *work*. If Jamal gets his head together and passes the ball to Tully, I'm fine with it. You and Tully can hump yourselves silly, for all I care."

"Jesus! Keep your voice down," Billy whispered. "I don't want to fuck Tully."

"Then he can fuck you."

"That's not—Jesus Christ, Mike."

"I know what I saw."

"I don't go for everyone who turns me on. I'm not like Jason."

"That's different."

Billy felt his stomach clench. "How so? Jason's got a new girl every Friday night, and you don't give him any shit."

"That's different," Mike repeated.

"How is that different?"

"He's—I don't have to share a locker room with him."

Billy felt like he'd been punched in the gut. "That makes no sense." He had to get away from Mike. He shoved Mike's legs. "Let me out."

"Where are you going?"

"Just let me out, will you?" He shoved Mike's knee.

"Quit that. Where are you going to go?"

"Move, asshole, or I'm going to climb over you."

"No! There aren't any more seats. Just cool it."

"*Get the fuck out of my way!*" Billy braced himself and shoved hard, sending Mike sprawling into the aisle of the bus.

"What'd you do that for?"

"What's going on back there?" Digger called from the front of the bus.

Mike scrambled to his feet. "Nothing."

Billy shoved past and staggered toward the front of the bus. Unfortunately, it seemed like Mike might be right, the only free seat he could see was with a member of the coaching staff he didn't know.

"Sit down, Billy," said Digger, "and stop fucking around."

Billy hesitated, already feeling stupid for letting things get out of hand with Mike.

A head popped up ahead of him. "Over here, Grandpa." It was Jamal, who'd been sprawled across two seats, apparently asleep, when Billy had passed him getting on.

Billy settled into the offered seat with relief.

"You and Whirlpool got a problem?" asked Jamal.

Billy's belly clenched as he thought about Mike's comment about the locker room. "Maybe."

"People say stupid shit all the time without meaning it."

That was the problem. Billy was pretty sure it was the truth that had slipped out, whether or not Mike had meant for it to.

"You want me to talk to him?"

Billy stared at Jamal, surprised at the offer. Jamal looked back steadily, his brown eyes warm. Every time Billy talked to Jamal, he ended up more confused. He felt like he'd taken a seat in the bleachers and found himself surrounded by the opposing team's fans when they stood to cheer a score.

"No, it's okay."

"You know I got your back."

When had he and Jamal become friends? He'd had the same feeling when he and Jonah had talked for the first time, and he'd realized that he didn't just feel sorry for the guy because he was getting hassled, but he genuinely liked him.

"Likewise. You think we can win today?"

Jamal shrugged coolly. "We got it in the bag."

JAMAL'S CONFIDENCE might have been mostly braggadocio on the bus, but win they did, by six points. Spurred by a crowd of enthusiastic fans, Jamal played with an intensity Billy hadn't seen on the practice court. More importantly, Jamal acted like Tully was a teammate instead of an enemy. Billy even got to play in the second half when they were ahead, and Coach Rocker gave Jamal a break. Billy didn't make any points, but he kept the ball moving where it was needed and sent a couple of passes in Tully's direction that won him assists. He wanted to protest when the coach put Jamal back in, but was amazed to find he'd been in for most of the half.

If Billy's teammates wondered why Billy kept twisting around to look into the seats, they didn't ask. Jonah had promised to be there, but Billy didn't figure out where his friend was until he stopped moving for a free throw and caught a glimpse of a short, tow-headed figure jumping up and down in front of his seat and waving like a ten-year-old at a Fourth of July parade. He looked away quickly, afraid of the distraction. But for the rest of the game, he felt Jonah's eyes on him like a hand on the back of his neck.

Jonah texted while Billy packed his duffle in the locker room. At the bonk from his phone, he trotted into a corner to get away from the happy noise of his victorious teammates.

Jonah Winfield: He shoots, he scores. Congrats
Billy Preston: Thks
Jonah Winfield: Meet 2 eat?

The team was scheduled to stay overnight in Muncie and drive home Sunday morning.

"Hey, Grandpa, we're gonna get some food. You coming with?" Tully marshaled a milling group of players toward the door. A few steps to one side, Mike watched Billy silently, his hands stuffed in the back pockets of his jeans. He looked away when Billy caught his eye.

"Nah, man, my family's here. I promised Mom dinner." The lie fell from his lips naturally, as though he'd planned it in advance. The truth was his dad had announced they would drive up for the first regular season game in November. He didn't see the point of making the drive for an exhibition game that didn't even count toward the season.

"Well hell, boy, that dog won't hunt," said Tully, rolling his hips suggestively. "I'll miss you."

Billy turned to go and nearly ran into Jamal and Otter. Jamal glared at Tully, lips pressed together in disapproval. He spun and slammed his palm into the crash bar of the door. Otter followed, a resigned slump to his shoulders.

A bonking sound from Billy's phone reminded him that he hadn't yet responded to Jonah's text.

Jonah Winfield: ?
Billy Preston: Hilton lobby 10 m
Jonah Winfield: C U

The team roomed at the Comfort Inn, not the Hilton. But the Hilton was nearby, a few blocks away. Billy figured if his family had come, they might have stayed there, so it wouldn't look odd for him to hang out there. Eight minutes later, he bounced his legs impatiently in a leather chair in the lounge part of the Hilton lobby. The potted plant-bordered space was hideously decorated in the colors of Ball State University, with red carpet, angular white armchairs, and chrome and glass coffee tables.

A businessman in a gray suit with a carry-on between his feet caught Billy's attention and gestured at the furnishings. "I guess this place gets a lot of Ball State business. Still… wow."

Billy laughed. "I'm lucky our team colors don't lend themselves to this kind of travesty."

The man took in Billy's jean-covered legs. "Let me guess… basketball? You played Ball State today? I didn't realize the season had started."

"Exhibition game."

"Ah." The man nodded, distracted by the arrival of an airport shuttle. "There's my ride. Good luck to you." He nodded and lit out for the revolving doors, his carry-on dragging through the carpet like a reluctant puppy.

A minute later, Jonah pushed in through the revolving door. He looked different than Billy remembered: taller or something. He was still lightly built and shorter than average, but he seemed older, more confident. He strode to the center of the lobby and looked around, a tentative smile on his face. Billy jumped up, and Jonah broke into a high wattage grin that took Billy's breath away.

"Jonah! Man, you look great." Uncertain whether to go for a hug or handshake, Billy opted for the latter and held out his hand. Jonah had dropped him, after all. Whatever they were to each other, they weren't boyfriends.

Jonah's face fell, but he clasped Billy hand firmly. "It's so good to see you."

Billy would have killed to make Jonah's grin come back. Jonah's hand was as he remembered: thin, but surprisingly strong. It was probably the piano playing that gave him the muscle.

"How was the trip up? You driving yet?"

"Nah, Rascal gave me a ride. He's waiting in the car."

"Oh… cool." Billy tried not to show his dismay. "It'll be great to see him." He'd really wanted to talk with Jonah in private.

Jonah laughed out loud, the merry sound causing the clerk at the desk to look up and raise her eyebrows.

"Don't worry, Rascal's gonna drop us off and head back to the hotel. I told him he'd be bored with our sports talk. We can take a taxi back."

"It'll be good to say hello."

Jonah laughed again. "Come on, big boy, I'm hungry."

RASCAL DROPPED them off at a restaurant that specialized in organic local produce and grass-fed meat. The decor was utilitarian, but the food was not. Jonah's Vietnamese Pho soup brimmed with fresh-cut leafy greens. Billy went for a pork belly sandwich with fruit on the side. He wanted fries, but listened to Jonah's order and sighed. He was in training after all. The conversation was sparse until they'd demolished all but scraps. With his stomach pleasantly full, Billy's thoughts turned to a harder emptiness to fill.

"I missed you. E-mail and text messages aren't enough." Billy searched Jonah's face for any sign that he'd felt the same way.

Jonah produced a wobbly smile. "That's why we can't be boyfriends. You should be free to—" He took a breath. "—to be with someone when you need it."

Billy's belly went from comfortably full to bloated. "I don't want someone else," he said tightly. "Did I do something to give you the impression I *wanted* to be free?" He knew his bitterness about Jonah's Dear John e-mail colored his words, but he couldn't help it. "You never asked what *I* wanted."

His response avoided the live wire issue of whether he could be attracted to someone else. Tully had left him no room for self-delusion there.

Jonah lost any pretense of a smile. "I didn't need to ask. You're in college on a basketball scholarship, which makes you a public person. I wasn't the only one watching you this afternoon. You can't afford to be seen hanging out with a high school student, much less a guy, and you know it. And if you don't believe me, I'm sure your coach will be happy to explain the facts of life to you."

"I don't need you to explain my situation," Billy hissed.

"Then don't pretend this can work."

"So why are you here?"

Jonah dropped his gaze to his hands, which were clenched together on the table before him. "Because I missed you too, and I'm too fucking weak to let go."

"Jesus, Jonah, what do you want from me?"

"Nothing," Jonah whispered bleakly. "I just wanted to see you."

The pain in Jonah's voice so mirrored his own that Billy had to work to keep his composure.

"How did you persuade Rascal to give you a ride up here, anyway?"

"I begged shamelessly. And I told him I had to see you in person to apologize for dumping you via e-mail."

"So are you?"

"Am I what?"

"Apologizing for dumping me via e-mail."

Tears glinted in Jonah's wide eyes. "Yeah, I am. It was wrong, but I didn't dare see you because I thought I wouldn't be able to go through with it in person."

"I wish you hadn't."

"I had to. You'll meet someone, and I can't—couldn't handle that."

Jonah's change of tense wasn't lost on Billy. But Billy thought Jonah wasn't nearly as committed to not being boyfriends as his words suggested. He also knew how stubborn Jonah could be. If he confronted him about his feelings, Jonah would simply close up and retreat to his music and his adopted family in Glen Falls. But if Billy waited, if he showed Jonah that he *could* wait, Jonah might come around.

"Okay, Jonah. Have it your way. I have to get back to the hotel. We have a 10:00 p.m. curfew tonight because we're playing again tomorrow."

"That's earlier than my mom's."

"Yeah, well, we're athletes. We have to get our beauty sleep."

"Can I walk you back to the Comfort Inn? I can catch a cab from there." Jonah's tone was diffident. Mad as he was, it still pained Billy to hear Jonah sound that way with him.

"Sure." Billy signaled for the waiter to bring their check.

Billy kept his thoughts to himself on the short walk back. Jonah shoved his hands firmly into his pockets as though to restrain them. Billy had to school his own body to maintain a suitable distance and to keep from outpacing Jonah. He felt as though the two of them were attached by an invisible rubber band that kept pulling them together until their differing statures and uncertain relationship stretched them apart again.

AFTER THE team returned from Muncie, Billy couldn't concentrate on basketball or coursework. He'd told his mother before coming to Hoosier State that he felt like he was living someone else's life. The truth was less complicated. He felt lost. In the past, he'd never really had to think about the future. Planning his career, his life, all that had been his dad's province. Billy'd had little say in the matter. Now, with his father a three-hour drive away, Billy found himself questioning everything he'd assumed was set in concrete. He wanted to talk to Jonah, but Jonah had stopped responding to his messages.

He felt like he'd gotten on a tethered balloon ride at the zoo, only the balloon had broken loose and he drifted helplessly away from everything familiar.

Billy's roommates veered between welcome distraction and depressing distance. Monday morning, Mike was civil and even invited Billy to join him for breakfast in the dining hall, but the connection they'd shared at the start of the term was gone, and their conversation was stilted. That night, Jason entertained them with a convoluted tale of girlfriend swapping among his teammates. Billy was grateful for the distraction, but the content of the story added to his alienation.

Usually, when he was down, he turned to basketball, the game transformed from entertainment and career goal to balm for his nervous agitation. On Wednesday, he caught both Jamal and Tully watching him, as though he played some part in their drama, only he'd misplaced the script and didn't know his lines. Jamal seemed to have decided he and Billy were friends, and he more than once patted Billy on the arm or threw an arm around his shoulders like an older brother. Jamal's attention and warmth calmed Billy, and he responded by throwing himself into Rocker's drills.

Thursday night, Jonah again refused his call, so he went to the rec center after dinner to find a free court and shoot some baskets to blow off steam. He lofted one after another from the free throw line, trying unsuccessfully to emulate Mike's Zen calm, but he missed as many as he hit.

"Whoa there, Grandpa. You better get your head screwed on before you break something."

Billy spun around. Jamal leaned nonchalantly against the court door. "I didn't see you come in."

Jamal grinned and let his South Side Chicago out. "Maybe you be needin' glasses or somethin', old man, 'cause it don't look like you seein' the basket too good."

"Damn." Billy sank to the floor where he was in the middle of the court.

Jamal's smile faded. "You okay, man?"

"I'm fine. Just beat." There was no way Billy could tell Jamal about Jonah. He had nobody to talk to. It took all the self-possession he could muster to shrug like it didn't matter.

Jamal loped out and dropped onto the polished hardwood next to Billy, then crossed his legs Indian style. "You want to tell me what's going on?"

"Can't."

"I been here three years now. Not much I ain't heard. Too early for you to be flunking out. Somebody die?"

"No."

"Okay, apart from that sad sad display you was putting on a minute ago, you been playing okay, so it ain't that. You know what that leaves."

Billy pulled up his legs and hugged his knees to his chest.

"Girlfriend asking for pickles with her ice cream?"

Billy laughed. Judging from the frequency of that question, he was beginning to wonder if he shouldn't check the bleachers for a row of miniature teammates next game.

"No way." But his voice cracked.

"She dump you?"

Billy didn't answer.

"I know how you feel."

"No, you fucking don't." Billy glanced up.

"Maybe I know better than you think." Jamal's expression had lost none of its warmth, but his tone was bleak.

Some skinny white guy Billy had never seen before stuck his head in the door. "You guys gonna shoot hoops or what?"

"This court is reserved for the basketball team," said Jamal without looking.

"Yeah, I know, but the guys usually let us use it if they're not."

Jamal shrugged. "You wanna come to my room and keep me company for a while? I got the place to myself. Otter's with his girlfriend."

Billy knew he should say no. The danger he would use the wrong pronoun or blurt something stupid was too great, but he wanted someplace quiet to get himself together before he went home to face Mike and Jason again.

"Come on, I'll even spot you a beer."

"I shouldn't. I'm not even—"

"Come off it, Grandpa. One beer ain't gonna kill you."

Jamal dragged Billy to his feet and turned to the skinny guy at the door. "Seems you're in luck."

"Hey, thanks!"

Billy followed Jamal to his dorm. "Maybe I should pick up some laundry." As jokes went, it was pretty lame, but Jamal chuckled anyway.

"My mama took in laundry when I was little. I saw enough dirty shorts to last a lifetime."

"Shit. I didn't know."

"Nah, it's funny. You and that giant bag. I'd never of known if you hadn't brought everyone else's shit."

By the time they reached Jamal's dorm, Billy felt more in control of his feelings. Jamal shoved open the door and ushered him into the double he shared with Otter. The suite consisted of a small living room/kitchen, a single bathroom, and two tiny bedrooms. They'd somehow levered a giant couch into the tiny room to face the wall where they'd mounted a large flat-screen television.

"How do you get any work done?" Billy asked, nodding at the flat-screen.

Jamal grinned. "Got to watch the games, man. Know thine enemy, right? Take a load off." He went over to the window and pulled up the sash. A row of beer cans nestled between the storm and inner windows. He tossed one to Billy. "Relax, it's just us chickens here."

"Thanks."

"You wanna watch something?" Jamal asked, plopping down on the couch and grabbing a remote from the crate that sat in front of it. "I got ESPN."

"Our setup sucks compared to this."

Jamal shrugged. "You get little more court time, and the alumns gonna wanna set you up." He seemed oblivious to the fact that more court time for Billy would probably mean less for him.

"You mean, like recruiters."

"Nah, man, fans, old guys went here before they went gray. You know, businessmen who like to see the team win. They'll tell you it's good for business, but—hey, you haven't opened your beer." Jamal grabbed the can from Billy and popped the top before handing it back. "Drink up."

Billy sipped, not wanting to be unsociable. "Aren't the Bulls and Celtics playing tonight? Can you get the game?"

"Damn straight." Jamal stabbed at the remote until he found the game.

They settled in to watch. Jamal got up a couple of times for more beer, so the can in Billy's hand never seemed to empty. It was like there were two Billys in the room, the guy who was getting quietly and obliviously drunk watching a basketball game, and the guy who knew Jamal wanted him drunk and was okay with that. The one who was paying attention noticed that each time Jamal got up for beer, he sat down a little closer until his shoulder pressed Billy's. The other Billy just watched the game and laughed at the announcer's stupid comments and didn't notice at all when Jamal's arm snuck over the back of the couch and landed with warm weight on his shoulders. Nor did he care when Jamal's muscular thigh pressed against his own longer leaner one, nor when Jamal's hand dropped into the crease between Billy's hip and thigh and rested there, as though that was a place where guys touched all the time, instead of a place that seemed constructed all of nerves instead of muscle and bone. Nor did he care when Jamal's touch sent twin charges up to the tips of his ears and bottoms of his feet and then back again to join forces at his cock—which was anything but oblivious to the goings-on. The Billy that watched said to the other Billy, *I thought so,* and then shut up, because Jamal lifted his hand and placed it directly on Billy's cock, which responded by trying to push up under the waistband of his shorts. And then Billy was only in one place, and that was drunk and in Jamal's suite, and Jamal was going to jerk him off or maybe suck him, and if any of the Billys who had ever been thought that was a bad idea, they said nothing.

When Billy failed to protest or say anything at all about the fact that Jamal's hand was cupping his cock, Jamal took that to mean things were proceeding in a mutually satisfactory direction, and he began to knead.

"Feels like you could use a little more room," Jamal murmured. He knelt on the floor between Billy's knees and reached for Billy's belt buckle. "Relax, man. I'll take care of you." He unbuckled Billy's belt and unzipped his fly. He cupped Billy's cock again through the strained fabric of his briefs. "Gonna get these out of the way, huh? Then you'll feel good."

Jamal lifted the waistband of Billy's briefs and pulled it down over the head of Billy's cock, which responded by springing up and outward. "That's better, ain't it, out in the cool." Jamal reached down to unzip his own fly and fished out his own thick, veiny cock. "Whole lot better."

When he thought about it later, Billy concluded the difference between what it felt like to touch himself and what it felt like when Jamal touched him was pretty amazing. Guys on his high school basketball team had insisted it was different when someone else did you, but he'd expected that was mostly bravado-fueled exaggeration. But when Jamal had placed his nose in the curly hair at the base of Billy's cock and sniffed, and his rough unshaven cheek brushed sensitive skin, Billy had nearly shot his load right then. Not long after, Jamal put his mouth around Billy's dick and sucked nearly its whole length into his throat, and Billy, gripping the cushions on either side of him for dear life, grunted a word of warning and shot his load in a long series of pumps that seemed to expel liquefied muscle from his thighs and belly along with the contents of his prostate, balls, and befuddled brain. Jamal hummed, unfazed, and merely swallowed repeatedly until Billy was done. Then the stimulation got to be more than Billy could handle and he yelled. Jamal relaxed his jaw and let cum slide out of his mouth and down Billy's shaft to soak into the nest of wiry hairs there.

Jamal rested his head on Billy's thigh. "You okay?"

"Guh." Billy tried to remember how to speak. "I'm good." It occurred to him that their activity had been one-sided. "Do you want me to…?"

"Been there, done that." Jamal pushed himself slowly to his feet. His T-shirt was spattered with cum. That was a revelation, that someone could get off just from giving a blow job. Billy'd always sort of thought of blow jobs as a duty someone performed in preparation for, or perhaps in thanks for, the main event. Now he wasn't certain what the main event was, at least when it involved two guys.

Jamal went into the bathroom. Billy heard him turn on the taps. After a moment he came out bare-chested and tossed a wet washcloth at Billy.

"Wipe off. It stinks like jizz in here."

Billy cleaned himself as well as he could under the circumstances, zipped up his jeans, and folded the washcloth into squares, unsure what to do with it.

"Toss it in the sink." Jamal jerked his head toward the bathroom. He picked up the TV remote from where it had fallen to the floor and dropped into the lawn chair that was the only other piece of furniture in the room. The physical intimacy Billy had enjoyed prior to the blow job was apparently done for the evening. Billy struggled to his feet, swaying, suddenly aware he'd had too much to drink. Jamal clicked the remote through several stations. Billy was uncertain what Jamal expected of him. He'd have liked to kiss or at least sit together awhile, even if it was impractical for him to stay the night. But Jamal's warmth had evaporated. He seemed more interested in the TV than Billy. Had Billy done something wrong?

Jamal stretched and glanced up. "Bulls won."

It finally dawned on Billy what Jamal expected: pretend it hadn't happened.

"Gotta go. Early clath—class tomorrow."

Jamal focused on the TV. "Catch you later."

Billy staggered to the bathroom and dropped the damp washcloth into the sink. He turned on the taps and splashed water onto his face. When he closed his eyes, the spins hit, and he gripped the sink tightly to stay upright. If he was going to be sick, he didn't want Jamal to see it. He rushed from the bathroom. Jamal didn't look up as Billy left.

"Hey, Grandpa, you all right? Lookin' a bit pale." Jackson, the team's power forward, who also lived in Johnson House grabbed his arm. He carried a heavy pack, like he'd just come from the library.

"Gotta home."

"Think you can find your way there okay?"

"Brooth—Brookhouse."

"Hold up a sec, cowboy. Here, lean on this." Jackson dropped his pack and snagged a plastic chair someone had left out in the hall. Beset by another bout of the spins, Billy let Jackson guide his hand to the chair, and he gripped it with both hands. Jackson trotted down the hall and stuck his head into a room. "Hey, Tully, one of your homies needs an escort."

Billy didn't hear the answer. Jackson disappeared into the room, pulling the door shut behind him. After a long wait, during which Billy swallowed bile more than once, the door opened and Jackson returned, Tully in tow.

Tully peered into his face. "Who been feeding you garbage, puppy dog?"

Jackson shouldered his pack. "You got him?"

Tully put an arm around Billy's shoulder. "Yeah, I got him."

The walk back to their dorm took twice as long as normal, because Billy stopped twice to throw up. The first time, they'd barely made it out of Jamal's dorm. Billy lurched to some bushes beside the concrete path and hurled into the leaves. Tully steadied him with an arm around his shoulders until he finished. The second time, Billy found a garbage can chained to a lamppost outside their dorm. Staring into the can's fetid depths, he thought about what he'd done, about what it could mean to the team and to his relationship with Jonah. Maybe Jamal was right to treat him like he did, because he was garbage.

"Hey, there." Tully shifted his arm and rubbed Billy's back. "Everyone gets sick. It's like a rule. Freshman gotta get falling down drunk and blow chunks. Nothing to cry about."

Billy spat bile and wiped tears from his eyes with the back of his hand because his fingers were disgusting.

"You didn't do this by your lonesome. Who you visiting, Grandpa?" Tully seemed to be speaking more to himself than Billy. "The guys I seen you hang with live there are Otter and Jamal, and Otter wouldn't...."

If Billy had been less drunk, he might have tried to head Tully off. Instead, he listened tiredly to the roar of the approaching train, unable to even try to get off the tracks.

Tully stopped rubbing his back. "Holy Jesus fuck." He leaned over to look into Billy's face. "You didn't let Jamal?"

Billy might have winced or something.

"That fucking bastard. He didn't force—"

"I thought he liked me."

"Oh, baby. So did I. So did I."

"COME ON, Tony!" Jonah smashed the phone to his ear, as if that would express the urgency of the situation. "The project is due Monday. We've gotta finish the website." He and Tony hadn't worked together for days. Whatever their issues, the project was still worth a third of their grade for the term.

Jonah heard Tony sigh over the phone. "My mom's gonna kill me if I fail history."

"You wanna meet at the café?"

"Can we do it somewhere else? I feel like everyone's watching us there."

That was news to Jonah. Until their last meeting, Tony had always seemed so confident in public. Maybe it really was all show—Tony'd called it his armor-plating.

"You could come over to the Music Box."

"What time?"

Jonah suppressed a flash of uneasiness at the eagerness in Tony's tone. "Four? I'll ask Davoud if you can stay for dinner."

"Davoud Avakian?"

"I usually eat with Davoud and Paul when Mom and Rascal are out of town."

Tony was silent for a second. "Him and Mr. G, they're like a real couple, aren't they? I mean, you've mentioned them before, but I didn't think of them eating together and everything."

Jonah tried to keep the impatience from his voice. "Of course they eat together."

"I've never met a real gay couple before."

"Holy Christ! They're just people. You can't come over if you're gonna treat them like an exhibit at the zoo."

"Keep your pants on. I think Mr. G is rad, even though I only had one class with him."

"Okay, so I'll see you at four."

"See you."

WHEN THE front door intercom buzzed at 3:58, Jonah jumped to answer it. "Yeah?"

"It's Tony."

"I'll buzz you in. Use the second elevator. Close the cage before you press the button for two."

When the elevator creaked to a halt at the second floor, Jonah waited for Tony to slide open the cage. "Welcome to the Music Box."

"This place is cool. I didn't realize it was so old."

"It was a hotel in the '20s before Davoud's family bought it. Come on, we can work in Davoud and Paul's place until dinner."

"Huh?"

"Davoud's got a better couch."

Tony's jet black eyebrows slid up, and he grinned. "I like the sound of that."

"You're relentless, you know that."

Tony smirked. "Yup."

"Come on. It's this way."

After he got Tony settled in the velvet monstrosity, Jonah carefully lowered himself into the far end.

Tony rolled his eyes. "I'm not gonna bite you—although I wouldn't mind a nip here or there."

"We're here to work. And Davoud will be home to start dinner soon." They had an hour and a half until Davoud closed the music store, but Tony didn't need to know that.

"Whatever."

The next hour was all business, although Jonah noticed that Tony gradually inched closer on the sofa. But since they had their computers on their laps, and the talk was all about the website, Jonah figured it was okay. Tony found a cache of interesting photographs on a history website, and they liberally sprinkled them throughout the essays they'd written. By five, the site was looking pretty slick.

Eventually Tony shut his laptop and leaned back. "It's in the bag. Are we not, like, the best team ever?" He raised a fist to bang against Jonah's.

Jonah felt himself grin in response to Tony's enthusiasm. He banged fists and then closed his laptop and set it on the coffee table. "Yay, team rainbow."

Suddenly Tony's arm was around his shoulders, and Jonah was at the receiving end of a noogie.

"Quit that." Jonah's protest sounded weak, even to his own ears. Tony's arms were warm and heavy on his neck. He squirmed around until he was lying on his back looking up at Tony's face. The naked desire there startled him, and he froze. Tony leaned over and kissed him on the lips. Tony's lips were warm and full, and for an instant Jonah responded, allowing Tony's tongue to caress his teeth. Then he realized what he was doing. High as the kiss ranked on his internal hotness scale, Tony wasn't the person Jonah dreamed of kissing. He rolled off the sofa and scrambled to his feet.

Tony slumped. "Shit."

Jonah trudged to the window and pretended to stare out so Tony couldn't see the tears in his eyes.

"Please don't say anything. I'll go."

"You don't have to." Why couldn't Tony just leave things as they were?

"Yeah, I do."

"Can't we just pretend it never happened?" Jonah said desperately. It wasn't like he had gay friends to spare. Jonah heard Tony put his laptop into his pack as he tracked the passing cars on Main Street.

"Maybe you can. I can't."

Jonah turned around. "I'm sorry."

Tony shook his head. "See you around."

Jonah heard the elevator cage crash closed before he let go and buried his face in the depths of the velvet monstrosity.

ON SATURDAY, Hoosier State played the first game of the regular season against the Belmont Bruins in Nashville. Billy's excitement at playing a team Coach Rocker expected them to beat was tempered by his feeling that he'd screwed up any chance of making friends on the team. He avoided Jamal and Mike in the days leading up to the game. His parents driving down to watch didn't improve his state of mind. His mom was going to ask about his classes, which he could handle, but his dad would want to talk basketball, and Billy didn't know what to say about his teammates. He might distract his dad with stats or talk of their opponents, but his mom would know something was wrong. The mess he'd made of his personal life was too raw to discuss. Of his roommates, only Jason would make a suitable topic. Their resident Lothario would be good for a laugh so long as Billy didn't provide too much detail. Altogether, Billy's college career was shaping up to be a total failure. And while he could usually confess his failures to Jonah, there was no way he could tell Jonah about the encounter with Jamal.

The team spent most of the day in travel to and from airports. They arrived in Nashville only a few hours before the game. To Billy's surprise, Mike sat next to him on the plane and bus, although he said little. Billy had expected Mike to request a different roommate after their blow-up on the bus to Muncie, but he hadn't done that.

Billy considered asking about it, but it felt safer to focus on basketball. He made believe he'd met Jamal, Tully, and Mike on the court for a pickup game.

They could have won if Tully and Jamal had maintained the same attitude. But Tully was back to his old tricks and annoyed or distracted Jamal every chance he got. Billy doubted anyone watching from the stands noticed. Tully's tricks were almost invisible unless you knew what to look for: a wink as Jamal set up for free throw, a pat on the butt that felt, judging from Jamal's flinch, more like a grope. Whether they understood the cause or not, everyone saw Jamal's distraction. They also saw his refusal to acknowledge Tully's presence on the court. Billy was pretty sure he understood Tully's anger at Jamal; he had his own reasons for disliking the guy. But Billy wanted to win more than he wanted revenge against Jamal, and he determined to play a clean professional game.

Coach Rocker reached a boil by the end of the half and sent Billy in to replace Jamal at the tip-off. Tully and Jamal's antipathy had bought them seven turnovers and a sucky percentage at the free throw line. Despite his irritation with Tully for getting him off the bench for the wrong reason, Billy played with rare focus. He gave up only two turnovers in the half, and gained a bunch of assists. He and Mike operated with the precision of a top-ranked pair at an ice skating competition. Mike's accuracy from beyond the three point line caught them up and nearly won them the game. Unfortunately, Tully and Jamal's feud had done too much damage, and Hoosier State lost the race from behind 87 to 89.

Despite the disappointing loss, Billy's teammates happily slapped Billy on the back and butt repeatedly on the way to the locker room. Wrapped up in the moment, Billy was shocked when a reporter thrust a microphone at him before he'd even wiped the sweat from his face.

"That was quite a show you put on in the second half, Billy. Do you think you'd have won if the coach had put you in for the first half?"

Billy froze, the microphone and the inflammatory question leaving him momentarily speechless. When he didn't answer, the reporter continued.

"White had seven turnovers in the first half. You had two."

"Jamal is a great basketball player. I'm sure Coach Rocker knows what he's doing. Mike did a great job today too."

"You mean Mike Brooks, the freshman shooting guard. He seemed to find his mark in the second half, when you were there to get the ball to him."

"But it wasn't his fault Jam—"

"There you have it. Billy Preston, the up-and-coming freshman point guard who nearly turned the game around for Hoosier State."

BILLY ESCAPED from the noise and commotion of the locker room and his still energized teammates and found his mom and dad waiting for him beyond the security gate.

"Billy, over here!"

Sighing inwardly, Billy trotted over to his parents, regretting already that he'd promised to let them take him out to dinner. His mother held out her arms, and he leaned down to lift her off her feet. He squeezed until she protested, and then let her down to coo over him for a minute before extracting himself to shake hands with his dad.

His dad started right in. "What the hell is wrong with Rocker? Jamal White couldn't hit the broad side of a barn. Do you know he made one in five free throws during the game?"

"I was there."

"White didn't play half the game you did, boy."

"It wasn't all his fault. Tully was—"

"Tully Sam? What does that flaming show-off have to do with it?"

Billy might as well have set the trap and stepped right in it. God, he had to learn to think before he spoke.

"Tully can be hard to get along with. He and Jamal don't—"

"Why are you defending him? You outplayed him. Rocker should have put you out there in the first half. If he had, Hoosier State would have won. You gotta learn to stand up for yourself, boy. Nobody's gonna do it if you don't."

"Dad, it's more complicated than that."

"What the hell is wrong with you? Why won't you admit you're the better player?"

By this time, the argument had taken on a surreal quality. Billy was granted a temporary reprieve while his dad negotiated the traffic getting out of the arena parking area. He took the opportunity to check his phone for e-mail or text messages. A text from Tully asked where he was. The guys were going out to a club later and Tully wanted him to meet them. While he thought about his answer, another text popped up.

Jonah Winfield: U shoulda seen ur face

It was the first message he'd gotten from Jonah since the exhibition tournament.

Billy Preston: U saw game?
Jonah Winfield: Close ur mouth next time
Billy Preston: ?
Jonah Winfield: On TV

They must have played that thing with the reporter.

Billy Preston: Surprised me
Jonah Winfield: Got that. So did a million others lol
Billy Preston: Did I say something stupid?
Jonah Winfield: Charmingly humble
Billy Preston: Didn't know what 2 say
Jonah Winfield: Where are u
Tulane Sampson: Where are u
Billy Preston to Tulane Sampson: With P U
Tulane Sampson: C u later?
Jonah Winfield: Can u meet
Mike Brooks: Thanks for compliment
Tulane Sampson: Party my room later
Billy Preston to Jonah Winfield: No thanks

"Shit!"
"Is that language really necessary?" said his mom from the front seat. "Who are you talking with?"
Billy started typing furiously with his thumbs. His phone pinged before he finished.

Billy Preston to Jonah Winfield: Sent 2 wrong person
Jonah Winfield: I want to see u
Billy Preston: Where are u

Billy Preston to Tulane Sampson: No thanks
Billy Preston to Mike Brooks: U deserved it

"Why does your phone keep making that noise?"
"Incoming texts."

Jonah Winfield: Nashville

"Holy shit!"
"Billy! What did I just say to you?"
"You don't complain when Dad says hell."
"I don't believe in Hell."
Billy glanced up. "But you believe in shit?"
His dad made a grunting sound suspiciously like a laugh.
"It's a reality I prefer not to hear about when I don't have to."

Tulane Sampson: Ur loss
Billy Preston to Jonah Winfield: With parents. Meet later?
Mike Brooks: Say hello to your parents

"Billy! I'm talking to you. I asked what you want to eat." His
mom sounded more amused than angry. "Don't your thumbs get tired?"
"What? No, my thumbs don't get tired. Anything's fine.
Someplace close. I'm starving."

Billy Preston to Jonah Winfield: Can't talk now
Billy Preston to Mike Brooks: Ok
Jonah Winfield: Sending address

Billy tapped the address and pulled up a map on his phone. The
address Jonah had sent was across town from the team's hotel. He'd
have to take a cab. But first he'd have to escape his parents. How in
hell had Jonah gotten down to Nashville? And what was he doing here?
Billy stared out the car window at the passing lights. It didn't matter,
did it? Billy knew he'd come whenever Jonah called.
"Billy! Your mother asked you a question."
"Sorry, Mom."
"Barbecue okay? Your dad googled a place at the hotel."

"Fine. Anything's good."

His mom twisted around in her seat. "You used to like barbecue. Is there something you'd prefer?"

"Barbecue's fine, Mom. Really. I'm just a little distracted."

"If you'd turn off that damn phone while you're talking to your mom, it would probably help," said his dad, glancing over his shoulder.

"Sorry, Dad."

"Is everything okay at school?" his mom asked.

"Sure, things are just a little more complicated than I expected."

"You know you can call anytime."

"Yeah, Mom. I know."

THE PLACE Jonah selected turned out to be a blues club with a restaurant and bar. They couldn't get into the bar because they were both underage, but no laws kept them from ordering a meal in the restaurant and listening to the music from there. When Billy yanked open the door, Jonah jumped up from a bench near the hostess station. Before he'd thought about it, Billy'd run over and grabbed Jonah in a hug. Jonah's compact form in his arms felt wonderful. He held on until Jonah started to squirm.

"Jesus, Billy. Somebody might—"

"I don't care," Billy whispered into the blond brush on Jonah's head.

The hostess cleared her throat. "You boys gonna eat or what?"

Billy wasn't really listening. "Huh?"

Jonah started to giggle. He escaped from Billy's arms and turned to the hostess. "My cousin and I haven't seen each other for a while."

The hostess, a middle-aged woman in a blond wig and heavy makeup, raised her eyebrows skeptically. "Bless your hearts. I'm sure y'all have lots to talk about. Your table is this way."

Billy motioned for Jonah to go ahead of him. The springy way Jonah walked on the balls of his feet when he was happy always made him look like he was suspended from an invisible bungee cord.

"Y'all enjoy yourselves," said the hostess, guiding them to a table near the railing that separated the bar from the restaurant. Their table had an unobstructed view of the small platform where a band was setting up. "The band will start a set soon." She handed them plastic-covered menus.

Jonah grinned at Billy excitedly, bouncing in his seat. "What do you think? I looked up the best places online. Everyone said the band here is really good."

"It's great, but what are you doing down here? I mean, it's great to see you. But—"

"You were surprised."

Billy wasn't sure whether he wanted to admit it or not. He opted for honesty. "Yeah, I was. You didn't answer my e-mails."

"I'm sorry. I kind of needed to get my head together."

"You haven't told me what you're doing here."

Jonah rolled his eyes like Billy had said something stupid. "I came to see you play, but I couldn't get a ticket, so I had to watch on the TV in my hotel room."

"But your mom wouldn't let you—"

"Everyone thinks I'm down here to audition at the Blair School of Music. It's part of Vanderbilt University. Actually, I *am* auditioning tomorrow, but that isn't really why I came."

"They bought that?"

"I think Paul knows something's up, but he didn't say anything to my mom or Rascal. It was pretty funny 'cause Rascal couldn't figure out what the hell I want to come to Vanderbilt for. I mean there's probably nothing wrong with their music program and all, but Tennessee? That had him really confused. The place is not exactly a bastion of gay pride."

Billy couldn't believe Jonah had planned the whole thing just to see him play.

Jonah laughed. "You really gotta stop leaving your mouth open like that. It makes you look like some kind of mouth breather."

Billy closed his mouth, his face warm.

A shaggy-haired, narrow-hipped young man in a black waiter's apron came over to their table, his gaze flicking curiously between them.

"You guys want something to drink before you order?"

Billy shook his head.

"The water's fine," said Jonah. "You ready to order?" he asked Billy.

Billy decided not to mention that he'd already had a full dinner of barbecued ribs, baked potato, and collard greens.

"I'll have the Caesar salad," said Jonah, barely glancing at the menu.

"Can I have an order of fries?" said Billy.

The waiter rolled his eyes. "You guys are killing me."

"Sorry," said Billy. "I'll have an ice tea too."

The waiter closed his eyes. "One Caesar salad, one order of fries, and one ice tea. Y'all sure I can't bring you anything else, like maybe some food?"

"No thank you," said Jonah politely.

The waiter rolled his eyes again and left.

Billy caught Jonah's attention. "Jonah, why are you really here?"

Jonah lost his grin. "I told you. I came to see you play."

Billy widened his eyes to a glare.

"Jesus fuck, give me a break with the fish eyes," said Jonah.

Billy stared until Jonah looked away. "Okay, so I met this guy."

Those weren't words Billy wanted—or expected—to hear. His stomach, always prone to fits of instability, staged a protest against the whole concept of food.

"Wait, it's not like that," said Jonah quickly. "Just listen for a second. I met a guy in my history class when we had to work together on this project, and he turned out to be really cool."

Whatever Jonah thought he was doing, it wasn't helping Billy's digestion. A series of thumps and clicks announced the return of the band to the stage. He turned his chair to watch so Jonah wouldn't see his expression.

"Okay, I better say this fast before your head explodes or something. Tony—that's his name—is really cool and it turns out he's gay, too, and kinda hot. And he kissed me."

Jonah stopped, apparently waiting for Billy's reaction. Billy risked a glance. Jonah had this kind of hopeful smile on his face like he'd said something good. Billy replayed the words in his head.

"Maybe I'm stupid, but I'm not sure what you're telling me."

"So Tony kissed me—"

"Not any better the second time."

"And he was pretty hot."

"Also not better the second time."

A chord from the band crashed from the speakers on either side of the bandstand. The band broke into a bluesy rendition of an old country song Billy recognized without knowing either the name or the original artist.

Jonah raised his voice to yell. "He was a good kisser."

Reanimated barbecued ribs tried to escape Billy's stomach. He swallowed acid hastily. He and Jonah had only kissed once last year, and he knew it hadn't been anything to write home about. Jonah had caught him by surprise, and he hadn't been ready to deal with the possibility that he liked boys yet. He'd run away before they'd had a chance to try again.

"But I stopped him, because he wasn't you."

Billy's stomach unclenched slightly.

Jonah continued yelling. "I wanted it to be *you*. I want to kiss *you*."

Billy gulped, trying to get the contents of his stomach back where they were supposed to be. Jonah wanted to kiss him. He wondered fleetingly whether Jonah's revelation meant he should tell Jonah about his encounter with Jamal. *Fuck no, you're not that stupid.* That mistake was never, ever going to see the light of day. He glanced at the bandstand. The singer, an old black guy with a gray beard, grinned at him.

Billy took a deep breath and found Jonah's gray eyes. He mouthed the words slowly over the ringing chords of the guitar. "I want to kiss you too."

THE RIDE back to Billy's hotel felt like the countdown to the opening game of the season. He and Jonah jammed together in the back of the cab, unable to resist pressing against each other, but agreed through some kind of Vulcan mind meld that their first real kiss should not be shared in sight of the cabby's rearview mirror. When the taxi pulled up in front of his hotel, Billy handed the cabby a ten-dollar bill.

"Wait a sec, and you can take my friend to his hotel."

"Y'all take your time."

Billy grabbed Jonah's hand and dragged him around the corner of the building away from the lobby windows. Now that he had the chance to do what he'd been dreaming about since last summer, he felt unaccountably shy.

"Okay, hotshot," he said, faking self-confidence he didn't feel.

Maybe Jonah was shy too. "How come you guys got such an early curfew?" he asked. Billy was pretty sure Jonah didn't care about the team curfew.

"Most of us are under drinking age. The university is probably afraid we'll get drunk and wake up in an alley somewhere. Lawsuits and all." Jonah's hand felt hot and a little sweaty in his own. He leaned down to get in range of Jonah's lips.

Jonah closed his eyes and stood on tiptoes.

Their lips had just brushed when Billy's phone rang. He straightened. "Shit, that's Mike's ring. He's probably checking to see where I am."

Jonah groaned. "Tell him to fuck off. You're busy."

Billy fished his phone from his pocket. "Just a sec. Hey, Mike, 'sup?"

"Where are you? You're due back in... like thirty seconds. Digger's about to do a room check."

"Shit! Be right there." Billy hung up and leaned down to kiss Jonah again. This time his mouth stayed on target. Jonah's lips were warm and surprisingly soft. Then Jonah made a faint whimper, and Billy felt Jonah's tongue invade his mouth and brush his teeth. The muscular touch sent a shiver the length of Billy's body. His cock, which had felt heavy and thick ever since Jonah had first mentioned kissing, tried to escape from his pants. He groaned and pulled Jonah to his chest, but their height difference made it hard to keep their mouths aligned.

"Wait." Jonah took a step back and leapt into Billy's arms.

Billy grabbed the firm globes of Jonah's ass and lifted him easily, startled by how light he was. Jonah always seemed bigger when he was talking. They went straight to dueling tongues this time. Billy tasted the after-dinner mints their waiter had left with the check. He ground into Jonah, wanting to rip off his clothes and press Jonah's skin against his own.

"Easy there, Stretch. A boy's gotta breathe," Jonah panted.

"I could kiss you forever."

As if in answer, Billy's phone rang again. "Crap." He lowered Jonah back onto the concrete. "If I don't get back up there, the coach'll have a cow."

A car horn sounded from the front of the hotel.

"It's a goddamn conspiracy," Jonah swore.

"I gotta go."

Jonah sighed and disengaged. "I know. Call me later." He spun around and trotted round the corner of the building toward the taxi.

Billy took a second to adjust his raging hard-on and limped quickly into the lobby. He reached an elevator just in time to watch the elevator doors slide shut. Afraid waiting for another elevator would take too long, he sprinted to the stairs and up four floors, emerging from the stairwell to see Digger leaning against the corridor wall next to the door to his room, chatting with Mike.

Digger held up his watch and tapped on the crystal. "You're late, Grandpa."

"Sorry, cabby took a wrong turn."

Digger raked his gaze up Billy's length and chuckled. "Tell me another, Romeo. Don't make this a habit, or Rocker will bench you so long you'll be shitting doll furniture."

After a pause to decipher the image, Mike's mouth fell open.

Billy laughed and pushed into the room, eager to escape Digger's knowing smirk.

"Nighty night, boys."

Mike followed, shutting the door in Digger's face. "You're flushed."

"Ran up the stairs."

"And your lips are swollen."

"Allergic reaction."

Mike stared. "Yeah, and the Pope's shit don't stink. Who were you with?"

"My parents."

"Not unless you were making out with them."

"That's sick."

"Who were you really with? Tully?"

"Tully!" Billy burst out, amazed.

"Why not? I know he turns you on."

Billy's unexpressed anger about the bus incident got the better of him, and he shoved into Mike's space. "It's none of your damn business. You wouldn't want to hear about it anyway."

Mike bit his lip and looked away. "I'm sorry about that, okay? It was a stupid thing to say. But you could cut me some slack, you know. This isn't easy for me."

"Easy for you? When did this become about you?"

"Maybe when you decided I wasn't worth—" Mike stopped to breathe, and his nostrils fared. "I make one stupid comment, and you decide I'm not worthy of your friendship. I thought we connected, that we could be pals. Guess you didn't." Mike's cheeks were flushed and his light brown eyelashes held tears, but he glared defiantly until Billy turned away in embarrassment. Maybe he had been unfair. Mike had grown up in Indiana, hadn't he? Not exactly a hotbed of gay liberation there either.

"Jeez. How am I supposed to stay mad when you go all soft on me?" Billy opened his arms for a hug. "Forgive me?"

Mike gulped visibly and moved to accept the embrace.

Billy laughed and stuck out a hand instead. "Relax, dude. Just testing."

Mike grabbed his hand firmly and shook three times.

"Your dad taught you that, didn't he?"

Mike's eyes widened. "Yeah."

Billy sighed. "Mine too. You sure you want to know who I was with?"

"I'm trying to understand. How am I supposed to know what it's like if you won't tell me anything?"

Billy glanced around the tiny hotel room, which was largely taken up by two queen-size beds. There wasn't anyplace comfortable to sit, and the day had begun to catch up with him.

"Tell you what, let's go to bed, and I'll tell you about Jonah."

Billy caught a telltale flicker in Mike's expression. He rolled his eyes. "Mine." He pointed. "Yours."

Mike relaxed visibly. "Who's Jonah?"

"Doofus. I gotta shower. Tell you when I'm out."

BILLY SWITCHED off the light and relaxed into a stack of pillows. "You sure you want to do this?"

Mike rolled onto his side on the other bed. "Do you have to be such a jerk?"

In the dark, Mike was just a faint blob on the darker bed. In a way, it was easier that he couldn't see Mike's face. "This isn't exactly a piece of cake for me either. Jonah's the only guy I've ever told before."

"Good."

"I don't—"

"I like that I'm the first straight guy you're telling."

"So, it's all about you again."

"Maybe I should just shut up."

"Maybe *I* should."

"Can we not fight? This is about both of us, okay? About being friends… teammates."

Billy remembered lecturing Jonah once about the responsibilities of being a friend. Now the shoe was on the other foot, and somebody had reached out to him. It was a good thing Mike couldn't see him blush.

"Okay, so I like guys. You already know that."

"Yeah, I got that from the giant hard-on when Tully humped you on the dance floor."

Billy was silent.

"Okay, so I think maybe I talk too much when I'm nervous." Mike sounded apologetic.

Mike was nervous. That was kind of a revelation from the guy with the Zen concentration on the basketball court. "Um, so Jonah, he's the first guy I ever felt—no, he's the first guy I ever felt so strongly attracted to I couldn't ignore it, and then he kissed me and I—"

"How long have you known?"

"Known what? I like girls, too, or I think I do." He sighed and tried for honesty. "But I gotta say I've never met one who made me feel like he does."

Mike didn't answer, and Billy wondered if he'd fallen asleep. "You got nothing to say about that?"

When Mike did reply, he sounded thoughtful. "I probably don't want to hear this—it's kind of like hearing about your parents' first date—but somehow I'm compelled to ask. *How exactly* does he make you feel?"

"I think about him all the time. Like I'm sitting in economics and the professor is talking about Adam Smith and the dude's wig reminds me of Jonah's hair."

"Your economics professor wears a wig?"

"No, Adam Smith's wig."

"Please tell me Jonah's not some perverted graybeard you met in the park."

Billy ignored him. "I want to tell him everything—unless it would hurt him. Because I can't bear that. His dad died last year, and it about killed him. I dream about him. About touching his hair, his skin, about the smell of his—"

"Enough of that. There are things I don't need to hear."

"I'm just getting started."

Mike sighed.

"I'll shut up if you tell me about your family." Billy had a pretty good idea Mike's family was a sore spot from the way he'd always shied away from talking about them.

Mike moved restlessly in the dark. "This is private, right? You won't tell the other guys."

"I won't tell anyone—well, except Jonah. I might tell Jonah."

"Rub it in, why don't you?"

"He's my...." He'd been about to say boyfriend, only Jonah wasn't because he didn't think long-distance could work. Billy didn't know what Jonah was.

"Whatever."

"Tell me about your family."

"I grew up in a small town, right? The kind of place where church is a really big deal, because it determines who you are. Anyway, my parents, they're born again, and they've got these really rigid ideas about what's right and wrong. They're good people, or they try to be. But they don't understand how other people can be different and still okay."

"So why are we talking? I've got to be the devil's spawn to them."

"I'm not like my parents, or I don't want to be. They judge *everyone*. If you don't believe in God, or if you think maybe the Bible was just a book with some good stories in it, you're going to Hell. That's all there is to it."

"You don't believe in God?"

"I didn't say that. I don't believe God burns people in Hell for eternity because they think the Bible shouldn't be taken literally. It's a book of stories, and stories are all about metaphors and analogies and symbols. That's how we understand stuff. We feel a connection, an understanding with our gut, not just our head.

"And it's not like the Bible's consistent, is it? I mean, there are all kinds of weird things in it. Lot's daughters lie with him and become pregnant, but Lot was just and righteous. God is a warrior. God is a consuming fire. But God is also love. They don't like it when you question how stuff like that is supposed to work because it's disrespectful."

"You were disrespectful, I take it."

"Until I figured out it was pointless to argue with them."

"And the gay thing? They think I'm going to burn, right?" It occurred to Billy that he'd never before referred to himself as gay. He'd have to think about that later.

"Pretty much. Yes."

"And you? Do you think that?"

"I'm trying to think for myself."

"That's not an answer."

"I don't believe you're going to burn in Hell because I don't believe in Hell."

"You're still avoiding the question."

Mike threw back his covers, and Billy heard him pad over to the window. He held open the blinds just enough to peer out at the lights of downtown Nashville.

"I don't know any gay people besides you. Gay people leave my town. I want to understand, but it's hard because there are things, you know, things you get taught or you absorb when you're a kid that you don't even realize you picked up until you find yourself judging someone."

"Like me and Tully."

"You know, it wasn't so much that you're both guys. It was the public thing. *Straight* couples make me uncomfortable when they kiss in public."

Billy didn't know what to say. "Maybe we should talk about something else. Like, do you have a girlfriend?"

Mike let the drapes fall back into place and returned to sit heavily on his bed. "I've never had a girlfriend. I've never had sex at all."

"Surely you've burped the worm? Based the ham? Peeled the sausage?" Billy knew Mike was uncut from seeing him in the shower and locker room.

Mike made a choking noise, and Billy wasn't sure if he was laughing or trying not to gag. Billy hoped it was the former.

"Polished your knob? Varnished the flagpole? You've got to have shot your wad. What about wet dreams?"

Mike's sounds increased in volume. Fortunately, it seemed he was laughing. "Please stop," he choked out. "You're killing me."

Billy couldn't resist. "Shot the moon? Wagged the dog? Made the bald man cry?"

"Please, Grandpa. I had no idea there were so many ways.... When I was thirteen, and I figured out that touching myself felt really good, I started using my socks, okay? And my mom must have noticed when she was doing the laundry—"

"Crusty socks. Dead giveaway."

"—and she said something to my dad, because he called me into the garage to have a talk about it. Only he couldn't say the word—"

"Which word? You mean masturbate?" Billy was probably enjoying this way too much.

"I get that you don't have the same problem," said Mike dryly. "Anyway, he told me it was a sin, and that I should try thinking about other things when I get aroused."

"Did it work?"

"No, I just bought my own supply of socks and threw them away when they got too skanky."

"Eew! Wasn't that expensive?"

"Dad thought I was spending my allowance on junk food. I was a growing boy, after all."

"Every night, I bet."

"Please, Grandpa." Mike sounded plaintive.

"So you really haven't had sex—with anyone else—yet?"

Mike's answer was barely audible. "No."

"You know we'll have to fix that."

"Please don't try to set me up."

Billy cackled evilly.

CHAPTER 5

Stats

~~Girls I'm pretty sure wanted to kiss me. 5 12 10,012~~
Girls I've kissed: 3
Boys I've kissed: 1

If Dad ever finds this, I'm dead—like broken spine, belly slit, and guts slithering out all over the floor dead.

Boys who've dumped me: 1
Boys I would kneel on the floor and worship as a basketball god: 1
Stupid nicknames: 2
Public boners: 1
Teammates I'd like to knock some sense into: 2
Different kinds of underwear worn by guys on my floor: 5
Basketball players on the down-low: 1

Points Scored this season: 12
Assists: 7
Turnovers: 2
Games Won: 1

Games Lost: 1

Blow jobs received: 1
Blow jobs given: 1
Sexting sessions: 0
Assholes I'd like to kill: 1

TRANSCRIPT

Billy Preston: You awake
Jonah Winfield: Yeah
Billy Preston: Want 2 try something
Jonah Winfield: Ok
Billy Preston: What are u wearing
Jonah Winfield: PJs
Billy Preston: Never mind

AFTER THE meet-up in Nashville, Jonah obsessed about finding a way to get to Hoosier State to see Billy. It was hard because he didn't drive and couldn't afford a three-hour taxi ride or even a round-trip bus ticket. He considered asking Rascal again, but Rascal would tell his mom. He really wasn't ready to explain to her why it was so important he see Billy, and she was too sharp to risk lying to.

On the weekend of State's game with Missouri State, he decided to hitchhike there on the Saturday before the game. He figured it would be okay because he could just swing the bus ticket home, so he wouldn't have to solicit a ride in the dark after the game. He e-mailed his mom that he was spending the weekend with Tony. She didn't know he and Tony had kept their distance since turning in the history project.

That was how Jonah came to be kicking gravel by the side of the interstate entrance ramp outside of Glen Falls with his thumb out. It was just after one, giving him plenty of time to travel one-hundred eighty miles to Hoosier State before the evening game. The weatherman had predicted dry, but the sky was slate gray and the wind chilly, so he had kitted out with his winter jacket and put a knit cap into his pack along with a bottle of water and a couple of candy bars for energy. He planned to take the interstate a couple of exits west, and then get off at highway 41. From there it was a straight shot north to Hoosier State.

Despite Jonah's worry that some busybody would see him by the side of the road and rat him out to his mom, the first part of the journey went surprisingly well. About twenty minutes after raising his thumb, a semi pulled out of the truck stop on the other side of the interstate and crossed the bridge in his direction. When it turned slowly onto the entrance ramp, he stuck out his arm, thumb high, half expecting the driver to ignore him like all the others had. But the truck ground to a halt with a chuff from its air brakes, so he dropped his arm and scrambled to grab his pack. Pulling open the door, Jonah climbed into the high cab. A middle-aged woman in a red flannel shirt glared at him from the driver's seat.

"*Söta Jesu moder*, what 'n heck ya doin' here?"

Jonah froze. "I thought you stopped…. You didn't see my thumb?"

"Saw it all right. I wanna know what y'think you're doin' hitchhiking in a place like this. Jesus, kid, anybody could pick y'up."

"I've got to get to Hoosier State to… to see my brother. It's a family thing." A lie seemed preferable to the truth. The woman was a complete stranger, after all.

She ran a hand through blond hair graying at the roots and stared for a moment. "Heck, better me 'n some pervert. Get in, you're lettin' all the warm out. I can take you to 41."

"Great, thanks. I'm Jonah, by the way."

The woman grunted. "Hilda."

After she'd merged the truck onto the freeway, Hilda leaned back and glanced at Jonah. "How old ya, kid?"

"Eighteen."

She whistled softly. "Course y' are. Don't know why I bothered. Your mama know ya thumbin' rides?"

Jonah didn't dare look at her. "Uh… my dad died…." He left the sentence unfinished, hoping she wouldn't pursue the topic.

"Sorry, kid. None a my beeswax."

Twenty minutes later Jonah saw a sign for the exit to State Highway 41. "Uh."

"I seen it."

A minute later, Hilda pulled the truck off at the exit for 41 and ground to a halt at the top of the exit ramp. "Now, you take care. Don't be hopping aboard the first somebody stops. Check 'em out first, *ja*?"

"Yes, ma'am."

That bought a full-throated laugh. "Ma'am? Ha! Happy trails, kid."

Feeling more confident than when he'd started out, Jonah climbed down and watched Hilda guide the truck across the highway and down the entrance ramp to the interstate.

An hour later, shivering as the wind pushed scraps of paper along the exposed gravel margin of the highway, he wished he'd worn a sweatshirt under his winter coat. Optimistic at first, he watched car after car whizz by. Too cold to stand still, he began walking north from the interstate toward the little town he knew was a couple of miles up the highway. Maybe he could find a gas station or diner to warm up in. The sign at the end of the exit ramp had indicated gas and food in this direction. There had to be something.

Twenty minutes after he started walking, Jonah heard the sound of a vehicle approaching from behind. He stepped aside and stuck out his thumb. A light blue pickup already slowed as the driver checked him out. The pickup's lights flashed on, and he threw up a hand to shade his eyes. The truck seemed to pick up speed as though it was going to pass. Then it slowed abruptly, throwing up a spray of gravel from its front wheels. Jonah jogged to the passenger side and peered into the window, remembering Hilda's directive.

The man inside leaned over and pulled the inside release, cracking the door. Jonah swung the door open partway. He wasn't very good at judging people's ages, but the goateed man who smiled at him from the driver's side looked about forty. He wore a baseball cap and a blue-and-white-striped dress shirt.

"Looking for a ride?"

"Thanks for stopping. I'm heading up to see the basketball game at Hoosier State. You going in that direction?"

The man's smile broadened. "Your lucky day. It just happens I'm heading that way. Hop in."

"Thanks, mister. It's colder than I thought out here." Reassured by the man's friendly grin, Jonah threw the door wide and jumped up, dumping his pack onto the floor between his feet.

"I bet." The man threw the truck into gear and rattled onto the pavement. When they were up to speed, he reached over and shoved the heater control lever into the red. "That ought to warm you up."

"Thanks."

"I take it you're a basketball fan?"

"I got a friend plays for Hoosier State."

"Yeah? That Tully Sam's a wild one. State's never seen his like before, have they?"

"I guess. B—my friend says he's pretty amazing."

"That's one word for it."

The man fell silent, and Jonah gazed out at the passing countryside. After a while, Jonah started to feel warm and he rested his head between the seat back and the window. Fields of corn stubble, soybeans, and hay bales melted into a haze of green and gold.

The next thing he knew, the rushing wind had been replaced by the ticking of the truck's engine as it cooled. Drowsily, he wondered why they'd stopped. A touch brushed the inside of his thigh, near his balls. He jerked awake, rubbing his eyes.

"Wha'?"

"Relax, kid. Feels good, don't it?"

Jonah had a brief impression of a parking area bordered by woods. Then the man's hand slid upward to grasp his zipper and yank down. Shocked at the invasion, Jonah froze, giving the man time to slip his fingers into the gap and grope Jonah's cock through the thin fabric of his boxer shorts.

"Wait! I don't—"

"Relax. You didn't think this ride was gonna be free, did you? All I want is a taste."

Jonah shied away, but he already pressed against the truck door. The man unbuckled his belt and unzipped his own fly. He fished the engorged head of his dick from the opening.

"Or you can suck mine. Your choice, kid."

"I don't want to." The passenger window felt cold against Jonah's neck. He reached behind him to find the door handle, simultaneously trying to shove the man's hand away from his crotch.

"Oh no you don't." The man hooked his fingers through Jonah's fly and yanked Jonah farther into the truck, ripping open the button at the waistband of Jonah's jeans. Jonah's jeans began to slide down his hips.

"Quit fighting. All I want to do is watch you come."

"No!" Jonah grasped the man's hairy wrist and tried to push it away, but the man was too strong. Changing tactics, Jonah let go and backhanded the man's crotch as hard as he could, feeling the heat of man's penis on the back of his fingers.

The man yelped and withdrew his fingers from Jonah's fly in order to protect himself. Scrabbling frantically, Jonah found the door handle and got the door of the truck open. He swung his feet out, but the man grasped the back of his jacket and began pulling him back into the cab. In desperation, Jonah shrugged off the jacket and stumbled from the pickup, holding his pants up with one hand.

The man jammed the truck into gear and rolled forward, keeping the truck between Jonah and the woods. Jonah changed direction and sprinted back along the side of the truck, cutting for the trees before the man could reverse. He jumped the parking barrier and crashed through low bushes and saplings into the shadowed woods.

Behind him, the man yelled, "Come on, kid! You want your pack and your jacket? All you gotta do is work with me a little. I promise!"

"Fuck you, asshole." When the man didn't follow him into the woods, Jonah slowed. Some kind of scratchy bush tugged at his bare arms and T-shirt. He took up position behind a large tree.

Heart pounding but safe for the moment, it occurred to Jonah to call for help. He slapped the pockets of his jeans, hoping against hope that his phone wasn't in his jacket.

BILLY OPENED his locker to hear the chime of an incoming text message. He dropped the towel he'd carried from the shower and fumbled to extract his phone from his bundle of clothes he'd stuffed into his locker before the game.

Jonah Winfield: Billy
Jonah Winfield: Billy
Jonah Winfield: Billy
Jonah Winfield: Please answer
Jonah Winfield: Pls answer
Jonah Winfield: So cold
Jonah Winfield: Cold
Jonah Winfield: Billy
Jonah Winfield: Cold
Jonah Winfield: Cld
Jonah Winfield: B

The first text had been sent at 5:26 PM, nearly three hours ago.

Billy Preston: What's wrong? U ok

There was a long pause. Finally the phone chimed.

Jonah Winfield: Need help
Billy Preston: Where are you?
Jonah Winfield: Trapped
Jonah Winfield: Ned ride
Billy Preston: Call me
Jonah Winfield: He'll hear

Billy's stomach clenched.

Billy Preston: WRU
Jonah Winfield: Rest stop
Jonah Winfield: Hw41 near Blakesville

What was Jonah doing at a rest stop? *Oh God.* The idiot must have tried to hitchhike to see him play. *Who* would hear if Jonah called? Fear burned through Billy's gut like a shot of 100 proof.

Billy Preston: Coming
Billy Preston: RU safe?
Jonah Winfield: No
Billy Preston: Call police
Jonah Winfield: No police
Billy Preston: Ambulance?
Jonah Winfield: I'm ok just come

Despite Jonah's reassurance, Billy felt like he'd drunk a cup of bleach.

Billy Preston: Coming now

The question was how to get there.

"You gonna dress or just stand there and text with your boyfriend?"

Something tapped Billy on the shoulder, and he jumped, almost dropping his phone. "Fuck! You startled me."

Mike, in jeans and a Bulls sweatshirt, craned his neck to see Billy's phone. "The guys are going out for pizza. You coming?"

"It's Jonah. Something's happened to him. I think somebody might be—" Billy swallowed, trying to keep down the acid that flooded his esophagus. "—might be trying to hurt him."

Mike glanced around to see if anyone was listening. "Jeez, he okay?" he whispered.

"I don't know. I have to get to him. Who has a car? You don't have a car. I need a car. He sounds bad. I have to get there. He can't be hurt. Mike, he can't—I've gotta—"

"Stop that." Mike's tone accepted no compromise. "Get dressed. I'll find some wheels." Mike reached into Billy's locker and retrieved Billy's pants. "Get dressed. I'll be right back."

Billy struggled to drag on clothes that seemed sized for a smaller person, possibly somebody without limbs. He checked his wallet for money. Then, with trembling fingers, he called up a maps application and searched for Blakesville. He found it forty miles south of the city on highway 41. While he was pulling up directions, his phone chimed again.

Jonah Winfield: Won't go away
Billy Preston: ?
Jonah Winfield: Man with my cot
Jonah Winfield: Freezing
Billy Preston: Hang on, we're coming

Jonah seemed confused. Billy's mind went back to the first weeks after Jonah's dad had committed suicide last year. Jonah had been volatile, sometimes okay and sometimes retreating into himself and refusing to speak to anyone. He didn't ever want to see Jonah like that again.

"What's up, Grandpa? Whirlpool says you need a ride." Tully looked uncharacteristically serious. Billy wondered what Mike had told him. For some reason, instead of one of his usual flamboyant outfits,

Tully sported a more subdued look: jeans and a black hoodie, like a banger from the hood. What had Mike told him?

"It's my friend, Tully. Something has happened to him. I gotta get to him."

"So what are we waiting for?" Tully glanced at Mike. "Let's go rescue your *friend*."

Mike had thrown on plain jeans and a windbreaker that made him look like he'd just walked off the set of *Leave it to Beaver*. Tully raised his eyebrows.

Mike looked steadily back. "You got a problem?"

Tully laughed at nothing Billy could understand. "And here I thought I had nothing but pizza to look forward to tonight. Come on, my ride's in the lot back of Brekerman Hall."

Billy and Mike jogged behind Tully to a sedan in the parking area. Billy didn't register the model, only that it was sleek and black. Tully hit the button on a key fob he pulled from his pocket, then jumped into the front seat. Billy took shotgun, and Mike slid into the back.

"Okay, where we goin', Grandpa?"

"South on 41." Billy held up his phone. "He's at a rest stop. I've got directions." He propped the phone on a raised lip in front of the radio.

"Nice ride, man," Mike called from the backseat. "This the HEMI model?"

"What do you take me for, a fucking poseur? Of course it's the HEMI. Five point seven liter, my man."

When they were on 41 heading south, Billy texted Jonah again.

Billy Preston: U Ok?
Jonah Winfield: Cold
Billy Preston: 30 min
Jonah Winfield: Faster

"Fuck, fuck, fuck."

Tully glanced at Billy, eyebrows raised. "You wanna tell us what we're getting into, Grandpa?" Tully flicked his eyes toward the back seat. "Or maybe it can wait."

"What? No, he's not—I thought Mike told you about Jonah."

Tully glanced in the rearview. "Will wonders never cease."

Mike raised a hand and waved, smiling sardonically.

"Jonah says there's a man... I don't know what happened, but Jonah's afraid of him. Keep your eyes open when we get there."

Tully laughed. "Four against one not good 'nough for y'all?"

"I don't know if he's armed."

Tully's laughter died.

THE REST stop consisted of a gravel pull-off in a wooded area with parking for seven or eight vehicles and a cinderblock box containing men's and women's rooms. Billy made out a couple of picnic tables in the darkness near the edge of the woods. A faded blue pickup truck idled in front of the restrooms, white vapor rising from its exhaust pipes. The telltale glow of a cigarette warmed the interior.

Tully nosed into the gravel turnaround.

"I think Jonah's hiding," said Billy, head swiveling.

Billy Preston: Where are u? In black sedan

Tully pulled up directly in front of the truck, and flicked his lights to bright.

"You think this is the guy?" Mike asked, pointing at the man shielding his eyes from the glare.

"Let's find out." Billy got out of the car and moseyed up to the truck's driver-side window. He tapped on the glass. Mike and Tully got out as well and went over to the passenger's side. The driver's window was rolled down a couple of inches to let out the smoke from the man's cigarette. From inside, Billy recognized the voice of a popular sports announcer on the post-game show from Hoosier State.

"Can I help you folks?" said the man, turning off the radio.

"Maybe. We're looking for a friend of mine. You seen anyone hanging around here?"

Mike cupped his hand on the passenger glass to peer inside the car. "There's a backpack on the seat."

The driver's side window rolled up suddenly, and Billy heard the truck clunk into gear.

"Watch out!" Tully yelled.

"Yeah, you better run, fucker!" Billy shouted, banging on the side of the truck with the palm of his hand.

The truck's tires spun, spitting gravel at Billy's legs as the vehicle accelerated backward.

"Motherfucking whore-son gonna ding my paint," Tully swore, brushing gravel from the legs of his pants. They watched as the pickup bounced over a parking barrier and careened out onto the highway.

Billy stared into the darkness under the stand of hardwood trees that sheltered the picnic area. "Jonah!" he called. "Where are you?"

"Over here!"

Billy followed the sound into the trees. "Keep talking. Where are you?"

"This way. I think I need help getting up."

Billy pushed through some kind of prickly bush. He retrieved his phone from his pocket and turned on the flashlight function. Holding up the phone, he saw Jonah crouched in the dark with his back to a tree, his arms clutched around his knees.

"Jesus, fuck, I'm cold."

"It's safe now. The guy in the pickup left."

"Fucker got ahold of my coat when I got out. Had to leave it. Bastard's got my pack too." Jonah tried to get to his feet, his limbs moving slowly. "Can't seem to...."

Billy dropped his phone into his pocket, slung an arm around Jonah, and pulled him up. Shudders racked Jonah's body. Billy wrapped his arms around him, shocked how cold he felt.

"You're warm," said Jonah faintly.

Someone crashed through the bushes. "You got him, Billy?"

"Over here, Mike. I'm not sure he can walk. Give me a hand, would you?"

Between the two of them, they maneuvered Jonah to the car where Tully waited.

"He okay?"

"I think he might be in shock or something. Help me get him into the back. Mike, you mind taking the front?"

"Holy shit, how long he been out here in that T-shirt?" said Tully.

"Too long. I'm going to kill the idiot when he's okay." Billy climbed into the backseat and pulled Jonah into his lap, unzipping his jacket so Jonah could warm himself on his body. "Turn up the heat," he said, rubbing Jonah's chest and belly.

Tully dialed up the temperature control and the heater fan came on. He pulled the car onto the highway.

"I suppose it's a dumb question, but shouldn't we be calling the police or something?" Mike asked. "I mean if that guy was—"

"No police," said Jonah, rallying a little. "Mr. G will kill me if he finds out about this. Rascal too."

"He'll have to stand in line," Billy growled.

Tully glanced at the rearview mirror. "Who in hell is Mr. G?"

"Music teacher," Jonah mumbled from under Billy's jacket.

"Sounds more like a mobster from some TV show."

Mike turned around in the front seat to raise his eyebrows at Billy.

"Long story," said Billy. "Friend of the family. Looks out for Jonah when his mother's out of town." He hesitated. "His partner owns Avakian Music in Glen Falls, and the building where Jonah lives."

"Whooee, Grandpa, you got some explaining to do," said Tully gleefully.

"Maybe we could start with introductions," said Jonah, twisting around to give Billy a hopeful smile.

"Hey, watch the ribs."

Billy had been so focused on helping Jonah, he hadn't even considered the potential consequences of letting the guys meet him. Tully could be a loose cannon. He had no idea how Mike would handle the situation. He hesitated long enough to see Jonah's expression dim.

Tightening his arms, he sent Jonah a reassuring look and cleared his throat. "Guys, this is Jonah. Jonah, meet the posse. The guy behind the wheel pretending he isn't enjoying this way too much is Tulane Sampson, otherwise known as Tully Sam. The throwback on the other side is Whirlpool—Mike Brooks."

Tully grinned into the rearview mirror. "How *do* you do, Jonah."

Jonah twisted around again, but not before Billy saw the grin that transformed Jonah's face and sent a flash of warmth through Billy's limbs. *I'll do anything to keep seeing that smile.*

"Shit! Tully Sam and Mike Brooks. I've seen you guys on TV. Billy says good things about you."

"He does?"

"Really?"

Jonah laughed. "Believe it or not, he does."

Tully chuckled, his grin matching Jonah's. "Our Grandpa is plum full of surprises today."

"The road's that way, Tully," said Billy, pointing.

Mike twisted around to face them in the back, his expression serious. "I'm pleased to meet you, Jonah." He extended a hand over the seat.

Jonah extracted his arm from Billy's coat and shook hands. "Congratulations on the win, by the way."

"How did you…?"

"What else was I supposed to do while I waited for you guys?" Jonah held up his smartphone. "Longest fucking game I ever watched. I kept hoping Billy'd foul out or something, get benched, and check his phone."

"Coach don't allow 'em at games," said Tully.

"Jesus," said Billy. "What if that guy had seen the light from the screen?"

"Fucker wasn't going to chase me around in the woods. He just thought he'd make me pay to get my coat."

"What happened, anyway?" asked Mike.

Jonah stiffened in Billy's arms. "Bastard thought I owed him something for the ride," he said flatly. "I preferred he fuck himself."

Tully drove on in the silence that followed. Billy knew that wasn't the whole story. He was pretty sure Tully and Mike did too.

"YOU NEED to tell someone where you are?"

Billy and Jonah lay side-by-side under a blanket in Billy's room, where they'd retreated for privacy. The effort of not demanding to know what the asshole in the car had done to Jonah made Billy tense. Jonah had finally stopped shivering. He seemed to take comfort from pressing his body against Billy's, but he gave no sign of wanting more. Billy was okay with that. Unfortunately Billy's cock didn't see this occasion as different from any other—in its primitive calculus Jonah equaled sex, so he had a more-or-less permanent hard-on whenever Jonah was around. If Jonah noticed the lump at Billy's center, he said nothing.

"Nah, I texted Rascal and told him I was staying at Tony's place. I'll be okay so long as I get back for dinner on Sunday."

Billy's restraint failed. "What the hell were you doing hitchhiking on your own? You could have been killed or—"

"Who the fuck are you to tell me what to do?" Jonah had something of a hair-trigger when it came to people telling him what to do. But his response sounded more rote than truly angry.

"Or something else could have happened," Billy finished determinedly.

"Fucking bastard wouldn't give me my coat back."

Here was real anger. Billy hesitated. "Was that all he did?" he asked, his lips close enough to feel the heat from Jonah's skin.

"No," Jonah whispered, his body tense.

Billy waited, his body vibrating with tension.

"It was really warm in the truck—I mean after standing around by the side of the road with my thumb out for-fucking-ever. I couldn't keep my eyes open." Jonah took a shaky breath. "Anyway, I fell asleep. When I woke up, we were at the rest stop, and the fucking pervert was groping me. I tried to get away, but he wouldn't let go of me. He kept saying I should relax. That I owed him for the ride. Fucking asshole. Relax... with his fucking hand in my fly?"

Billy's cock responded with typical disregard for propriety at the idea of getting into Jonah's pants, and hardened to a throbbing shaft in his jeans. Mortified, Billy started to roll away from Jonah.

"Please...," Jonah whimpered, grasping at Billy's hip.

"I'm sorry, Jonah. I'm so sorry." Billy rolled back and pulled Jonah's torso tight against his chest, unsure whether he was apologizing for his stupid prick or for his own role motivating Jonah to try hitchhiking. If he had accepted what Jonah had said at the beginning of the term and moved on, then Jonah would never have tried to come to the game, and this would have never happened to him.

"What have you got to apologize for? You're the hero who led the posse to the rescue."

"If I were a hero, I would have let go when you asked, and then you would never have—"

"I never wanted that."

Billy stiffened, unsure whether to push Jonah away or pull him tight. "What *do* you want from me?"

"Same thing I always wanted." Jonah twisted around and planted his lips on Billy's.

Jonah's lips were soft, but there was an urgency in their press that sent a series of shocks like lightning balls rolling the length of Billy's limbs. Jonah snuggled into his arms as if he'd been made for it. Billy ran his hands down Jonah's slender back, wishing he could make Jonah's T-shirt disappear. Jonah's tongue slid along his own, and he explored the taste and texture of Jonah's mouth. Jonah shifted, and Billy realized his rigid cock crushed against Jonah's equally determined hard-on. Was Jonah ready for this? Especially after what had just happened to him? Was he?

Jonah must have felt his uncertainty. He stopped kissing Billy long enough to murmur, "It's okay. I like that you want me."

"Are you sure?" Billy prayed Jonah was, because he wasn't sure he actually could stop at this point. Thank God they still had their clothes on. Any more skin-to-skin and he'd lose control.

"Take your shirt off."

Billy giggled.

Jonah stopped squirming and reared back to glare, a flicker of hurt mixed with irritation. "You think that's funny?"

"I'm sorry. I was just thinking it's a good thing we still have our clothes on."

"How is that a good thing?" Jonah demanded.

"If I take my shirt off, I'm not gonna be able to stop touching you."

"Did I ask you to stop?"

"Maybe you should. Are you ready for this?" Billy swallowed, his throat suddenly constricted. "Sex, I mean."

"Yes," said Jonah decisively. "I don't want to wait anymore." Jonah's body convulsed in a shudder. "And I sure as hell don't want my first to be some jerk in a pickup. Don't you want to?" he asked, suddenly vulnerable.

Billy preferred the sassy demanding Jonah to this vulnerable one. The idea of anyone hurting Jonah made the blood thunder in his ears. "I don't want to hurt you. I don't want to be like him."

Jonah raised his head from Billy's chest in surprise. "You're nothing like him."

"No, but I don't want you to feel like I pushed—"

"Nothing you do could ever feel like that. I love you."

Billy froze, and he waited in disbelief to see if Jonah would retract what he'd said.

After a second Jonah made a hurt sound and tried to climb off Billy, but Billy jerked to life and tightened his arms.

"No."

"No, what?" Jonah cried openly now.

If he hadn't been pressed into the bed under Jonah, Billy would have pounded his stupid head against the wall in frustration for making Jonah doubt himself. "Don't go. I love you too. Ever since you carried that stupid saxophone case into school with 'Faggot' painted all over it like you were some kind of superhero and that was your telephone booth."

"Telephone booth?" Jonah laughed through his tears, and Billy began to breathe again.

"So I'm not so good with words when you're rubbing your dick all over mine."

"Am I rubbing my dick all over yours?" Jonah squirmed some more. "Hello! Guess I am."

Billy lowered his hands and grabbed Jonah's ass.

"God, Billy. Does it make me some kind of slut that I really, really like it when you do that?"

"Nope."

"Will you *please* take off your shirt now?"

"Only if you do."

Jonah's shirt disappeared so fast Billy thought they might find pieces of it on opposite sides of the room in the morning.

After that, they kissed for a long time, running their hands all over each other. Then, by mutual consent, they shoved down their pants and underwear, and kissed some more, rutting frantically until Billy's cock was a swollen fire hose with Jonah's hand on the valve.

"Uh." He meant some kind of warning, but couldn't find a word. "Ahhh."

Jonah climbed on top of Billy, sliding his rigid erection up and down Billy's. Then, digging his fingers into the muscle of Billy's pecs, he rubbed a thumb over one of Billy's sensitive nipples. Billy tensed and groaned loudly, pumping thick gouts of white between their sweat-slicked bodies. Jonah yelled in wordless triumph, adding his own viscous ribbons to the mess.

When there was nothing more to pump, Jonah collapsed, heedless of the mess that covered Billy's chest. He sighed and seemed to lose consciousness instantly. Billy listened to him breathe for a few minutes, then maneuvered a pillow case off one of his pillows and dragged it between their bodies a couple of times to absorb the worst of the sticky wetness. Jonah whimpered but did not wake. Considering what Jonah had been through, it seemed a compliment to Billy that Jonah could relax so completely in his arms. Billy settled back to hold Jonah and listen to him breathe, already planning Jonah's introduction to the miracle of the blow job.

TRANSCRIPT

Billy Preston: I miss u

Jonah Winfield: I just left!

Billy Preston: !

Jonah Winfield: My mom's gonna maim me if she finds out about this

Billy Preston: Rascal won't let her maim his writing partner

Jonah Winfield: Bus is leaving

Billy Preston: Wave at me, dork!

CHAPTER 6

Stats

~~Girls I'm pretty sure wanted to kiss me. 5 12 10,012~~
Girls I've kissed: 3
Boys I've kissed: 1

If Dad ever finds this, I'm dead—like broken spine, belly slit, and guts slithering out all over the floor dead.

Boys who've dumped me: 1
Boys I would kneel on the floor and worship as a basketball god: 1
Stupid nicknames: 2
Public boners: 1
Teammates I'd like to knock some sense into: 2
Different kinds of underwear worn by guys on my floor: 5
Basketball players on the down-low: 1

Points Scored this season: ~~12~~ 61
Assists: ~~7~~ 31
Turnovers: ~~2~~ 5
Games Won: ~~1~~ 3

Games Lost: ~~1~~ 2

Blow jobs received: 1
Blow jobs given: 1
Sexting sessions: 0
Assholes I'd like to kill: 1
Parents who aren't talking to me: 2

GAME DAY. Billy woke on a Wednesday morning in November, a cold draft on his face from the window he'd left cracked the night before. Even the drumming of a heavy shower and the near-nighttime darkness wasn't enough to dampen his mood. Today was the day of the home game with Ohio State. The fact that the Buckeyes were considerably above them in the rankings didn't faze him. Even the fact that the midweek schedule meant Jonah wouldn't be there to watch was okay. Truth be told, Billy was relieved to focus on basketball and let everything else fall away for a few hours.

It amazed Billy how much fun basketball was now that he didn't have to go home and rehash every move he'd made with his dad. Of course, rehashing every move was exactly what the team did in the locker room after every game, but that was different. The guys could rag on each other about passes that flew out of bounds or free throws that bounced off the rim, and somehow it was about basketball, about what they'd done together. With his dad, Billy knew he could never run fast enough, jump high enough, or raise his free throw average high enough to suit his dad, because it finally wasn't about basketball or even Billy; it was about something his dad lacked.

Only with Jamal and Tully did criticism consistently cross the line and get personal. Coach Rocker's threats and imprecations were not wholly without effect. Jamal clearly knew that his place on the team and his future career depended on working with Tully Sam. But the tension between the two of them had reached the point where Jamal had requested a new locker assignment on the far side of the locker room from Tully. When Digger had told Tully, after practice on Monday, Billy happened to be passing by on the way from the showers, a towel wrapped around his middle, flip-flops on his feet. Digger leaned close to speak, and Billy saw the expression that flashed on Tully's face: *hurt*. Tully's usual grin replaced the expression so fast Billy would never have noticed if he hadn't been staring right at Tully's face.

Tully produced a booming laugh. "Well bless his heart."

Digger said something else, and Tully's grin stretched to something more like a grimace. "I don't give a fuck where he stores his shit." Tully thrust out a hip and flicked silver-painted fingernails as if ridding himself of a booger. "Hey, Billy! Got plans tonight? I'm in the mood to dance!"

Billy shrugged.

"You gotta come. Phi Sigma Kappa's got a soirée tonight. We are gonna par-tay!" Tully rotated his hips, ending with a suggestive thrust.

The idea of cutting loose had suited Billy's mood. "Yeah, what the hell. I could use a break."

It was only as he'd followed Tully out into the late-afternoon gloom that he'd caught Digger watching, an uncharacteristically serious expression on his face. Despite the rainy weather, Tully had worn skintight black jeans and an orange-and-black-striped tank top that showed off the voodoo tats on his shoulders. Over this, he'd thrown a silver-and-gray fur jacket, which he left unfastened. Back at the dorm, he disappeared into his room to return a moment later in a black top hat decorated with a skull and crossbones and knee-high white boots. He'd stuck out his tongue so Billy could see the silver wink of the stud piercing his tongue. Next to him, Billy felt like a clogger at a debutantes' ball.

Digger's odd expression had stayed with him while he danced at the party. He'd kept his distance, not wanting word of any dance floor indiscretions to get back to his teammates. Tully, on the other hand, had burned more brightly than ever, his movements liquid and unabashedly sensual as he bumped and ground with everyone who dared get within reach.

Later that night Billy had called Jonah to describe Tully's wild behavior. "He won't label himself for anyone, but he can't resist daring the world to do it for him."

"Does everyone have to fit neatly into a box? Why can't he just be Tully Sam?" Jonah had asked.

Stretched out on the bed listening to the drumming rain, Billy thought of Jonah and reached down to run a finger over the slit at the end of his cock, which thickened instantly. He might not be able to see Jonah often, but since Nashville, they'd established a habit of late-night phone calls and occasional sexting. He'd been more than a little surprised at Jonah's willingness to describe what turned him on while he touched himself. Their distance seemed actually to help him open up.

Billy pictured Jonah naked under the cool sheets of his bed and curled his thumb and forefinger around the head of his dick. He allowed the white noise of the rain, his excitement about the upcoming game, and his imagination to lull him into relaxed state of full arousal, his hand gradually moving faster over the sensitive skin of his cock. It was going to be a great day.

TRANSCRIPT

Billy Preston: What are u wearing

Jonah Winfield: Briefs

Billy Preston: What color?

Jonah Winfield: White

Billy Preston: Tighty whities? Really?

Jonah Winfield: Am I supposed 2 lie?

Billy Preston: Take them off

Jonah Winfield: Ok

Billy Preston: They off?

Jonah Winfield: Nature boy

Billy Preston: Ru hard

Jonah Winfield: Wait. Got 2 lock door

Billy Preston: No

Jonah Winfield: Rascal might come in

Billy Preston: Makes it hot

Jonah Winfield: Ur sick

Billy Preston: Want 2 stop?

Jonah Winfield: No

Billy Preston: Touch yourself

Jonah Winfield: R u naked 2

Billy Preston: Stark

Jonah Winfield: Does it reach ur bb?

Billy Preston: BB?

Jonah Winfield: Belly button!

Billy Preston: <smirk>

Jonah Winfield: Stand up and push it down

Jonah Winfield: Does it bounce back?

Billy Preston: Yeah

Jonah Winfield: Hot

Billy Preston: Touch the slit on yours. Wet?

Jonah Winfield: Is now used tongue

Billy Preston: OMG u can selfie
Jonah Winfield: Legs over head
Billy Preston: OMG
Jonah Winfield: What r u doing?
Jonah Winfield: ?
Jonah Winfield: Billy?
Billy Preston: Had 2 wipe face
Jonah Winfield: Licking myself and pretending its ur cum mmm
Billy Preston: OMG
Billy Preston: Running finger down my crack
Billy Preston: What r u doing
Billy Preston: Jonah?
Jonah Winfield: Sleepy now
Billy Preston: LOL

FANS PACKED the arena for the home game, their screaming so loud it shook Billy's gut and stabbed his ears. They broke out their blue-and-white T-shirts and jerseys and coordinated a series of waves that flowed back and forth across the seating like falling dominos. For the occasion, Tully had dyed his hair day-glow orange and painted his fingernails black. Rocker's eyes narrowed as Billy and Tully sauntered into the locker room before the game. He said nothing, but Billy bet the star center would get an earful about appropriate grooming before the next game. Personally, Billy didn't care what Tully wore or how he decorated himself, so long as he played well. Maybe he could have chosen the royal blue of State's colors for his nails—for the sake of the occasion.

At the whistle, the Ohio State center, a seven-footer with arms that stretched so long he could have been born of an El Greco painting, tipped the ball to his point guard. The Ohio player made a run for the basket, but Tully raced him down court and timed a leap perfectly to get a hand in front of the ball and bat it away. Tully's grace was mesmerizing. No matter how convoluted they were, Tully always managed to look like he'd rehearsed his moves in a ballet studio. Billy wasn't the only person in the arena to appreciate him. Every time Tully got the ball, the crowd noise pulsed in time with his movements. In contrast, Jamal's style was muscular, powerful, as if he were forcing the ball through water by sheer will. He was fascinating to observe as well, but exhausting.

By the end of the first half, the score was 43 to 40, Ohio State— not quite where Rocker wanted them, but within striking distance. At the buzzer, Tully and Jamal turned to head off the court together, but Billy saw Jamal pause rather than walk beside Tully. Tully must have caught the movement too, because his hips twitched and he stuck his butt out at Jamal before skipping off the court. Jamal stared, the muscles of his arms bunching, his expression thunderous. Otter offered a towel as he approached the bench, and Jamal ripped it from his hand. Détente was clearly over.

"Come on, man. It's just Tully Sam being Tully Sam," said Otter.

"Yeah, right. Wait till the faggot does it to you."

Billy turned to head for the locker room and found the coach behind him, his expression tense. "You ready to play, Preston?"

"Huh?"

"Get your head together. I'm putting you in after the half."

"Sure, Coach. I'm up for it."

After the tip-off, Billy lost himself in the pounding of his heart, the sting of sweat in his eyes, and the slap of his palm on the ball. He played to forget, to clear his mind of the stupid fight between Tully and Jamal—whose nature he'd not fully understood until that moment. He played to forget his aching incompleteness when he wasn't with Jonah, and he played to keep from thinking about his father's inevitable reaction to his inevitable announcement that he was gay. Through the second half, he played like he'd never played before, as though every point he allowed Ohio State brought his problems closer, and every basket he made wove a magical spell of protection.

They won. Tully focused in the second quarter, Jamal's absence apparently allowing him to forget as well. Billy and Mike worked the outside and Tully and Otter the inside, as if they'd grown up in the same neighborhood, catching games in the same playground. At the final buzzer, State's fans roared and beat their seats until Billy knew his ears would ring for hours. The ball was in his hands, and even though he was well beyond the three point line, he lofted the ball toward the Ohio State basket. He watched with calm satisfaction as it dropped through the rim as though sucked into the gravity well of a black hole. The basket didn't count, but the crowd roared in approval anyway.

Billy's teammates lifted him in their arms and carried him giddily off the court.

In the locker room, Billy escaped the arms of his teammates only to be corralled to the front of the line of players waiting to be interviewed. Where was Tully? This was usually his gig. He blinked as a burly guy with a TV camera on his shoulder aimed a light into his eyes. Somebody handed him a towel, and he wiped the sweat from his face. The reporter, whom he recognized as being the sports reporter from their hometown Fox News station, was the same woman who'd cornered him before.

"Congratulations, Billy, fantastic game. Keep this up and you'll be on your way to the NBA."

Billy wasn't sure if there was a question there or not. "I... yeah.... Tully and Otter—Otutu—played really well today. Mike too."

"People are saying Coach Rocker should bench White and start you from now on."

"I can't comment on that. Coach Rocker knows what he's doing."

"Speaking of rumors, Billy, what do you think of the story that's been going around that one of your teammates is gay?"

Billy opened his mouth to say something fire-retardant, but nothing came out.

"Would it bother you if one of your teammates was gay?"

"No, it wouldn't." He turned and shoved his way through the circle of people surrounding the TV crew before the reporter could ask anything more.

JONAH WATCHED Billy push his way through crowd as the camera followed him. Billy's face was drained of color. He pressed the button on the remote to turn off the TV.

"Hey, I was watching that."

"Sorry." Jonah tossed the remote to Davoud. "I got homework."

"It's Saturday night." Davoud put the remote on the coffee table and patted the sofa next to him. "Sit with me for a second."

Billy and Davoud had watched the Hoosier State game together. Paul was attending a PTA meeting and wouldn't be home until later. Rascal and Jonah's mom were in Chicago for the weekend.

"I really should work on my geometry."

"I'm sure it can wait a couple of minutes."

Jonah dropped back onto the sofa, but he kept his eyes to himself. He didn't need Davoud knowing how upset he was.

"How's Billy these days?"

"Okay, I guess. Cool game, huh?"

"Your friend is very good. You think he's got a chance at the NBA?"

"I don't know... if he wants to, I guess."

Davoud stretched out his long legs and rested them on the coffee table. "That reporter was obnoxious, dropping that question on him like that."

Jonah gestured at Davoud's legs. "My mom would kill me if I did that."

Davoud shrugged. "My house, my rules." His gaze stayed fixed on Jonah.

"Jesus, have you been taking lessons from my mom?" Jonah's mom was a trial attorney specializing in civil rights and discrimination cases. She was particularly good at cross-examination.

A corner of Davoud's mouth twitched. "Billy seemed a little upset."

"Why won't people just leave him alone? They should be asking about his free throw average, not about someone's personal business."

"She didn't ask if *he* was gay. She didn't say who might be gay. Things are better than when I was in school. Still, being a gay athlete has got to be a pretty tough row to hoe."

"Who said anyone's gay?" Jonah wasn't about to talk about Billy's sexuality. "That was probably just some bullshit she cooked up for the ratings."

"You don't think Tully Sam's gay?" Davoud cocked his head.

"Billy thinks Tully's probably bi." Jonah was happy to shift the spotlight to Tully Sam. He figured it was okay to speculate since neither he nor Billy actually knew anything for sure about the guy.

Davoud clasped his hands behind his head. "That was a pretty amazing piece of music you wrote for Billy."

Craptastic. Paul must have told him about Billy. Jonah flicked a speck of something from his jeans while he thought about what to say. Davoud was okay. He wouldn't say anything unless Jonah told him it was okay.

"Aida thinks you should use it for your application to music school. You thought about where you want to apply?"

Jonah wasn't sure he liked the idea of sharing the concerto. The piece was too personal. "I'm still checking out the catalogs."

"You know it's already late. You should be getting your applications together by now."

Jonah shrugged. "I'm not sure what I want to study."

Davoud examined him skeptically. "You've got such talent. You're not eager to find out what you can do with it?"

"I love playing with the Rascals and Mr. G. Don't you even care that I'll have to stop when I go to college?"

Davoud placed a hand on his chest. "You really know how to hurt a guy."

"Well, do you?"

Davoud's answer was a barely audible rumble. "You cannot imagine how much Paul and I will miss you. But we want what's best for you. And Rascal's getting ready to end his sabbatical anyway, and will be on the road again soon. You can tell by the way he twitches when he talks about the quintet."

"Do you think my mom knows?"

Davoud sighed. "She knows. She wants what's best for *him* too."

"Do you think they'll stay together?"

"I don't know. I hope so. She's good for Rascal."

It was hard for Jonah to imagine his mom being good for a man. But there was no doubt in his mind that Rascal was good for his mom. Since she and Rascal had gotten together, she'd grown softer and easier to get along with.

"Um… I really do have geometry, you know."

Davoud laughed. "Never in the history of the universe has there been a teenager so eager to do his homework." He pulled his legs off the sofa and rose to his feet. "Well, not in the Music Box anyway. Paul will be home from his PTA meeting soon. You want to join us for some ice cream later? He always needs cheering up after those things."

Jonah felt his mouth stretch to a grin. "Sure. I'll come down when I'm done." It wasn't like he was really that eager to do geometry.

"WHAT WERE you thinking, Billy, running away like that? Now everyone is gonna think you're protecting the faggot."

Billy stared at the phone in his hand and then at his roommates, who were watching TV while demolishing a bag of chips and a Tupperware container of guacamole Jason's latest had brought over after the game. Sally Jean—Billy wasn't sure, but he thought that was her name—had given up and gone home when Jason had shown more interest in the Bulls game than her. Billy mouthed the word "parents," and stepped into his bedroom, pulling the door closed behind him. He didn't need anyone hearing his father's bigotry.

"Are you listening to me?"

Billy thought about disconnecting the call but stopped, mad at himself for letting his dad get to him. "Hi, Dad, how the heck are ya? Fine weather we're having, ain't it?" Actually, it was raining again, gusts of wind spattering droplets against his window. "The guys at work treating ya okay? Still in the running for salesman of the month?"

"Don't you be smart with me, kid. I'm still your father. Don't think I won't come up there and kick your butt if you need it."

Billy laughed at the improbability of his dad's scenario. "Jesus, Dad. Do you have any idea how ridiculous you sound? I'm six inches taller than you."

Unexpectedly, his dad started to chuckle. "Okay, you got me there, buddy. I'm serious, though. What got into you? First you sound like a robot with that reporter, and then you run like you got something to hide."

"Pretty great that we won against Ohio State, huh, Dad?"

"Billy! I'm trying to talk to you."

Billy dropped onto his bed and kicked off his shoes. "What do you want me to say? I really *don't* care if someone on the team is gay."

"This is about that Jonah kid you used to be friends with, right? Just because he got teased in school, he's got you all PC about the gays. I'm glad you're done with him now that you're in college. You keep hanging out with fags like that and people are going to start thinking you're a limp wrist too."

"Dad, this isn't about Jonah." Billy heard the tension in his voice and hoped his dad didn't pick up on it. He didn't think he could talk about Jonah right now without saying something he shouldn't.

"That reporter was talking about Tully Sam, wasn't she? Why doesn't the coach just get rid of the pansy?"

"You know why. He's a great basketball player. I'm lucky to play with him. And pansy is offensive."

"Now you sound like a fucking robot again."

Billy heard a scuffle at the other end of the line, then his mom's voice. "I think you're right to protect your teammate. That kind of loyalty is rare. I'm proud of you, son."

"Hi, Mom. I'm not protecting anyone." *No more than I'm protecting myself.*

"Give that back," his dad said in the background.

"I mean it, Billy. You've got to think of yourself—how people are going to see you," said his dad, apparently having won back possession of the handset.

"Maybe I *am* thinking of myself." The rain had stopped, and his voice was loud in the silence.

"What are you saying?"

"Maybe I don't want to live in a world where people feel like they can do stuff to people like Jonah just because he's small and... and...." *And gay.* And awesome. And breathtaking when he smiles at me.

His dad's voice held only contempt. "That little sissy?"

Billy's stomach tensed like that instant before you vomit, when you feel it coming and there's nothing to do but open wide and hang on to the porcelain. "You can't talk about him that way! I *love* him."

Billy heard his dad breathing on the other end of the line. Billy's room was silent, suspiciously silent. What had happened to the TV? *Jesus, fuck.* Jason was out there. Couldn't he come out to someone on purpose for once?

"Look, I'm sorry. I know Jonah was your friend, but it's time you grew up and—"

Billy closed his eyes and tried to sound as strong and confident as he could. "Jonah is not my friend; he's my *boyfriend.*"

"I know you're just winding me up, Billy, but I'm serious. If it gets out that—"

"I'm gay, Dad."

After a few seconds, his phone displayed the disconnect screen. He threw it on the bed and slid onto the floor, his back to the door of his room.

"Fuck. Fuck. Fuck."

He'd barely had time to start cataloging all the ways he was fucked when someone knocked on his door.

"Go away."

The doorknob rattled. "Sorry to bother you, Billy." It was Jason. Could the day get any worse? The last thing he needed was another heart-to-heart with a disgusted roommate.

"It's not a good time, Jason."

The doorknob rattled again. "It's not what you think, Grandpa," Mike called through the door.

Billy sighed and got up. "I suppose you guys heard." He opened the door.

"It was kinda hard not to, dude." Jason held out a can of beer, his expression grave. "You're pretty loud when you get riled up."

Billy took the can automatically. God knew where it had come from. Jason must have been holding out on them. "Riled up? What do you think this is, a movie?"

"He's not making light." Mike leaned against the back of the couch, hands in pockets.

"Why don't you let Jason speak for himself?"

Mike shrugged and crossed his legs.

"I just wanted to tell you that I got your back," said Jason. "My uncle got married in Vermont last year. Pretty cool wedding, if you go in for that kind of thing."

Mike smirked.

After a moment, Billy realized his mouth was open. "Uh... that's great. Congratulations. I mean to your uncle and his... his...."

"Husband. Hey, you going to drink that? Because it's from my special stash, and if you're not—"

"Thanks." Billy popped the tab and took a long swallow. And then another. And then another.

DIGGER CAUGHT up with Billy as he laced his trainers after practice. "Coach wants to see you, Billy."

"What's up?"

"Didn't say. 'Just get him in my office,' he says, like I'm his secretary or something."

Billy looked up at Digger in surprise. "You okay?"

Digger's lips formed a thin line. "It's nothing. Just watch your back, right?"

Billy was pretty sure what was on the agenda. Bye-bye basketball for Billy. Good-bye scholarship. Hello, McDonald's. Tully Sam might be able to get away with flamboyant clothes and humping everything that moved, but he was a star and on his way to the NBA. Billy was just... Billy.

Billy stood and held out his hand. "Hey, it's been good while it lasted."

Digger took his hand reflexively. "What the heck are you talking about? You do something I should know about?"

"I haven't done anything wrong."

"Then go in there, listen, nod, swear you'll never do it again, and I'll see you tomorrow. Jeez, you'd think this was the frigging drama department." Digger stalked off.

Billy hoisted his duffle and placed foot ahead of foot until he could examine the paint chips on the doorframe outside Rocker's office. Regrettably, the door was open. Rocker glanced up and motioned him in.

"Close the door behind you."

Here it comes. Billy stood in front of the desk.

Rocker leaned back. "What are you standing there for? Quit hovering and sit."

Billy lowered himself reluctantly into the waiting chair.

Rocker examined him. "Your dad called this afternoon."

I am so fucked.

"You and him have a problem?"

"What do you mean?"

"He seems to think you've fallen in with a bad crowd."

People are going to start thinking you're a faggot. "He... uh...."

"You got some kind of problem I should know about?"

"No."

"Drinking too much?"

"No."

"Using?"

"Of course not."

"Do *you* think you've fallen in with a bad crowd?"

"What? No. The team's really great. Everyone's great."

Rocker smiled, the expression failing to reach his eyes. "I suggest you call your *dad* tonight and have a little heart-to-heart. Maybe suggest he leave the coaching to the professionals."

"He doesn't mean anything by it, you know. He just wants what's best for me."

"Does he? You've made a great start here, Billy. You're showing promise on the court and working well with your teammates. Don't let anything get in the way of that." Rocker stood.

Billy jumped to his feet so suddenly he knocked the chair over behind him. "Shit, sorry." He scrambled to set the chair back on its legs.

"See you at practice, Billy."

"Right. Thanks, Coach." Billy backed out of the office, resisting the temptation to bow as he went.

BILLY STRODE from one pool of lamplight to another across the gloomy quad in a rush to get supper at the dining hall before the line closed. He heard footsteps closing from behind and moved to the side of the path, expecting a runner to pass. A hand landed on his shoulder instead.

"Hey, Grandpa. Sup?"

"Jamal?" Billy twisted from under Jamal's grip.

"On your way to eat?"

"Yeah." Billy expelled the word reluctantly. Since the BJ in Jamal's room and Jamal's subsequent coolness, Billy had mostly avoided the guy. With Rocker putting Billy into games for longer and longer stretches, he doubted Jamal thought of him as his BFF.

Jamal fell into step. "Good, I'm starved."

Billy knew for a fact that Jamal usually ate with a group of seniors in the dining hall nearest his dorm. What was he doing over here?

"Gettin' the hang of the place?"

"Sure."

"Great game against the Buckeyes. I meant to say something, but you got snagged by that reporter."

"Thanks."

"Who you think she was talkin' 'bout, anyway?"

Had Jamal been giving so many blow jobs he was concerned about word getting out? "It's gotta be Tully, don't you think? The guy puts the drag queens in Boy's Town to shame."

Jamal chuffed like he'd been holding his breath. "Yeah, you gotta be right. Hey, you wanna come by and watch the game in my room?"

They'd reached the dining hall. Billy held open the door. "Some other time, maybe. I got a paper to write."

Jamal stepped into the hall but waited inside for Billy. "You work too hard. Gotta relax sometime."

Billy ignored him and zeroed in on a familiar vendor at the back of the huge space, heart set on a burger and fries.

Jamal followed him to the line, taking only a dried-out cup of fruit salad from the outward-facing cooler that formed an order counter. "I got the Bears game on the box too."

Billy ordered the double burger platter from a tired-looking student in a hairnet. Jamal finished checking out first. A bored checkout clerk swiped Billy's ID card without even looking up from her book. Billy glanced around the room for a free table. Jamal put his hand on Billy's neck and guided him to an empty table. Billy realized belatedly Jamal was hitting on him. He shrugged off Jamal's hand and took a seat across the plastic-topped table from him.

Jamal leaned close. "You got a girl somewhere I don't know about? I never seen you with no one. You gotta be horny by now."

"Maybe you ought to bother someone who's actually interested, Jamal."

Billy glanced around. Tully stood behind him, the tall center's attention focused on Jamal, his expression closed.

Jamal raised his head slowly. "What's your problem, faggot? I'm talking to Grandpa. Nobody invited you to the party."

Billy felt like the ball in one of those classic matches between John McEnroe and Björn Borg they still showed on ESPN. "This isn't a game, and I'm not a tennis ball."

"What?" Jamal frowned, his attention on Tully.

Tully looked at Billy. "You got somewhere to be?"

"The fuck?" said Jamal. "Billy and I are eating."

Billy stood, missing his burger already. "You know what, I'm not really hungry."

Tully leaned down and hissed at Jamal. "He's already got a *boyfriend*, asshole."

Jamal jumped to his feet, head moving side-to-side like a radar antenna. "Fuck, man, somebody'll hear."

Tully raised his chin and laughed loudly. "You think I give a fuck? You're the one on the down-low."

Billy took off for his dorm, leaving his teammates still facing off over his abandoned burger. Maybe he could drink dinner from Jason's not-so-secret-anymore stash.

TRANSCRIPT

"Hold on, Billy, I gotta get my earbuds."

[Click]

"You okay? Has your mom called?"

"Nope."

"That sucks."

"I think she will, once she gets used to the idea. My dad might even—"

"Love isn't always enough."

"I hate it when you say that. Your dad was sick."

"Everyone says that like it might help."

"Mike's mom isn't talking to him either. She's been giving him a hard time about Tully. She caught that fucking interview just like my dad did, and now she's on my case too. I don't know what Mike said to her, but she won't take his calls."

"Sounds a regular suckfest."

"I feel guilty about it."

"Don't you fucking dare. You said exactly the right thing."

"That doesn't make it feel any better."

"I wish I was there. I'd give you a massage or a blow job or something."

"There's a pleasant thought. Are you in bed?"

"Yeah."

"If you're wearing PJs, I don't want to know about it."

[Rustling sounds]

"Not wearing anything."

"You touching yourself, nature boy?"

"Do you want me to?"

"I'm not doing this by myself."

"Tell me what to do."

"I thought you liked to do that."

"Your turn this time."

"Uh... is your room warm enough?"

"The room is fine."

"Did you take a shower before going to bed?"

"Just get on with it, Grandpa."

"Eew!"

"Sorry."

"Lift your legs over your head, so your butt is exposed."

"Okay."

"I wish I was there to see it."

"You like butt holes?"

"I love yours. You're going to love it too, when I'm done with you."

"Big talk."

"Lick your finger. When it's nice and wet, run it down your crack toward your asshole."

"Eeek, cold."

"Work with me, nature boy. Now run your finger in a circle around your bud."

"Bud?"

"Asshole, asshole."

"Really?"

"Lightly, just around the edge."

"Oh, wow."

"Don't touch your cock!"

"Whoops."

"Hands where I tell you. Now take your index finger and press lightly against the muscle. Not enough to go in, just a little pressure. How does that feel?"

"Weird but good."

"Okay, now press a little harder. Circle around the rim."

"Umm."

"Hands off your dick, dick."

"Aw, you're killing me."

"Lick your finger again."

"Really? Gross."

"You took a shower, right? Lick your finger, then press in the center until the tip is inside."

"Uh."

"Wiggle it around a little. Don't go in too far."

"I hate you!"

"Wiggle it around some more. How does that feel?"

"Are you jerking off? 'Cause that's not fair."

"Never you mind what I'm doing. If it doesn't hurt, add another finger."

"It's pretty tight."

"Uhm."

"You're jerking off, aren't you?"

"Forget what I'm doing. Now take out your fingers and shove the middle one back in as far as you can reach."

"Oh God."

"Put your legs... [Panting]... put your legs all the way over and lick the end of your cock."

"Got to touch it to get it to my mouth."

"So touch it, already! Put it in your mouth and lick around the head."

"Mmmm...."

"Jonah? Jonah!"

"Do you like the taste of jizz?"

"Oh God. Ahhh!"

"Billy?"

"Crap, I think I got cum up my nose."

"I swallowed."

[Silence]

"Jonah?"

"Mmm."

"Good night, Jonah."

"Zzzz."

"Hang up the phone, doofus!"

BILLY WITHDREW his key and shoved the door to their suite open. Mike and a girl he'd never met before panted at opposite ends of the couch. Mike's face was flushed, and the collar of his button-down shirt was askew.

"Hi, Grand—Billy." Mike gestured. "This is Sunflower. I don't think you've met."

Billy knew he was staring, but he couldn't help it. Mike making out with a girl? It was like the fat lady had not only sung, but moved to Indiana and opened a massage parlor. Sunflower? Really?

"Hi, Billy. Mike's told me a lot about you."

The girl, young woman, looked to be of Native American descent, with straight dark hair, light brown skin, and a round face. Her smile began to falter as Billy stared, so he pulled himself together and plastered on his best smile.

"Pleased to meet you, Sunflower. I'm sorry I'm so—it's been a weird day."

"Sunflower is in my anthropology class." Mike failed to meet Billy's eyes. "We were just—"

"Whatever, dude. I'm not her father."

"Mike's kinda shy," said Sunflower. "That's one of the things I like about him."

"That's our Whirlpool, shy as a butterfly at a bullfrog convention."

Mike glared. "Thanks a lot, pal. Way to cockblock your BFF."

Sunflower chuckled, the sound deeper than expected. She slid over to put a small hand on Mike's thigh. Mike's leg twitched, and his breathing stuttered. Sunflower smiled sweetly at him.

It was fun to see Mike flustered. Then it hit Billy. BFF? Mike considered him his best friend? Before he could think what to say, Sunflower gave Mike's thigh a firm pat and bounced to her feet.

"Good to meet you, Billy. Unfortunately, much as I enjoy getting Mike all hot-and-bothered, I got a paper to write."

Mike jumped to his feet. "I should walk you home."

"Isn't he sweet?" Sunflower gazed at Mike fondly. "Sorry, bub, you're more of a distraction than I can afford tonight. You stick around and tell your best friend all about me, since I see you've been holding out on him." She grabbed a hugely overstuffed pack from the floor next to the couch. "See ya."

Billy jumped to open the door for her.

Sunflower sailed out, grinning.

"Wow." Billy closed the door. "You *have* been holding out on me."

Mike fell back into the couch. "Whew."

"For what it's worth, I think she's pretty."

Mike grinned. "Yeah, she is, isn't she?"

Billy dropped his pack and flopped onto the couch. "To coin a phrase, how long has this been going on?"

Mike shrugged. "Couple of weeks. I was going to tell you, but then there was the thing with Jonah and your dad and I didn't...."

"You seem happy."

Mike closed his eyes and linked his fingers behind his head. "She does these things that—she doodles on her notepad. That's how I noticed her. I sit behind her in lecture hall, and I was going past one morning when I noticed she'd drawn a picture of me in my uniform shooting a basket with this silly look on my face, and she caught me checking it out—here let me show you." He bent double and pulled a folded sheet of notebook paper from an inner compartment, unfolding reverently before handing it to Billy. The drawing was more caricature than portrait, but it captured perfectly the intense, slightly pinched look Mike got when he was trying a long shot from beyond the three point line.

"She's a real artist and scary smart."

Billy considered and thought better of pointing out that she probably wanted Mike to notice the drawing. So what if she had? Mike was dreamy as a kid getting his first glimpse through a telescope, starships and distant worlds crowding his thoughts. It was a good look on him.

"Yeah," Mike breathed wistfully. "She's too good for me. I'd have all the appeal of an accountant if it weren't for basketball."

Neurons in Billy's brain linked with a snap, and he fell back onto the cushion. "I feel that way all the time with Jonah. No way I'm good enough for him."

Mike opened his eyes to examine Billy quizzically, as if he were working something out in his head. "You do?"

"God, yes. Did I tell you how he can listen to a piece once on the radio—even something complicated—and work it out on the piano without written music?"

Mike jumped to his feet and began to pace. "Do you think married couples feel like this? Or are we just losers, doomed from the start?"

Billy thought of the adult couples he knew, married or not. According to Jonah, Paul still looked at Davoud like he hung the moon. Davoud was harder to read. Rascal, Davoud's brother, was a better example. He stared at Jonah's mom like he'd been bonked on the head and couldn't quite remember what day it was. Billy's parents were harder to assess, maybe because his feelings about his dad overwhelmed his judgment. Did his mom still think of his dad as the star jock he'd been in high school? He hoped not. He wondered how his revelation had affected them. Maybe his dad hadn't told his mom. That would explain why she hadn't called.

"I don't know," Billy answered. "But you gotta expect the best couples think pretty highly of each other. I mean, can you love someone you don't respect?"

Even as he said it, Billy's thoughts went to Tully and Jamal. He was pretty sure Tully felt something for Jamal, and Tully kept baiting Jamal because Jamal had rejected him. He couldn't respect Jamal's refusal to acknowledge his sexual preference. Whether Jamal felt anything other than contempt for Tully was an open question. The whole business with Tully and Jamal made him feel sad and out of control, like Jonah's father committing suicide. Jonah had loved his dad, and John Winfield had appeared to love his son, but that hadn't kept him from hanging himself from a beam in the master bedroom of their home. Jonah's mom said he'd been depressed about being out of work and the failure of their marriage. Maybe he'd also felt inadequate in the face of her success as a civil rights attorney.

"Don't sell yourself short," he said to Mike. "You're a good person. If Sunflower is worth anything, she sees that."

Mike stopped pacing and pursed his lips. "You think I'm a good person? Do you know I couldn't bear to stay in my room when you and Jonah were together? I slept in the lounge so I wouldn't have to listen."

Billy watched the conflicting emotions work Mike's face and thought his own must look pretty much the same way. "I think you could have complained, and you didn't. I think you could have applied for a new roommate at the housing office, and you didn't." Or he hoped Mike hadn't. For some reason, he thought about his dad. "We all have feelings. We all judge unfairly sometimes. What matters is what you *do*. If I ever do anything to hurt Jonah, you can judge me for that."

"Last time I saw him, he looked like you'd just carried him from a burning building."

"Jonah?"

"You think I wasn't watching? Asking myself if my parents and their people aren't right about you?" Mike's legs seemed to turn to rubber, and he dropped cross-legged to the floor. "But he looked at you like you were his very own hero."

"Yeah, he did." Billy didn't like to think about it too much, because it scared him. But it was true. "He makes me a better person. Everything I do, I'm always wondering, 'What will Jonah think?'"

"My mom and I aren't talking right now. She thinks Tully is unnatural and going to Hell, and that anyone who consorts with him is probably going there too."

"God, Mike, why didn't you tell me?"

"You had your own thing going with your dad. I didn't want to make it worse."

Billy got off the couch and knelt next to Mike. "I'm so sorry."

Mike shrugged. "I'm so stupid. I thought I didn't care what they think anymore."

"They're your parents, doofus, of course you care. It's like... hardwired." Billy squeezed Mike's shoulder.

Mike flinched, but he stayed where he was, a solitary tear making its way down his cheek.

BILLY WOULD never have noticed the figure if it weren't for the jacket, and for the fact that he'd been benched. He'd been irritable and off his game since the call with his dad. On the court he'd been stupidly aggressive, charging opposing players and using his elbows. Late in the second half, after using his last foul, he'd slunk to the bench and put his head in his hands, pretending to meditate or something, too embarrassed at his own idiocy to show his face. He had nothing against aggressive basketball, but getting yourself thrown out of the game made no sense. He didn't look up until Mike handed him a towel and yelled into his ear over the noise of the crowd.

"Chill out, dude, or I'm gonna change your nickname to Bubba."

Billy raised his head to ask where a guy from Indiana got off sounding like a surfer from Ventura Beach when he caught sight of the scarlet windbreaker emblazoned with the Glen Falls / Martin Luther King High School motto. As far as he knew, only two people had jackets like that. One was his high school coach. The other was his father. The jacket had hung on the hook by the kitchen door as long as Billy could remember. God knew who his dad had bribed to give it to him. Maybe he'd had it made himself.

Billy would have assumed that the guy in the stands was his former coach, Dean Presis, but it was Saturday, so Presis would be at his own game. What's more, the guy was a diehard Hoosier State fan. There was no way he'd be sitting over by the visiting team. That his dad was there could only mean one thing. He wanted Billy to see him. Why didn't he fucking call? Why play stupid games?

"What are you looking at?" Mike yelled.

He nodded at the other side. "I think my dad's over there."

"That's good, isn't it?"

"I guess."

When the game ended, Hoosier State having scraped by with a one point win, Billy evaded the press—why he'd want to answer questions about his uncharacteristic aggression beat the hell out of him—and rushed through a shower and change. He burst out of the locker room, scanning for his dad, but there was no sign of the windbreaker among the fans and family waiting beyond the security barricade.

"Damn it." He slammed the barrier in frustration.

"Looking for someone, Billy?" It was the same woman reporter who'd asked him about having a gay teammate.

"What? No. I thought I saw someone I knew at the game."

"You look upset."

Billy glanced at her. "What?"

Outside of the glare of the television lights, the woman looked less like a reporter and more like somebody's mom come to pick up her kid. She had her blond hair pulled into a pigtail behind her head. Deep creases fissured the makeup on either side of her eyes and at the corners of her mouth.

"I said you look upset. Is something bothering you? You were pretty aggressive on the court today."

In the back of his mind, Billy knew he was being questioned by a member of the press, and he should be careful what he said, but standing outside in regular clothes instead of his uniform, it didn't feel like an interview.

"It's nothing, I just... it's nothing. I just thought I saw somebody I know." He craned his neck to get a better look at the people crowding around the parking area.

The woman smiled sympathetically. "Somebody you were hoping to meet?"

"Nah, it probably wasn't him."

"Hey, Billy! What are you doing standing around? The bus is over here." Mike grabbed his arm and dragged him away from the reporter. "Do you have any idea what you just said to that vulture?"

"What? Let go of me. I was just trying to see if my dad—"

"Holy Mother of God, did aliens come down and remove your brain while I wasn't looking?"

"What are talking about? I told you, I thought I saw my—"

"You just told that reporter you were looking for a guy." Mike continued to drag him toward the bus, an arm thrown around his shoulder as if they were best buddies—which maybe they were—his other arm looped through the straps of a couple of sports bags.

"Would you let go of me!"

Mike dropped his arm, and let the bags slide off his arm onto a pile of bags and equipment waiting to be loaded on the bus.

"Jeez, man, get your head together! That was the same woman who asked you about having a gay teammate. God knows what she's thinking now."

"Oh shit."

"Was it your dad? Was he here?"

"I don't know. He wasn't around when I got out."

TRANSCRIPT

"Hey."

"Hey, yourself."

"Something we need to talk about?"

"Sometimes I wish you were a dumb blond—no thought in your head besides whether those jeans make your ass look big."

"Really? It's been that long since we've seen each other?"

"What?"

"I am blond."

"I know! That's the point! You're not stupid."

"When you first saw me, did you think I was a dumb blond?"

"How could I think you were a dumb blond? You were ripping through some Lester Young solo for Mr. G. I didn't even know who Lester Young was."

"Neither did I."

"Maybe you are a dumb blond."

"If I were, would you tell me what's bothering you?"

"You know my name really is Billy, not William? I'm not sure my parents realized they were naming me with a diminutive."

"Whoa! That's a big word coming from a jock."

"It's like my dad wanted to make sure I couldn't be anything but a dumb jock."

"Jocks aren't the only people with nicknames. If I ever work the jazz clubs, you might have to start introducing me as Baron Winfield."

"What the fuck are you talking about?"

"Duke, Count, King, Emperor, Prince—they've all been taken. Although Prince probably shouldn't count. Technically, the name's free now, so—"

"I think my dad came to the game."

"About time. I don't know how long I could have kept that up. Did you talk to him?"

"He didn't stick around afterward. I looked for him, but...."

"Even so, it's a good sign, right?"

"I don't know. He sat on the other side. Maybe that was a message."

"Forgive me, but I don't think your dad is that subtle."

"So why did he come?"

"He's obviously trying to reach out to you."

"So why didn't he stay to talk?"

"He will."

"What makes you so sure?"

"Who could bear to give you up?"

"Gah! Don't make me vomit."

"Seriously! I'm on the damn phone with you, when I could be spooning with the boy next door. Call me stupid, but I can't imagine anyone so brain-dead as to give you up."

"He's my dad, not my boyfriend. There's a boy next—"

"Yeah, he's your dad, so he really shouldn't... shouldn't give you... shit. I hate it when I do this."

"Fuck! Jonah, listen to me. Your dad loved you. I know he did. He was sick and he did something desperate. That doesn't mean he didn't love you."

"I'm a bad boyfriend. I'm supposed to be making you feel better."

"You don't have any idea what it means to me to hear your voice every night. And that's not counting the boner I get when you answer the phone."

"You get a boner when I answer the phone?"

"Uh-huh. Just like one of Pavlov's dogs."

"Pavlov's dogs got boners? Have you been reading again? No wonder your game's slipping."

"My game is not slipping, and I'm not a dumb jock."

"No, you're my jock. Billy?"

"Say my name again. I'm almost there."

"Billy? You're jerking off! You should have told me."

"Ahhhhh."

"Fuck! Let me know next time, so I can—"

"Just a sec, I gotta... do you like the smell?"

"Of jizz?"

"Yeah, never mind, here's what I want you to do."

"Uh-oh."

"Did I say you could talk?"

CHAPTER 7

Stats

~~Girls I'm pretty sure wanted to kiss me: 5 12 10,012~~
Girls I've kissed: 3
Boys I've kissed: 1

If Dad ever finds this, I'm dead—like broken spine, belly slit, and guts slithering out all over the floor dead.

Boys who've dumped me: 1
Boys I would kneel on the floor and worship as a basketball god: 1
Stupid nicknames: 2
Public boners: 1
Teammates I'd like to knock some sense into: 2
Different kinds of underwear worn by guys on my floor: 5
Basketball players on the down-low: 1

Points Scored this season: ~~12 61 206~~ 260
Assists: ~~7 31 60~~ 87
Turnovers: ~~2 5~~ 11
Games Won: ~~1 3~~ 6

Games Lost: ~~1~~ ~~2~~ 4

Blow jobs received: 1
Blow jobs given: 1
Sexting sessions: ~~1~~ 4
Assholes I'd like to kill: 1
Parents who aren't talking to me: ~~2~~ 1
Crazy boyfriends: 1

THERE WASN'T much to distinguish the house from the one next door. Somehow Jonah had expected Billy's childhood home to be special in some way, if for no other reason than that Billy had grown up there. Square, two-story, with white vinyl siding and contrasting gray shutters didn't qualify. He was reaching for his phone to check the address again, when he noticed the stack of firewood that partially blocked the garage door behind the regulation-size basketball hoop. Clearly the family car never saw the inside of that shelter. The driveway had been widened and lines painted on it like a basketball court. He put his phone back into the pocket of his parka. Taking a deep breath, he marched up the steps and rapped smartly on the door.

"Hold your horses, I'm coming," someone yelled from within.

The door opened. The man behind the screen door wore a jacket as if he were preparing to go out. If the Glen Falls / Martin Luther King High School motto emblazoned over the left breast pocket of the jacket weren't enough to identify him as Billy's father, the man's lanky build and straight brown hair were. Unfortunately the pinched furrow between his brown eyes suggested he might view the world rather differently than his son.

"What the hell are *you* doing here?"

"Hi, Mr. Preston. I don't know if you remember—"

"I know exactly who you are."

"Dave, who's at the door?" A woman appeared in the dim foyer behind Mr. Preston.

"Hi, Mrs. Preston." Jonah put up a hand to shield his eyes from the midday sun and tried to make out the woman's features. "I'm Jonah Winfield. I don't think we've ever met."

"Jonah! You're the one Billy—"

"Yes, he is. And if you don't mind, I'm trying to figure out just what the fuck he thinks he's doing here."

In fact Jonah wasn't entirely sure what he was doing there. Coming to this house might be the stupidest thing he'd ever done. But he hated seeing Billy hurt, and he felt like he had to do something.

"I was hoping you might give me a ride."

Mr. Preston's mouth dropped open, and for a second his open astonishment made him look rather more like his son.

"I heard that you might be going up to Hoosier State to watch Billy play. Although you and I will have to agree to disagree if you're going to sit on the wrong side again."

"Is that where you went last week, Dave? Why didn't you tell me?" Mrs. Preston shoved her husband bodily out of the way and pushed open the screen door. "It's cold outside. You better come in before we let all the heat out."

"I… it doesn't mean what you think it does," Mr. Preston said to his wife.

"You can pretend all you like, dumbass, but I know exactly what it means, and I think Jonah does too."

"I do not want that… that—"

"Be careful, Mr. Preston. Any label you apply to me might just as well be applied to your son."

"You and my son have nothing in common."

"David Preston! We are not going to discuss this with the door open and all our neighbors—"

"We are not going to discuss this at all." With a murderous look, Mr. Preston stepped in front of his wife and yanked the screen door shut.

"Fine. You stay home and fume like a spoiled child. But if you can go see him play, I can too. You wait right there, Jonah."

Mrs. Preston disappeared from sight, and Mr. Preston took the opportunity to slam the heavy inner door in Jonah's face. Jonah heard urgent voices from within, but he couldn't make out the words. He'd have left, but Mrs. Preston's instruction had been clear, so he wandered over to the driveway and paced the free throw line, setting one foot before the other as though he were on a balance beam.

"Jonah?"

He spun around. Mrs. Preston, in hat, gloves, and quilted winter coat, waited by the car parked in front of the house.

"Mrs. Preston?"

"What are you waiting for? You wanted a ride, right? Well I'm going to see my son play basketball. You're welcome to come if you like."

"Uh…. Mr. Preston?"

"My husband can't find his ass with both hands."

Jonah didn't know if laughing was allowed. "I don't—"

"Come on, I don't want to miss the tip-off."

THE CROWD at the security barrier had diminished significantly by the time Billy left the arena, duffle slung over his shoulder. Better yet, no reporters waited to pounce with a question he didn't want to answer. Today, the press had focused their collective attention on Tully, who had played a spectacular game, scoring 31 points and guiding Hoosier State to a 104 to 99 win over Loyola. If anyone had noticed that Billy and Jamal spent nearly equal time on the court or that Billy returned to his usual style of play, their thoughts had probably been overshadowed by Tully's performance. It had been a relief not to face the heat of the television lights. Billy set out for the team bus but stopped short at an unexpected call.

"Billy! Over here! Billy!"

He glanced over at the usual crowd of family, fans, and general hangers-on who waited beyond the security barrier, stopping dead at the unexpected sight of his vigorously waving mom. Amazingly, Jonah grinned by her side. Billy dropped his bag, shocked to see the two of them together, and trotted over. He'd scanned the stands every chance he got during the game, but he'd been looking for his father's distinctive jacket, not his mom's winter coat. Jonah's presence surprised him in another sort of way. After Jonah's hitchhiking adventure, he'd made Jonah promise to tell him when he planned to attend a game. Stupidly, this last thought captured his mouth first.

"You promised you'd call first."

Jonah blinked. "Sorry. Your mom and I were so busy talking, I guess I forgot."

The disconcerting picture of the two of them gossiping like a pair of old ladies that formed in Billy's mind left him momentarily speechless.

"Billy?"

His mom's tone was more tentative than he liked, and it broke Billy loose of his imagination. He pulled himself together and leaned over the barrier to give his mother a one-armed hug.

"Mom! It's great to see you. I didn't think… without Dad…."

"Do you have time to talk a little?"

Billy glanced over his shoulder to see if anyone had followed him out of the sports center. "Hey, Otter! Tell the guys I'll see them later."

Otter waved. "No problemo, Grandpa."

"Grab my bag, would you? I'm gonna say hello to my family."

"Grandpa? Did he just call you grandpa?" his mom asked, eyebrows raised. "I thought your friends called you Billy Goat."

Billy ducked under the barrier. "Yeah, well, new school, new nickname."

She smiled. "I'm not sure which I like less. Do you know, they called your dad Socks in school. When we moved to Glen Falls, he made me swear not to tell anyone that." She winked at Jonah.

"My lips are sealed, ma'am. I don't need to give your husband another reason to hate me."

Her smile lost some of its shine. "The car's this way, Billy. Do you want something to eat?"

Billy wondered whether his mom would say anything about his dad's absence, or whether she would pretend nothing was wrong. "Sure, Mom. I'm starved."

THE RESTAURANT they chose had framed pictures of local high school and college sports teams, players, and coaches mounted all over the walls. Billy wondered if his picture would ever show up there. Maybe it was already here? He couldn't help checking as they followed the hostess to their booth.

Jonah caught him looking and grinned.

Busted. Sometimes the shrimp was just too damned smart for his own good.

"Your waitress will be with you shortly." The hostess handed them each menus.

His mom shrugged off her coat and tossed it onto the bench seat next to her. Her soft white hat and leather driving gloves followed. Jonah and Billy slid onto the vinyl bench across from her.

"Anything you want, boys, it's on me," she said, giggling self-consciously. "I always wanted to say that." Billy's dad always ordered on the rare occasions they went out for dinner together.

Billy knew it would be better manners to wait until they'd eaten or at least until they'd ordered, but the flutter in his gut was only going to get worse until he got some answers. If he was going to eat, he needed to ask now.

"So, how—" He pointed back and forth from his mom to Jonah. "—and where's Dad?"

Jonah grinned and high-fived Billy's mom. She slapped hands and then sighed and set her menu on the table. "You have a remarkable friend in Jonah."

Billy examined her face to see if she was serious. "Yeah, I do."

"Do you know he came to our house and asked your father for a ride to the game?"

Billy swiveled to stare at Jonah, unable to comprehend what thought process had led Jonah to think *that* was a good idea. Jonah smirked like he'd laid out an eighty-point word score in Scrabble.

His mom laughed out loud. "Close your mouth, buddy. You look just as stupid as your dad does with your mouth hanging open."

"What did he say? I mean, he didn't come, right?"

Her laughter died as quickly as it had come. "No, he didn't."

"He declined the opportunity to bask in my fabulousness," said Jonah dryly.

"Holy fuck," Billy breathed.

"Language," said his mom mildly.

Their waitress, a plump brunette with crooked teeth and blond streaks in her hair, picked that moment to interrupt the conversation. "Hi, I'm Cindy. I'll be serving you today. Can I get you something to drink to get you started?"

Billy's mom nodded in acknowledgement. "Hi, Cindy." She was the only person Billy had ever met who always addressed strange waiters by name. "I'll have a frozen margarita. Coke or something, boys?"

Still reeling from the idea of Jonah asking his father for a ride, Billy was thrown further off-balance by his mom's order. She rarely drank, usually claiming she didn't need the extra calories.

Jonah stepped into the breach. "I'll have a diet. Grandpa, here, will have unsweetened iced tea." Jonah knew Billy didn't like sweet drinks when he was in training.

Cindy didn't bat a false eyelash. "One frozen margarita, one diet, and an unsweet for Grandpa. I'll be right back with your drinks and to take your order."

Billy shook his head. "I can't believe you did that."

"I presume you're not speaking of my choice of beverage."

"You're lucky he didn't haul off and—"

"Your father is not violent," interrupted his mom.

"No, he's just a bigot."

Billy's words hung in the air for a moment while his mom examined her menu.

"Your father is not perfect, but I didn't come here to listen to you badmouth him."

"So why did you come?"

"I wanted—" His mom's voice cracked, and she cleared her throat before trying again. "I wanted to get to know the boy my son says he loves."

It was Jonah's turn to look like a stunned calf. "You told them you love me?"

If there had been anything in Billy's stomach, he would have lost it then. He'd left that part of the conversation out when he'd told Jonah about the disastrous call with his dad. But he had the presence of mind to know that there was only one course open to him now.

He took a shaky breath. "Yep, I did."

Jonah stared, wide-eyed. "Did you mean it?"

His mom's eyes went back and forth with the rapt attention of a referee at a tennis match. Out of the corner of his eye, Billy saw his mom wasn't their only audience. Their waitress stood frozen a couple of steps from their table, a serving platter of drinks balanced on one hand. *Why does everything important have to happen to me in public?* It was shaping up to one of those moments you tell stories about for the rest of your life. Billy saw himself at a bar, a line of empty whiskey glasses lined up before him, pouring out the story to a balding bartender, the man's sagging face fixed in an expression of pity. Shaking his head, Billy wiped the scene from his mind and formed another: a table laden with a Thanksgiving feast, the balding bartender replaced by his and Jonah's combined families. The story he told had frayed edges, but it was the wear of happy retelling.

Billy refocused. Jonah's wide gray eyes held the glint of tears. His chin trembled almost imperceptibly.

"Yes, I did," said Billy. "I love you."

"Oh." Jonah looked down at his menu. "I wasn't sure. Does that make me a bad person?" Then, almost as if it were an afterthought, he looked into Billy's eyes and smiled. "I love you too."

Cindy dropped a martini in front of Billy's mom. "Okay, glad we've got that out of the way. Wave when you're ready for another. I expect you'll need it."

Billy tore his gaze from Jonah. His mom had tears in her eyes as well. "It'll be okay, Mom. You'll see."

"I'm supposed to be the one saying stuff like that."

"It's okay. You've had a shock, right? You don't have to say anything."

"I think I do."

Billy hid his hands under the table to keep his mom from seeing them shake. Was this the moment when he'd find out she felt the same way as his dad and she'd only come to tell him in person? Or would she tell him that gay was okay so long as he never actually touched anyone like some stupid preacher? Maybe she couldn't stomach the idea of him and Jonah together. He gripped Jonah's hand under the table. Jonah squeezed in return with the same fingers that could make the old Martin Luther King High School upright ring like a concert grand or tinkle like a child's toy. Their wiry strength gave Billy the courage to meet his mother's direct gaze.

Her chin jutted. "It's not what I imagined for you. I saw girlfriends. Later, much later—" Her eyes flared. "—some young woman you couldn't bear to give up. Marriage. Children. Grandkids I could spoil. I don't know what this means for—"

"I want children too," Jonah interrupted.

This was totally out of hand. Was it too much to expect that Billy and Jonah talk about stuff like having kids in private before sharing with the entire world? Billy realized he was crushing Jonah's hand. He loosened his grip, but Jonah merely tightened his own. Billy felt like a witness in a trial. Only he wasn't sure whether he was the defendant or a witness for the prosecution.

He cleared his throat. "Do I get to play basketball for a while first? Or do I get any say in this at all?"

"I don't—" said his mom.

"Maybe." Jonah grinned. "But it will cost you."

Improbably, given the circumstance, Billy's dick chose to perk up at the promise in Jonah's tone. He slid his butt down the vinyl bench.

His mom shook her head. "You're both so young. It's too soon for this. You don't even know who you are yet."

Billy had the feeling she wasn't talking about marriage and children anymore.

"You know it's not a choice, right, Mrs. Preston," said Jonah earnestly. "Sexual preference isn't—"

"Don't you dare lecture me about my—"

"Stop." Billy used the voice he normally reserved for the times when Tully goofed off on the court. Surprisingly, it worked. His mom sat back in her seat. Jonah extracted his hand from Billy's and flexed his fingers. "Mom. Jonah and I gotta make decisions for ourselves now. We *have* to. I'm asking you to respect that." He took a breath. "I love Jonah. I love you and Dad. I want you all in my life."

His mom's eyes widened. "Oh, honey, you didn't think I'd... you're my baby. I couldn't...."

Billy felt something loosen in his chest.

"Your mom and I are cool," said Jonah. "She gave me a ride up here, right?"

That left the elephant in the room. Billy pictured his dad as an elephant with floppy ears and a long trunk for a nose. He shook his head free of the image. Sometimes his imagination got the better of him.

His mom sighed. "Your dad will come around. Give him time. He has a lot of words to swallow." She laughed unexpectedly. "It's going to take a while."

The elephant chewed a giant wad of green leaves. Billy joined in his mom's laughter, while Jonah looked from one to the other as if they'd both lost their minds.

TRANSCRIPT

"I can't believe you and Mom—"

"I don't want to talk about your mom. I mean she's rad, but...."

"Somebody's horny."

"It sucked to see you and not be able to kiss you."

"When I saw you standing there, I wanted to rip your clothes off and lick you all over."

"I hate this."

You hate sex talk?"

I love sex talk. But I want more. You think your mom will give me a ride up again?"

I'm still in shock she brought you the first time. No way she needs to know about our sex life."

"Forget your mom. Talking isn't enough."

"So let's kick it up a notch."

"You gonna tell me what to do again?"

"Yeah, but this time you're gonna be thinking about me all day."

I already think about you all day! I daydream so much my teachers probably think I'm stealing Valium from the nurse's office."

"A game of dare. I dare you to do something hot. If you do it, then you get to make me do something."

"Uh... what exactly...."

"Go commando for a week."

I'll get a boner!"

"Exactly how I like to picture you."

I have swim class. I can't go into the locker room like that."

"So bring some briefs and put them on in the boy's room before class."

"So if I do this, I can make you do anything?"

Yep."

You're gonna regret this."

I already do. Please don't get me arrested."

IT WAS past time for Jonah to quit letting everyone else determine his fate. More precisely, it was time he got his driver's license. He was eighteen. He didn't need anyone's permission. With a license he could drive to Hoosier State to see Billy whenever he felt like it. The main obstacle in the way of driving lessons was his class schedule, which had no room for driver's ed. Another problem was that the school district only offered driving classes in the summer. He hadn't been ready then. So now he had to find someone else to give him lessons. Mom was out. Literally, since she was out of town on an extended trip to DC. Rascal was in Europe for a few weeks of solo engagements. That left Paul or Davoud, his stand-in dads. While Paul might agree, his emotionalism didn't strike Jonah as helpful in a driving instructor. That left Davoud.

Jonah slipped into the Music Box just as Davoud closed Avakian Music for the day.

"Hi, champ." Davoud locked the door behind Jonah. "Were you wanting the piano?"

"Maybe later. Actually, I want to ask you something."

"Oh?" Davoud flipped the Open sign over. "What's up?"

"You know I'm eighteen now, right?"

"I wasn't *that* drunk at the party."

Jonah grinned. "You were there? Maybe I should have refused that last toke."

"Very funny, smartass. You mind following me upstairs? I want to put a chicken in the oven for dinner."

"Sure, no problem."

Jonah waited for Davoud to close out the register and then followed him up to his and Paul's apartment.

"You want to chop for the salad?" Davoud twisted the oven temperature knob to preheat.

"What do you need?"

"How about a couple of tomatoes and some red onion? Lettuce. Avoid the slimy stuff."

Like you would ever let anything rot in your refrigerator. While Jonah collected salad ingredients, Davoud washed a chicken and used a meat cleaver to cut it into pieces. Jonah washed and dried the vegetables, then laid them in the dish rack to dry.

"So I'm eighteen, right?"

"I think we established that."

Jonah transferred his salad ingredients to the chopping board.

"All the guys at school are driving now."

"Uh-huh." Davoud retrieved a bag of flour from the cabinet where he kept baking supplies.

"If I could drive, I could help out with errands. You know, grocery shopping and stuff."

Davoud dumped some flour into a dredging bowl and added salt, black pepper, and a pinch of mustard powder. "Not to mention what it would do for your social life."

"Well, maybe, but that isn't...." Jonah let his sentence trail off when he realized he didn't want to explain his real motivation. He would have to tell Davoud and Paul the extent of his feelings for Billy sometime, but he wanted to get his act together first. Too soon, and he'd be fielding questions about logistics for which he had no good answer.

"Then there's that newfound love of basketball. It'd be nice to get up to Hoosier State for a game or two, wouldn't it? I might even hitch a ride sometime." Davoud dumped a piece of still wet chicken into the dredging mixture and pushed it around until it was coated. His face was oddly devoid of expression.

"Um... yeah, well, that'd be great, but I need somebody to help me practice before I take the test."

Davoud put the chicken into the oven and took up position leaning against the counter. "Just whose car do you plan to subject to this little experiment?"

"It's not like my mom is using hers."

"Don't you think you better ask before you start counting your chickens?"

"I thought she'd be more comfortable with the idea if she knew you'd be the one teaching me."

Davoud loosed a guffaw. "That the plan, eh?"

"Please, Davoud, will you do it?" Jonah finished chopping lettuce and started in on some scallions he'd found in the crisper. "I can't afford to pay for lessons from a driving school."

"But you think you can afford to drive? You looked into insurance yet?"

"Mom can add me to her policy."

"You think she'll go for that?"

"Let me worry about that, would you? Please, Davoud, I'm desperate."

Davoud lifted a stack of plates from a cabinet. "Well, in *that* case."

"You'll do it."

Davoud grinned. "God help me."

Jonah put down the knife carefully before leaping to envelop Davoud in a bear hug.

"I'm pretty coordinated, you know—for a gay boy."

Davoud laughed. "Give me a break, Romeo. I already said yes."

"I knew you wouldn't let me down." What was with the Romeo?

"You know you have me wrapped around your little finger," said Davoud, smiling. "Ugh, I can't breathe."

PRACTICE ON Friday was tense. Saturday's game was with Missouri State, the top-ranked team in the conference. Rocker worked them hard, spitting out comments like they hurt his mouth. They ended with a practice game in which Jamal and Tully faced a team led by Billy and Otter. It went well enough until Tully lost control of a pass and Jamal lost control of his temper.

"Get your head out of your ass, faggot."

"What was that you called me?" Tully asked calmly, as though he'd failed to hear.

Otter stopped dribbling and held the ball in front of him like a bowler.

Jamal's gaze narrowed, and he stepped into Tully's space. "That's what you are, right?"

Rocker, who was at the other end of the court, started to jog in their direction.

"Christ, guys, can't you take it off the court?" said Billy.

Jamal turned to look at Billy. "Yeah, 'cause that's where you like to take it. Right up the ass."

"Jesus, man," said Otter. "Leave Grandpa out of this. He ain't done nothing to you."

Tully glared at Jamal. "You're one to talk, cocksucker."

Jamal's fists clenched. Billy knew what Jamal was going to do before he did it, but he was too late to stop it. Jamal's fist connected with Tully's face with an audible smack. Otter and Billy moved at the same time, grabbing Jamal's arms. Tully staggered and spun, but kept his feet. When he faced them again, bright red rimmed his nostrils. He licked his upper lip and grinned. Then he stepped over and kissed Jamal on the mouth.

Jamal's limbs went slack for a frozen instant. Then he went berserk, trying simultaneously to head butt and knee Tully. Billy and Otter hung on for dear life. Tully danced out of reach, his booming laugh filling the gym.

"Break it up!" yelled Rocker, putting his body between Tully and Jamal. "Jesus Christ! What is wrong with you people?"

"Get the fuck off me," said Jamal, trying to yank his arm from Billy's grip.

Digger ran up. "Get out of here, Tully," he said, shoving Tully toward the gym exit.

Rocker pointed toward the locker room and coaches offices. "Jamal, my office now."

Jamal ignored him and lunged at Tully. "Gonna kill the faggot. Gonna kill him."

"I got him," said Digger, taking Billy's place. Rocker took Jamal's other arm from Otter. Together, they dragged him toward Rocker's office. The locker room door slammed, leaving the players staring at one another in the sudden quiet.

It wasn't until then that Billy noticed a guy standing by the gym exit holding a smartphone shoulder level like he was taking a picture.

"Hey, you!" he yelled, jogging toward the guy. "What are you doing?"

The guy carried a winter parka over his arm, and wore jeans and a Hoosier State sweatshirt like a student, but he could have been anyone, even a reporter. The last thing they needed was a video of Tully and Jamal showing up on the evening news. Before Billy could get there to interrogate him, the guy disappeared through the exit. Billy followed into the main corridor of the athletic center, but the guy must have slipped into one of the rooms that lined the hall.

"Shit." Billy turned to find Otter behind him, his face contorted with worry. "Do you think he got much?"

"Don't know," Billy answered. "I didn't see him until Digger got hold of Jamal."

"I'm sick of this crap!" Otter rubbed his face. "Those two don't give a fuck about anyone or anything except yanking each other's chains. You got to do something, Grandpa."

The fuck? "Why me?"

Otter shrugged. "You're the only guy on the team who still speaks to both of them."

"What about Rocker?"

"If he had anything to offer, he'd a done it by now."

SATURDAY MORNING, Rocker announced that Tully had declined to press assault charges. It hadn't occurred to Billy that Tully could do such a thing. Rocker went on to say that Jamal was suspended from the team for three games. He would return on probation. Any further violence, and he would be off the team. Billy's reaction, when he heard the news was to tear up, out of frustration, sadness, or something else, he wasn't sure. He kept his head down until the strange rush of emotion subsided. He sympathized with Jamal's desire to keep his private life private. But Jamal's self-loathing—for what else could you call it?—both saddened and angered him. A contemptuous voice in the back of Billy's mind, sounding suspiciously like his dad, suggested both players were out of line. In truth Billy couldn't understand either of them. Let it go, he wanted to tell them.

The other players' reactions were largely along party lines. Jamal's friends ranged from stoic to openly bitter. Tully's entourage seemed mostly relieved, some apparently having been afraid the coach would punish Tully for provoking Jamal, even though—as far as Billy knew—nobody had told the coach what either player had said before the kiss. The kiss, of course, had come *after* Jamal punched Tully. Billy couldn't see Rocker trying to explain giving Tully disciplinary action for sexual harassment to the press or his colleagues in the athletic department. Tully himself was uncharacteristically quiet, his long fingers drifting up repeatedly to rub his swollen nose.

Mike's comment that night at the student union was succinct. "I guess Rocker doesn't equate kissing with sexual harassment."

He and Billy shared a plate of greasy nachos with Sunflower and Jason.

"Tully's too important to the team," said Jason. "You know Rocker would never do anything to jeopardize the season."

"Hasn't he already?" said Sunflower. "I mean by not dealing with their crap. What's their beef anyway? What was that kiss about?"

Billy raised his eyebrows at Mike. *You want to take that?*

Mike took a chip and turned it to wind up a long string of melted cheese. "It's your story to tell. Sunflower won't tell anyone if you don't want her to."

Billy caught a flicker of pleasure in Sunflower's eyes as Mike spoke. *That'll buy you a kiss—at the very least.*

Jason shrugged and mimed zipping his mouth shut when Billy caught his eye.

Billy sighed. "Jamal is on the down-low, and I think Tully has, or had, a thing for him. But it's probably more hate than love at the moment."

"Holy shit!" said Sunflower, spitting salted caramel mocha back into her cup. "What are the chances of *three* gay guys on one team?"

"Actually, I don't think Tully's gay," said Billy. "More like bi."

"Jamal is gay?" said Jason. "How do you know?"

Billy's face heated.

"Oh my God!" said Sunflower. "You guys are more fun than daytime television."

"I can't believe you—does Jonah know?" Jason asked.

The blood drained from Billy's face as fast as it had collected there. "You can't tell him. We were—he broke up with me, so it wasn't cheating—but it would kill him! He wouldn't understand. It was just—"

"Sex," said Jason, scooping salsa and melted cheese with a corn chip.

"Not even that. He only… I mean we didn't…."

"Whoa, boy. Nobody here is judging you," said Sunflower. "We've all done things we regret, right?"

Mike's eyes narrowed. "Like what, exactly?"

"Down boy, I have a past. Let me spell that for you, in case you weren't paying attention, P-A-S-T."

Mike subsided, frowning.

"Jealous a little, are we?" said Jason, his mouth full.

Billy gladly let the spotlight pass to someone else. The idea of Jonah finding out about the incident with Jamal filled him with terror.

"So what are you going to do about them?" Sunflower asked Mike.

"Who, Jamal and Tully?" Mike caught Billy's eye. "Beats me." He pointed at Billy. "He's got a better chance of…."

Billy sighed. "Why does everyone seem to think it's *my* problem to fix? They're so—the whole thing is just epic."

"Operatic," said Jason, earning him looks of astonishment from his roommates. "What? You think I got no culture?"

HOOSIER STATE steamrolled up the ranks toward the conference title. In their late-night phone calls, Billy rarely mentioned the team's progress, nor did he obsess about player and team stats like so many sports fans and TV commentators—not with Jonah. He reserved their phone calls for less brainy pursuits. But Jonah couldn't escape the reality that Billy was good and getting better, and he thrived in the high pressure vessel of the Hoosier State basketball program, despite his teammates' ongoing strife.

Billy's athletic success created a dilemma for Jonah. At the start of the school year, Jonah had fantasized that Billy might drop out of the athletic program, relieving Jonah of the need to attend a local music school. But Billy's love of basketball had only grown, so it was time for Jonah to confront his fears and solve the problem of his and Billy's physical distance. What Billy apparently didn't realize, and Jonah was reluctant to tell him, was that one of the best music schools in the country was located an hour's drive from Hoosier State, at Indiana University Bloomington. Some rankings put the Jacobs School of Music second in the country, after the Eastman School of Music in Rochester, New York. Jonah didn't tell Billy about Bloomington because he was convinced he wasn't good enough to get in. His unconventional musical education, his lack of a proper piano teacher to recommend him, and his interest in inappropriate musical genres would all count against him. The thought of going through the involved application process and failing tied his lungs in knots.

The week after Thanksgiving, Jonah spilled his fears to Aida, matriarch of the Avakian musical dynasty, retired opera singer, and informal piano coach. Billy was actually the first to use the term coach to describe Aida. Aida wasn't a pianist, so she couldn't really be Jonah's piano teacher, but she rocked the opera stage, and she'd insisted they schedule time together almost since Jonah had come to live at the Music Box. Billy had nodded sagely on hearing Jonah describe their sessions. "Oh, so she's your coach. That's cool."

Jonah had planned to tell Aida about Billy, but until T-day, events had always intervened. A rant about scales finally triggered his confession. Aida insisted he begin every lesson with a progression of scales in various keys.

"They must be familiar as your own body," she said with a vague gesture in the direction of his crotch.

"Gross! I can't believe you said that. How am I supposed to take you seriously when you joke like that?"

Aida frowned, her whole body sagging in despair. "I cannot be both funny and serious? This is terrible. How am I to live?" Her eyes widened to a glare. "Play the scales!"

They were in the back room of Avakian Music, at the Steinway grand that never sold, despite occasional inquiries from well-heeled customers.

"I hate this. Scales are boring. I used to like playing the piano. Hearing something on the radio and working it out was fun. This is mind-numbing."

Aida's nose rose into the air, and she glared down its length. "Yes, you sacrificed basic skills for a game. Now you must be serious, if you are to be all you can be. Play them again."

Jonah sighed and began the progression again, wondering whether Aida intentionally echoed the Army slogan. She would make a good sergeant.

"Again."

Jonah's irritation and underlying worry overwhelmed him. "What's the point? I'll never be as good as the students who've had proper teachers. They'll never let me in."

He had to give it to Aida. She might have the ego of a diva. She could make a scene with the best of them, but she never let her emotionalism distract her from what was important. With typical focus, she ignored his dig at her teaching skills and honed in on the thing he hadn't meant to say.

"Who will not let you in? Where?"

He couldn't meet her gaze. "No place special. Music school."

Aida tapped a foot impatiently. "Music school is special. Few are so privileged as to attend one. But I do not think you referred to just any music school. Where have you decided to go?"

It was so like her. One decided to go and went. Simple.

"I haven't really. I just—"

"Do not lie to me, young man."

"Maybe I don't wanna talk about it."

Aida folded her arms over her chest and glared.

"Jeez, Aida. You're worse than my mom."

"Your mother is an amateur. Tell me."

He swallowed. "Bloomington. The Jacobs."

"Ah, very good. I know many there. But why not Juilliard or the Curtis, which are in cities where there are more of your kind?"

My kind? Jonah knew that Aida knew he was gay—the events of the past year had made for a very public coming out—but he'd never actually spoken to her about it. While she might be more like his grandmother than his real grandmothers in Chicago, he wasn't sure he wanted to share that part of his life with her.

"My kind?"

"Gay people. You must not be like my son and wait so long to find a husband. I will not live so long, and I wish to see you happy."

"But I don't need to find anyone. I already—" *Whoops.* His cheeks warmed.

Aida dropped onto the piano bench next to him and examined his face thoughtfully. "This sudden interest in basketball on the TV. I knew it wasn't natural. But I thought you just liked long and tall. Now I think…."

She had to feel the waves of heat coming off his face by now.

"Yes. The boy who used to bring your schoolwork. B… Bobby, I think? He was tall. You like tall. Does he play basketball at Hoosier State?"

Had his family nothing better to do than speculate about his love life? Watching her work it out was like a train wreck, only in slow motion. Each freighted car slammed into place accordion-style, until there remained only the rush of silent dust to choke him. What he wouldn't give for seven or eight brothers and sisters to distract her. There was nothing for it but to confess. She would only pester him until he told all.

He sighed. "Billy. His name is Billy Preston."

Aida grinned. "Rascal told me there was someone. I thought here at school."

Jonah lowered his forehead onto the keys. "Ahhhh! It's like living with the mafia."

Aida patted him on the back. "I made a mistake with Davoud, leaving him to find his own way. I won't make that mistake again."

"What are you talking about?"

"Is it so bad, knowing you have family who wish you to be happy?"

Jonah glanced at her from the corner of his eye. "No, of course not. I just… you know, a little privacy now and then."

"Very well. We shall not discuss what you do with your underwear at night."

Jonah buried his face in his arms, the piano crashing as he landed on the keys. "Oh my God!"

Aida patted his knee. "Young people are so sensitive. You must invite Billy for Christmas. I wish to meet him."

"I'm already having nightmares."

Aida huffed. "We are a nice family. He will like us."

Jonah raised his head. "That's what I'm afraid of."

Aida smiled serenely. "So you want to go to Bloomington to be near this boy." She slid off her stool to pace around the piano. "It won't be easy, but it is not impossible, I think."

Something loosened in Jonah's chest, and his eyes began to burn.

Aida stopped pacing. "What are you sitting there for? You must practice if you are to go to Bloomington! Play the scales again."

Regrettably, unclouded vision wasn't necessary for scales.

FROM THAT day Aida drove him relentlessly in their sessions at the Steinway. When Rascal returned from his tour of the continent, she browbeat him into offering Jonah a series of catch-up lessons in music theory to fill in the gaps left by his hit or miss musical education. She even encouraged him to put together a portfolio of pieces of his own composition.

In addition to the usual college application forms, test scores, and essay, the piano department at the Jacobs School of Music required that Jonah prepare a recording of a fixed list of pieces selected by the faculty. Jonah could play the pieces, especially after he'd hunted down recordings and listened to them. The memorization wasn't a problem—he was expected to perform them without a score—but he continued to obsess about his technique, which could never match that of students who'd had proper teachers since their hands had grown large enough to span the keys.

When he voiced his concerns to Aida, she pooh-poohed the issue. "Technique you can learn. That is what school is for. Your ear, your feeling, they are what makes you a musician." So Jonah kept his worries to himself. He said nothing about the application to Billy.

TRANSCRIPT

"Do you have any idea how raw my dick is?"

"How many times a day have you beat off?"

"You're sick, you know that."

"How many?"

"Don't think I can't hear you smirking. Four, pervert. Four times yesterday."

"That's one thing you and Dad agree on."

"I'm nothing like him!"

"Sorry."

"Send me a pair of your jeans."

"Huh?"

"Rev—" [Coughing] "—for your dare. I promise to send them back."

"What are you going to do to them?"

"Never mind, just send them."

"What was I thinking?"

"You were using your little head."

"Who's calling me little?"

"Sorry, you were using Mr. Potato Head."

"More like it."

"Careful you don't get a swollen head."

"Too late. I told you what happens when you call."

"We can't talk five minutes without getting off."

"You don't want to?"

"Did I say that?"

"You still have pants on?"

"Yeah."

"No underwear?"

"I promised, didn't I?"

"Good. Leave your pants on."

"Am I gonna have to do my own laundry again?"

[Evil laughter]

"JONAH YOU'RE a bar late." Davoud let his bow drop. "I'm surprised you're having such trouble remembering when to come in—it's your piece." Had it been Jonah talking, it would have come out snarky, but Davoud managed to make it a sound like a gentle inquiry about Jonah's health.

"Sorry, I'm just...." Jonah straightened up on the piano bench and tried to look attentive. He nodded at Paul to start again.

Paul raised an eyebrow and took a breath. He subsided at a warning look from Davoud. Shrugging, he bent over his guitar and strummed the dissonant opening chords. The trio for piano, guitar, and string bass they practiced was one of the pieces Aida had convinced Jonah to include in his portfolio for music school.

On the second run-through, Jonah hit the entrance, but flubbed a chord a few bars in.

Davoud rubbed his chin. "Why don't we break for a few?"

Paul set down his guitar. "I've been meaning to ask why 'Macaroni and Cheese'?"

He referred to the title Jonah had scrawled across the top of the sheet music.

"Don't know. Seemed to fit."

In fact, the piece was a tribute to Jonah's dad. While he wasn't sure he'd ever really be able to forgive his dad for taking his own life, Jonah tried to spend the anniversary of his dad's death doing something more productive than bawling. The piece was his attempt to turn anger and grief into something positive.

Jonah's dad had loved to cook for Jonah. He'd actually had a broad repertoire of dishes, but macaroni and cheese was Jonah's favorite, his comfort food. In the trio, he'd tried to capture the feeling of coming home from a crappy day at school—last year's bullies had gifted him plenty of those—and hanging out in the kitchen while his dad made dinner. The dissonant guitar opening conveyed his agitation after school. The piano added layers of anger and relief at having survived a fight with the bullies. Davoud's bass brought comfort and warmth, resolving the jangling nerves and strong emotion of the first section into the warmth and comfort of... well... his dad's macaroni and cheese.

"I'm okay. I promise I'll get it right this time."

This time, they actually made it through to the end of the piece. But something wasn't right, and Jonah wasn't sure how to fix it. Usually, he'd ask Rascal, his writing partner, but Rascal had taken his mom to dinner, probably in an attempt to distract her on the anniversary. Jonah was grateful. He and his mom weren't very good at comforting each other, even if their relationship had lost some of its adversarial quality.

"Earth to Jonah." Paul sounded concerned.

"Sorry. Can we take the last—no, there's no point. There's something wrong with the middle section, but I'm not sure...." Jonah dropped his head into his hands. "It's too cheesy. I don't know how to fix it."

Davoud and Paul started to laugh.

"What?"

Paul rolled his eyes at him. "Cheesy? Macaroni and cheese?"

"God." He grimaced. "I'm so out of it today, I didn't even realize...."

Paul put his guitar in the stand and joined him on the piano bench. "Don't be so hard on yourself." Jonah leaned into his warmth, glad he'd finally reached the point where he could let Paul comfort him without losing it.

Davoud set his bass down and leaned on the piano. "We can wait for another day."

"No, I'm okay, and I need to finish this. Aida wants it next week."

"Then I have a suggestion. The part where I come in and fix everything? It's too easy." Davoud grinned. "Easy cheesy."

Paul snorted.

"It needs some back and forth. Might be a good time for variations. Use your own experience. It takes time to accept that you have a right to be comforted."

"Fuck, you're right. Why didn't I see that?" It was obvious in hindsight. He'd been too eager to show the good part about his dad and had forgotten that things that come too easily lose their value.

"Um." Jonah hesitated. "There's something I've been meaning to ask you." His relief at identifying the problem gave him the strength to address the other problem on his mind.

"Me?" Davoud asked.

"Both of you. It's about Billy."

Paul let out a puff of air, as though he'd been holding his breath. "Yeah?"

Davoud raised his eyebrows but said nothing.

"Billy and I… you know we talk a lot."

"We have some inkling," said Davoud dryly.

"Like, he came out to his family a while ago, and his dad hasn't spoken to him—" Paul began vibrating like a tuning fork. "It's not as bad as it sounds. I mean, he's been going to Billy's games, so I think he'll eventually come around. And his mom's okay with it."

"But…." Paul hadn't stopped vibrating.

"Well, Christmas is coming soon and winter break, and I want to make sure he has someplace to go for the holiday. You know, where he won't be judged."

Davoud squeezed his shoulder. "Of course he can stay here. Aida's got a spare room he can use, if he doesn't—"

"Um, that's great, but…."

Paul laughed suddenly. "I think what slick here is trying to say is that he'd like Billy to stay with him, right, Jonah?"

This was something of a switch. Jonah had expected Paul to fly off the handle, especially after he heard about Billy's dad. Instead, it was Davoud's hand on his shoulder that suddenly felt heavy.

Davoud cleared his throat. "Isn't he a little young to—"

"No." Paul turned around on the bench to look up at his partner. "They're both over eighteen."

"Mother will—"

"Aida already knows about me and Billy."

Davoud's hand was going to leave a mark. "What, exactly, does she know about you and Billy?"

"That we're… you know."

"If you can't even say it, I'm supposed to believe you're ready to have sex with the guy? That's what this is all about, right?"

Paul stood up and took his partner's face in both hands. "Give him a break, Stretch. Did you *ever* reach a point where you could talk comfortably about sex with your parents?"

"I certainly did—" Davoud loosened his grip. "—not."

Jonah jumped up from the seat. "If you can't cope, we can find another place to—"

"No way." Davoud's tone could have cut steel. "We've only just started getting this place working the way it should. Christmas is for family."

Paul's hands dropped, and he pulled Davoud against his body. "Shush. It's okay, baby."

"I want—I *need* you here, Jonah," Davoud growled.

Jonah glanced up, shocked at the glint of tears in Davoud's eyes.

Jonah had never seen Davoud cry. Not ever. "Oh wow, I didn't mean to... that's what I want too, Davoud. It's just that Billy and I hardly get to see each other and I—"

"Hush, both of you." Paul pulled Jonah into his embrace. "Billy can stay as long as he wants to, Jonah. If Aida won't put him up, we will. But it's your mother's call whether he stays in your room or not."

"Mom?" Jonah squeaked.

"Esmé?" Davoud protested, as gobsmacked as Jonah.

"Hush, honey. I know what I'm doing," Paul said.

That's when it occurred to Jonah that he hadn't yet told the hardest person of all about him and Billy. He ducked from under Paul's arm so he could glare at him better.

Paul smirked complacently.

"MOM, CAN I talk to you?" Jonah poked at his dinner of vegetarian lasagna, green salad, and garlic bread, certain he'd vomit if he tried to eat before he got this conversation over with. It was just him and his mom tonight, in the third floor apartment across the hall from Aida's place. He glanced around the dining room at the framed paintings and battered sideboard filled with his grandmother's china set, not quite sure how to begin. They'd finally moved some of the furnishings from their old house, mostly Jonah figured, to protect the priceless Persian carpets and antique furniture that Davoud's family had left behind, so the place seemed homier than before, without being too much like the house they'd abandoned.

He might not eat after he told his mom, either, but that was getting ahead of things. His mom sported an elegant silk blouse and tailored wool suit, even though she'd just made dinner. That meant she planned to return to her office and work. While she telecommuted, and her home office was only a floor below in one of the Music Box's spare apartments, she always wore business clothes in case she had to video conference with a client or colleague about a case.

"Always, honey."

Jonah sighed and tried to focus on his mom. "It's kind of important."

Her hands dropped to her lap. "I'm listening."

"It's about Billy."

She was too good an attorney to show much on her face, but Jonah noticed her breathing was unnaturally steady, as though she were timing it.

"He's your friend from last year, right? How is he?" Her voice had a teasing quality he didn't understand.

"He's fine. He's at Hoosier State now. Actually, that's partly what I wanted to talk to you about."

"Yes?"

Why did talking to his mom always feel like he might come away bleeding? Some of his confusion must have showed on his face, because she reached out to touch his hand.

"It's okay, honey." She smiled. "I already know about you and Billy."

"How?"

"Have you forgotten who pays your phone bill?"

Actually, he had.

"It didn't take an investigation to figure it out, given the calls to Hoosier State—and your sudden interest in basketball. Billy's tall, isn't he? I was surprised, because people usually pick somebody who's not too far off in height, but I guess you found a way around that?"

Jonah felt stupid. Of course, she'd known all along. She was his mother, the lawyer. The facts never escaped her. He forked lasagna to cover his confusion. Maybe the height *would* be a problem. He and Billy had only kissed a couple of times. But he was still growing, unlike most of the seniors at school. What would Billy say when he realized Jonah was a whole two inches taller than he'd been last year? Actually, that was an easy one. He'd make a lewd joke about Jonah being a growing boy.

"What's so funny?"

"I was thinking about Billy."

"That's good. He makes you laugh."

"Yeah, he does."

"How else does he make you feel?"

"Safe." Jonah surprised himself with the ease with which he answered the question, but then nothing about this conversation was going as he'd expected.

"He stood up for you last year, didn't he?"

"He did."

His mom smiled. "I knew I liked him."

"You did? Why didn't you say anything?"

She took a sip of wine. "Maybe I should have, but you were so contrary then. I was afraid you'd drop him just to spite me."

"Oh." He had to admit she had a point.

"So what did you want to talk to me about?"

He told her about Billy and his dad and Christmas. She listened, nodding when he paused. He took a breath and plunged on. "So I want him to stay here for Christmas, with me… in my room." Before she could answer, he went on. "I talked to Davoud and Paul. They're okay with it, if you are."

"They are, huh? Nice of them to leave it to me."

Not for the first time, Jonah wondered if his mom resented the pseudo-parental role his substitute fathers played in his life. But she still smiled, so maybe she was okay with it.

"If you're asking what I think you're asking, do *you* think you're ready?"

He didn't hesitate. "Yes. The only reason we haven't already, is that it's so hard for us to get together with him up there and me down here."

She seemed a little taken aback at his openness. But he figured if there was ever a time for honesty, this was it.

"Okay. Do we need to have a conversation about being safe?"

"No, Billy and I already decided to use condoms until we live together. In case one of us gets lonely and does something stupid."

Her eyes popped at this. "That's uncommonly… rational of you."

"I figure I get it from you."

She nodded and reached for her wineglass.

He hadn't entirely meant that as a compliment, but she didn't seem to take offense. On the other hand, the level of wine in her glass had dropped precipitously in the last few minutes.

"I don't suppose Billy's parents have anything to say about this."

"We're not asking them."

"I see." She cut a small square off her lasagna. "I suppose I should be thankful you're asking me." She cocked her head. "So I take it, what you want to know is whether he can stay in your room—not whether it's okay with me if you have sex."

Jonah gulped and looked her in the eye. "Right."

"It seems you've already made the important decisions. I'd be tilting at windmills to refuse you, knowing you'd just go somewhere else to—" She paused to take another sip of wine. "—do it." She finished the wine. "Don't you think?"

His mom's comment struck Jonah as something of an evasion. He found he really did want to know her opinion of what he planned with Billy. "Come on, Mom, I…." He had difficulty finding words.

"So you really *do* want to know what I think."

She knew him pretty well. *Here comes the bleeding part.*

"What I want is for you to be happy, to have someone in your life you love and who loves you. What I think is that Billy has proved a pretty good choice so far. Has he given you any reason to doubt him?"

Jonah thought about his long-distance relationship and how hard it had been. Billy had to have felt the same, at least a little, but he'd never suggested they give up. "No, he hasn't." He rubbed his hands on his jeans. "I miss him so much." She had to know he wasn't talking about conversation.

"I imagine you do." She lifted her napkin to dab at her eyes. "Damn, I'm going to have to fix my makeup." She smiled at him through glistening eyes. "I think I'm blessed with a son who knows his mind better than most and who's been forced to grow up a lot faster than is right. I trust you to do what is right for you and for Billy."

Jonah wanted to thank her, but didn't think he could speak without losing control, so he nodded instead.

CHAPTER 8

Stats

~~Girls I'm pretty sure wanted to kiss me. 5 12 10,012~~
Girls I've kissed: 3
Boys I've kissed: 1

If Dad ever finds this, I'm dead—like broken spine, belly slit, and guts slithering out all over the floor dead.

Boys who've dumped me: 1
Boys I would kneel on the floor and worship as a basketball god: 1
Stupid nicknames: 2
Public boners: 1
Teammates I'd like to knock some sense into: 2
Different kinds of underwear worn by guys on my floor: 5
Basketball players on the down-low: 1

Points Scored this season: ~~12 61 206 260~~ 421
Assists: ~~7 31 60 87~~ 149
Turnovers: ~~2 5 11~~ 14
Games Won: ~~1 3 6~~ 8

Games Lost: ~~1~~ ~~2~~ 4

Blow jobs received: 1
Blow jobs given: 1
Sexting sessions: ~~1~~ 7
Assholes I'd like to kill: 1
Parents who aren't talking to me: ~~2~~ 1
Crazy boyfriends: 1
Families: 2
Boys I love: 1

JONAH TROMPED down to the post office on Main Street the week before Christmas to send his screening tape by registered mail to Bloomington. Only a few days before the winter solstice, the sun had already dropped behind the line of late-nineteenth century buildings lining the Glen Falls business district. The orange glow of the sodium street lamps warmed the buildings' long shadows. Last-minute shoppers desperate to ship presents to absent friends and family in time for the coming holiday packed the lobby of the post office. The longer he waited, the lower Jonah's mood fell. By the time he'd shuffled his way up the slow-moving line to the counter, Jonah had convinced himself his efforts were futile. The faculty would see right through him. They would sneer at his compositions, laugh at his vain attempt to cut the waiting line into their rarified company.

"Happy Holidays. May I help you?" said a rosy-faced clerk in a Santa hat.

Jonah opened his mouth to inform the clerk he'd made a mistake, but the address of one of the packages stacked in the canvas-and-metal wheeled cart awaiting the next shipment caught his eye.

William Ball, 24 Addison Hall, Hoosier State University

Was this William another Billy? Or did his family call him Will? *His* Billy might not get presents this year. What if his father wouldn't let Billy's mom send anything? In his foul mood, he would believe anything of the man who couldn't bring himself to speak to his gay son. How could Jonah face Billy if he hadn't had the courage to try to get into Bloomington?

"Did you want to mail that?"

The wait for Billy's visit stretched before Jonah like a child's hours before Christmas. He ached for Billy. He wanted to plaster himself against Billy's skin, bury his nose in the hollow below Billy's clavicle, and breathe him in.

"Sir?"

"Yeah. Registered mail please."

The transaction finished, Jonah turned to make his way back to the Music Box. It would be a kind of relief if he didn't get into Bloomington. Hoosier State had to have some kind of music program. What did it matter really where he went to school? He would be with Billy.

TRANSCRIPT

"You get the jeans?"

"Yeah. What did you do to them?"

"You haven't worn 'em yet?"

"No, they just got here."

"Put 'em on."

"Jesus! What did you do to the pockets?"

"Ventilation."

"You don't expect me to—"

"You will walk across campus wearing the jeans with no underwear."

"I'll get a hard-on."

"Welcome to the club. You started this."

"And now I'm gonna regret it."

"Just listen. In a public place of your choice, you're gonna put your hand in your pocket and think of me."

"You're diabolical."

"Pathological."

"You're gonna get me arrested."

"Or mobbed by fan girls."

"I don't have fan girls."

"You've never been in the stands while you're playing."

JONAH'S ADOPTED family did everything they could to make Billy feel welcome in the run-up to Christmas. Billy suspected they must have consulted with Jonah about the gift-giving thing. Either that or they'd guessed how precarious his finances were. Anyway, after Jonah's enthusiastic suggestion that he spend the holiday at the Music Box, he'd received a stately invitation from Aida Avakian requesting that he spend Christmas with the Avakian family. At the bottom she'd added a handwritten note explaining that he shouldn't contemplate presents for the adults, but nobody would mind if he wanted to exchange gifts with his own generation. Therefore he needed only to find something for Jonah and for Amir Avakian's little girl, Zhara. He was embarrassed to have his personal finances so bluntly assessed, but at the same time reassured to know what was expected of him.

But even the prospect of seeing Jonah wasn't enough to keep Billy from thinking that it would be the first Christmas in his life he'd spent apart from his parents. He might not have always seen eye-to-eye with his dad, but they shared the same attitude about Christmas: more was better. More lights. More tinsel. More frosted sugar cookies cut in the shapes of Santa, elves, Christmas trees—and in accordance with a particular Preston family tradition—ice skates. As Grandma Preston told it, the ancient tin cookie cutter shaped like an ice skate had been formed by her grandfather for her grandmother after she'd won in a race around the pond at their family farm. In any case, white-frosted ice skate cookies were a firmly entrenched family tradition.

Only Billy wouldn't be licking the frosting off any sugar cookies this year because Dad was still being a dick and fighting with Mom about their sissy son. She finally called a few days before he left Hoosier State to tell him she would be spending Christmas this year with Grandma Miller and he should join her there. Grandma Miller was a gray-haired farmer's daughter whose social life revolved around quilting and the Methodist Church. Billy didn't know whether his mom had told Grandma he was gay, but she didn't have to say anything for him to know Jonah wouldn't be welcome there. He felt churlish refusing to meet her, because he knew she was hurting as much as he was. Nevertheless, he told her he'd be spending Christmas with Jonah at the Music Box.

"At the Music Box? You mean the Avakian building."

"Jonah's been living there since... since last year."

"We don't even know the Avakians, but you'd rather spend the holiday with them than your family?"

"I want to be with Jonah. They're okay with that. You know Davoud Avakian is Mr. G's partner."

"Mr. Gaston from Martin Luther King High School? That Mr. G?" She sounded surprised. He'd always assumed she knew Mr. G was gay, but he guessed people saw what they wanted to see.

"Yeah. They live together now."

"I had no idea. Good thing your dad didn't either. He'd have made you drop Jazz Ensemble."

"Has he said anything to you about—"

"We're working on it." Her clipped tone didn't welcome more questions.

It was probably stupid, but Billy felt guilty for causing a rift between his parents. "Um, you want to meet for dinner or something, after Christmas?"

"I'll be damned if I'm going to mail you your presents."

They agreed to meet for dinner at a restaurant in Glen Falls the day after Christmas.

THE GLEN Falls Greyhound station was a ten-minute walk from the Music Box. When the driver pulled his bag from the luggage compartment, Billy texted Jonah to tell him he'd arrived. The streets were wet from the cold drizzle that had speckled the bus's windshield all the way from Hoosier State. It was eerily quiet for a midweek afternoon. Billy held the door for a man as he backed out of the drug store, his arms full of packages. Everyone probably huddled around the fire with their families, as befitted Christmas Eve. At the Music Box, he caught a flash of movement inside the dim foyer. The door burst open, nearly catching him in the face. Jonah grabbed Billy's duffle and dragged him into the building.

"You're here. I thought you'd never get here. Everyone's watching football at Aida's place, but we don't have to go up if we don't want to. I thought we could put your bag in the room and then maybe—are you hungry? I could make something, although Davoud's been cooking all week and Paul too, so there are cookies and stuff everywhere. Or we could get leftovers from Aida. She made this gigantic ham yesterday, so we'll probably be eating that all week...." Billy followed Jonah upstairs, bemused to find his boyfriend chattering like a crack-addict. When Jonah offered to take back a perfectly good set of clean towels and change it for another "because the other set would match the color of your eyes," Billy finally dragged Jonah from the bathroom to ask what the fuck was wrong with him.

"Nothing, I just want everything to be perfect."

Billy's unruly feelings about his family had him sufficiently out of kilter to sharpen his answer. "Well, that ship has sailed. Perfect would be my dad talking to me."

Jonah bit his lip. "I meant here at the Music Box—with me."

"Shit, Jonah. I'm sorry." Billy pulled Jonah in for a kiss, but he pulled back when Jonah's tongue slid against his own, glancing up and down the hall to see if anyone had noticed.

Jonah pressed his groin against Billy's thigh so Billy could feel the bulge there. "You don't have to do that, you know. They know about us."

"What do you mean?"

"They know we're together. How I feel about you." Jonah blushed. "They're even okay with us sharing a room."

Billy wasn't entirely sure *he* knew how Jonah felt about him. Late-night booty calls and lazy conversation were one thing, but didn't a real relationship require other shared experiences? They'd had precious little time together in the months since he'd left Glen Falls. One night of mutual blow jobs—an experience he admittedly wanted to repeat as soon as possible—wasn't a substitute for time hanging out. What if they weren't a good fit physically? What if they had incompatible expectations about public displays of affection? Spending Christmas with someone else's family was bad enough, but now he was going to spend every meal wondering what the Avakian across the dining room table thought about him.

"Great. That's just great."

"What's wrong? I thought you'd be pleased."

Billy tried hard to put himself in Jonah's shoes and to stay patient. "It's a lot of pressure, okay? Now I gotta not only look good as a friend but as the dude who's—" He wiggled his hips. "—you know, with their precious wunderkind."

Jonah's eyes narrowed. "Wunderkind?"

"Adopted son, whatever."

"You don't want to sleep with me."

"I didn't say that. But it's Christmas. I miss my family. I want to be with you, I really do. I'm just—fuck. I don't know what to say."

Jonah turned his face away, but not before Billy saw the tears in his eyes. "I thought this was our big chance, you know, to be together. But you don't…."

Billy rubbed a tear from Jonah's cheek. "I do care. I want to be with you, Jonah. I just… I just need a little time to get my head together."

Jonah shoved him back. "So we're taking a break, then?"

"Jesus fucking Christ! Please stop putting words into my mouth." Billy held out a hand. "Just give me a few minutes to get my head together."

"Fine." Jonah ignored Billy's outstretched hand. "Take all the fucking time you need." He stamped over and pressed the down button on the elevator.

"Where are you going?"

Jonah held a hand to his ear with his forefinger and pinky extended like a disappointed bride. "Call me when you got your head together." He slammed the elevator cage shut.

Billy went to their room and threw himself on the bed, already kicking himself for not realizing how much the visit meant to Jonah. An hour later he woke from a nap he hadn't meant to take and went to find Davoud.

Davoud smiled and swung open the door to his apartment. "Billy! We wondered what happened to you. Did you have a good trip down?"

"It was fine. Listen, Jonah's a little pissed at me right now. I think he went down to the shop. Can I borrow a key?"

Davoud nodded and lifted a set of keys from a hook inside the door. "You know he's been looking forward to your visit…."

"I know. I gotta talk to him."

"Good luck."

Billy found Jonah furiously running scales on the Steinway, right hand chasing left until they reached the high notes and reversed direction to rush downhill again.

He nuzzled Jonah's neck.

Jonah's shoulders twitched, but he continued to play. "How'd you get in?"

"Davoud gave me the key."

Jonah grunted.

"Do you think you could stop long enough to kiss me?"

"Maybe that ship has sailed."

Billy latched on to the word maybe. He stopped kissing Jonah's neck and flicked the tip of his tongue into Jonah's ear. "I said I was sorry."

Jonah's scale faltered. "Did you? I must have missed that."

"All the way down here, I couldn't think about anything but seeing you."

"The whole elevator ride, huh? I actually told my mom we'd be sleeping together."

"I meant the bus ride." What Billy would have given to be a fly on the wall during that conversation! He resumed working on Jonah's neck, trying to imagine what it would be like to have such a conversation with his mom.

Jonah's hands skipped across the keys to land in his lap. "Please...."

"Please what?"

"Please don't stop."

Billy laughed. "God, you're fickle."

Jonah slid off the bench and turned to face Billy. "Can we start over?" he pleaded. "I wanted—I want your visit to be special. I'm sorry about your mom and dad and Christmas and everything. I'd give anything to make that right for you."

Billy thought his smile probably looked a bit crooked. "Me too, short of giving you up."

Jonah leapt into Billy's hug with a half sigh, half sob. "I didn't think this would be so hard."

Billy grabbed Jonah's butt with both hands and lifted until he could nip Jonah's neck. "Hard, I can handle."

Jonah blew a raspberry in Billy's ear.

THAT NIGHT, Aida took Amir and Dorothy's daughter, Zarah, to her room for a bedtime story. Billy and Jonah watched "It's a Wonderful Life" on the thickly carpeted floor of Aida's living room with their backs to the big sofa, in between the older couples: Rascal and Jonah's mom, Davoud and Paul. Billy slipped an arm around Jonah's shoulders. Amir and Dorothy Avakian snuggled in the big leather armchair they'd dragged over from the corner.

At the final scene where everyone in town has come over to support George Bailey and his family, Jonah announced, "See how the whole town shores up the heterosexual hegemony."

Billy stared at the alien being that had replaced his boyfriend. "Heterosexual hegemony? I don't even know what that means. The townsfolk support him because he's a good man who helps people, not because he's straight."

Jonah responded, deadpan. "But would they be there if they didn't perceive him as a family man who meets their preconceived notions of normalcy?"

Paul kneed Jonah's arm. "Shut up, professor, I want to hear the bell ring when Clarence gets his wings."

Jonah cracked a grin and began to giggle. Billy shook his head in relief.

The movie over, Paul stretched out his legs, toppling Billy and Jonah onto the top layer of Persian carpet. "Okay, it's time you two go to bed."

"What!" said Jonah's mom. Billy's stomach tensed in response. Esmé might have agreed to their arrangement, but she clearly wasn't so comfortable as to acknowledge it publicly.

Davoud chuckled into the silence. "What my oh-so-diplomatic partner meant to say was that we need the room to complete some last-minute preparations."

"Oh, good. 'Cause I'm pretty tired," said Jonah, dragging Billy to his feet.

"Jonah, can I speak to you for a moment?" Esmé asked.

Billy watched, his gut rumbling, as she led Jonah to the kitchen. After a moment, Jonah came back to the living room to take Billy's hand in his own, face red but head high. Esmé surprised Billy on their way out by pulling him into a brief hug.

"Don't you dare hurt him," she fiercely whispered into his ear.

"I couldn't," he answered truthfully.

Billy followed Jonah across the hall to 3B. "What did she say to you?" he asked as Jonah opened the door.

"She's gonna stay with Rascal tonight. On the second floor."

"Oh… wow."

Billy followed Jonah across the hall to other apartment. "I guess she is okay with it."

Jonah hesitated at the bedroom door. "I think she's afraid of hearing us."

Billy bumped into Jonah. "Anyway, it's pretty cool of her." He put his arms around Jonah and sniffed his neck. "God, I love the way you smell. Like apricots and fresh cut… something."

"She also asked if I had condoms and lube."

Billy laughed, unable to help himself. "Oh my God."

"I told her they're in the bed stand."

"Good, because mine are in my suitcase. Which is too far away." The bag in question rested on the bureau on the other side of the room.

"So we're really doing this?" Jonah sounded vulnerable, for all his determination to get Billy into the same room with him.

Billy rubbed Jonah's belly through his T-shirt. "I hope we're doing something. But we don't have to do anything you don't want to—condoms or not."

"You know I've never been with anyone. I don't know—"

"Shush."

"But you have, haven't you? With a girl? It's okay, I mean, it's better somebody knows what they're doing, right?"

"I never did anything more than make out with a girl."

Jonah twisted around in Billy's arms to face him. "But you had a reputation."

"Carefully constructed from innuendo and outright falsehood."

Jonah's eyes narrowed. "I don't like to think of you as being that, that…."

"Conniving?"

"Dishonest?" Jonah grimaced as he said it, as if he were afraid he'd gone too far.

Billy sighed. He had been dishonest with the girls he'd dated, and he hated himself for it. Even if he hadn't totally come to terms with his own sexuality, he'd known he wasn't interested. "I did just come out to my family. Don't I get any credit for that?"

"I suppose," said Jonah, dragging out the word.

Billy relaxed at the smile tweaking the corners of Jonah's mouth and decided it was time to stop talking. He bent down and sealed Jonah's mouth with a kiss. Jonah opened his mouth and slid his tongue along Billy's teeth. Billy loved the way Jonah could be vulnerable and courageous at the same time. He vowed silently to follow wherever Jonah led, now and forever. Then Jonah's tongue, the softness of his lips, and the press of Jonah's body against his own left no more room for thought. Wanting Jonah's skin against his own, Billy grabbed the back of Jonah's T-shirt and yanked it up to get his hands under it.

Jonah hummed inarticulately into Billy's mouth and slid both hands under Billy's sweatshirt, enthusiastically grinding his erection against

Billy's. Billy found the gap he'd opened and slid his fingers into the crack of Jonah's ass. Jonah moaned in response, and tried to completely encircle and swallow Billy's tongue.

Billy pulled back to catch his breath. "Take off your clothes. I want to feel you."

Jonah's T-shirt flew over his head and across the room. Yanking at his fly, he nearly ripped the button from the waistband of his jeans. Free of his jeans, Jonah's boxers tented. He gave Billy no time to appreciate the sight, but shoved them down. His unencumbered cock bounced up at Billy. Billy's mouth flooded. He wanted to taste that.

"You too," Jonah growled, stepping out of reach. "I want to see you."

Billy's clothes had gotten way too tight anyway. He tossed sweatshirt, jeans, and underwear after Jonah's.

"Socks too," said Jonah imperiously. "I like your feet."

Billy bent over to comply. He'd hardly straightened when Jonah plastered himself over his body. Because of their height difference, Jonah's cock slid between the sensitive skin of his inner thighs, its upward curve lifting his balls. His own dick strained upward between his belly and Jonah's sternum. The sudden press of skin to skin nearly made him come on the spot.

"You're taller," he panted.

"I thought you'd never notice."

"Keep wiggling like that, and I'm gonna jizz all over you."

Jonah grinned. "Okay. We got all night."

The idea of his cum on Jonah sent a jolt through Billy's nervous system. He grabbed the firm globes of Jonah's ass in both hands and lifted. Finding the top of Jonah's ear, he licked, the taste salty on his tongue. Jonah wrapped his legs around Billy and flexed his hips, the ridged muscles of his abdomen increasing the friction on Billy's cock.

Billy cried out and slid his fingers into Jonah's crack, kneading and separating Jonah's butt cheeks.

An inarticulate sound escaped Jonah, and his delicious movements accelerated. Billy lost control and bucked frantically.

"Come for me, Billy."

Hearing the words took Billy over the top, and he pumped silky strings onto the gap between Jonah's pectoral muscles. Jonah cried out and came in hot spurts that coated Billy's balls and dripped from his perineum down the insides of his thighs.

Billy trembled from the strain of holding Jonah and the strength of his orgasm. "I gotta…."

Jonah found his voice. "That was…."

Billy collapsed slowly to the carpet, his back against the bed, Jonah still in his arms.

"Intense." Jonah leaned backward to rest on his back, and spread his legs, wantonly displaying his crotch.

Billy eyed Jonah's balls and the intriguing shadow behind them. "Next time, we could try the bed."

Jonah ran a finger along the ridge of skin that separated the halves of his scrotum, eyes on Billy.

"I think I could get into that."

Billy's cock, which had only softened slightly, perked up.

Jonah grinned.

WHEN HIS heart began to slow, Jonah lifted his legs off Billy and rolled to his knees. "I need a washcloth."

Billy grunted and stretched his arms over his head.

Jonah stood, taking care to keep the puddle of cum on his chest from dripping onto the antique Persian carpet. He stopped to take in the long lean lines of Billy's torso and legs. They'd waited so long to be together. The holiday would be over all too soon. He wanted to burn every detail into his mind, from Billy's tangled hair to his puffy mauled lips, so that he'd be able to call them up when they were apart.

Billy's eyes danced. "You're kinda making me self-conscious."

"I wanna fix this—you—in my mind."

"Don't know about you, but I'll be seeing you lying back with my spunk on your chest when I'm ninety and the only thing I can get up is my memory."

"Creepy." Billy was right, as usual. There was no way Jonah could ever forget this.

In the black-and-white tiled bathroom, he wiped the cum off his chest, then ran hot water over a washcloth and wrung it out thoroughly.

In the bedroom, Billy pulled the sheets down on the bed. He pointed at the washcloth. "Can I borrow that?"

Jonah shook his head. "Let me."

Billy's eyes widened.

Jonah laughed. "Put your foot on the bed." Billy complied, looking surprised as if Jonah had offered to trim his man-brush. Jonah reached under and wiped Billy's tackle.

Billy twitched when he ran the warm washcloth back over Billy's perineum and up the crack of his ass. "Oh wow. That's…."

"Feels good, huh?"

"You keep surprising me."

Jonah stopped. "Is that bad?"

Billy gazed at him with open adoration. "I love it."

"Good." Jonah dropped the washcloth onto the bed stand and shoved Billy onto the bed. "I'm not done with you yet."

"Promises, promises."

This time Jonah determined to take things a little slower so he could explore more of Billy's body. He pushed Billy onto his back and started with the hollows above his clavicles, licking as he went, and moved on to the tiny nipples that decorated Billy's defined, but not overly inflated pectoral muscles. Licking there, he delighted to see them harden to sharp buds.

Billy cleared his throat. "Do that some more."

Jonah complied, and felt Billy's cock nudge his belly. He made note of the direct connection between Billy's nipples and his groin. He slid down to lap at the dips inside Billy's hip bones, taking care to avoid Billy's cock. Billy squirmed and took a fistful of Jonah's hair, his other hand clutching at the sheet. Jonah liked the gentle tugging sensation at his scalp. He nosed the coarse hair at the base of Billy's cock and sniffed, reveling in the scents of clean sweat and male. He licked Billy's balls, and then sucked one into his mouth. Salt and bittersweet spunk. His dick, already hard, throbbed.

"God, Jonah, you're killing me."

"You ready?"

"Anything."

"I want you to fuck me."

Billy tugged his head upward for a kiss that started soft and lasted until they both panted. "I love you."

"I love you too. Now will you please fuck me?"

"You're sure?"

Jonah fumbled for the bed stand, impatiently. "I've been practicing." He glanced back to see the expression on Billy's face and repressed a laugh. "With a dildo, doofus."

"Oh... right. You've been holding out on me."

"I ordered it online and had it delivered to Davoud and Paul's place, just in case."

"Didn't you have to have a credit card?"

"Mom's. Told her the charge was for school supplies."

Billy laughed in amazement. "Give me those." Billy took the condom and lube from Jonah.

"Hey, I was gonna get you ready," Jonah said.

"I don't think that's a good idea. I want to last longer than that. How do you want to do this?"

Jonah flipped onto his elbows and knees and wiggled his butt, looking over his shoulder to check Billy's reaction.

Billy flushed, eyes wide. "Another sight I won't have to work to remember."

Jonah heard Billy squirt some lube from the bottle. He felt Billy kiss him in the hollow of his back. "So hot," Billy murmured.

Jonah felt something wet and slightly cool touch the rim of his opening, and he shuddered.

"Too cold?"

"Get on with it. Use a finger until I relax."

Billy rubbed a circle around Jonah's pucker and then pressed gently.

"It's okay. Push harder."

Billy kissed him again, and smoothed a hand over his butt. Then Jonah felt the pressure increase until the finger popped through the ring of muscle with a burning sensation. He pushed back and groaned. The finger started to withdraw. "No!"

Billy froze.

"I'm okay. Move it around."

Billy pushed the tip of his finger in farther and twisted it.

After a moment, the burning abated.

"That's good, do it some more."

The pressure increased. Then Billy curled the finger, and Jonah gasped.

Billy froze. "You okay?"

"Do that again," Jonah panted. "Nerves there, I guess. Oh God, that's good. Add another finger."

Billy withdrew and Jonah whimpered at the loss. He heard the squirt of the lube bottle again and then the pressure was back, this time Billy kept it up steadily until both fingers slid in. The burn was sharper, but not worse than the dildo.

"You're really tight."

"Give me a second." Jonah pressed back and concentrated until his muscles relaxed. "Okay."

Billy wiggled his fingers.

Jonah gasped. This was nothing like having the bigger, but inanimate, dildo inside him. "Do that thing you did before."

Billy curled his fingers. Jonah's groaned out of pure pleasure. "God, that's good."

Billy curled his fingers again, this time scissoring them a little at the same time. Jonah cried out wordlessly. Billy repeated the action until Jonah gasped out, "Stop!"

"What's wrong?"

"I want you in me when I come."

Billy pulled his fingers out. Jonah heard a wrapper tear and the lube bottle again. Then the pressure was back, this time blunt. He wanted to scream, "*Yes, yes, yes. Put it in!*" but he was afraid Billy would think him a slut. The pressure increased and with it the burn of stretching muscle. "Gah."

Billy froze again. "Should I stop?"

"No, keep going. Just slow."

Billy grasped Jonah's hips with both hands and pressed steadily until Jonah's muscles gave and the head of his penis slid through.

"Oh wow, you're big. No, don't stop, it feels good."

Billy pressed in until his balls were snug against Jonah's butt. Jonah felt full, the heat of Billy's cock amazing. That was another thing he hadn't felt with the dildo. Billy leaned over and kissed Jonah's back again. "You okay?"

"Move."

Billy slid out a little and pressed forward again.

"More," Jonah grunted. "Fuck me."

Billy complied, establishing a slow rhythm. Jonah whimpered. Billy increased his speed, pulling out a little farther with each stroke until the heat and friction became overwhelming and Jonah cried out again wordlessly.

Billy's motions became frantic and uneven. "Gonna come," he panted. "You're so hot and tight. Please come for me."

Jonah's world had contracted to the sensations in his ass, so he cried out in shock when Billy reached around to grasp his cock and stroke him firmly. Jonah's body lit up like a fireball and he pumped a great spout of cum onto the sheet. Billy shuddered and rammed deep into Jonah's body. Jonah felt his cock jerk, then Billy's weight pressed him onto the bed. After panting for a minute, Billy shifted and pulled out carefully.

Jonah sighed.

"You okay?"

Jonah tried to answer, but all that came out was a kind of contented slur. "Yush."

Billy hummed and rolled off.

Jonah whimpered.

"Come back."

"Gotta get rid of the condom."

The bed shifted and creaked. Billy returned and lay down on his back next to Jonah. The semen under Jonah's belly started to cool, so Jonah rolled over and plastered himself on top of Billy's warm body.

Billy sighed contentedly and wrapped his arms around him. "Was I okay?"

Jonah took inventory. His butthole ached and he thought he might have bruises on his hips. None of it mattered. "How long do you think before we could do it again?"

Billy stared, a little dazed. "You're awesome."

CHRISTMAS MORNING, Billy worked himself carefully from under a soundly sleeping Jonah, found jeans and sweatshirt, and wandered into the living room of Jonah's apartment. He gasped. A pair of large red stockings hung from the mantelpiece, one with his name embroidered on the cuff. When had they delivered those? He adored Jonah's unexpected tendency to vocalize when aroused, but he worried about scandalizing Santa.

Taking down his stocking, Billy dumped it out on the coffee table: packets of trail mix, an orange, a cellophane-wrapped pack of cards, and a set of wood and metal puzzles he knew would be easy to take apart and much harder to put back together. Packed in the toe, he found a packet of basketball-shaped chocolates wrapped in orange foil. Laughing out loud, he grabbed Jonah's stocking and carried his bounty back into the bedroom.

Jonah had kicked off the covers and curled to a ball in the center of the bed, the engorged tip of his morning wood peeking between his legs. Billy climbed onto the bed.

"I woke up and you weren't here," Jonah grumped, eyes closed.

Billy rubbed blond spikes.

Jonah's eyelashes slid up. "And you're wearing clothes—in bed. There ought to be a law about that."

"I brought chocolate."

"Okay, so I might forgive you." Jonah rolled over and snuggled against Billy's side, his erection poking Billy in the thigh.

Billy unwrapped a chocolate and fed it to Jonah.

"Mmm, good." Jonah wiped chocolate from his mouth and rubbed Billy's lips. "You're not having any."

Billy walked his fingers down Jonah's bare chest toward his belly. "I had another breakfast in mind."

Jonah glanced down and shrugged. "Oh, that. Won't go away unless I jerk off."

"I bet I can make it go away."

"Only if you take those clothes off."

A COUPLE of lazy hours later, Billy and Jonah lounged on the bed in their underwear. Someone pounded on the apartment door. "Anyone alive in there?"

"Just a sec, Rascal," Jonah yelled, popping one of the last chocolates between brown-stained lips.

Billy scrambled off the bed and retrieved his jeans from the corner where he'd kicked them. He watched Jonah pull a T-shirt over his head.

"What?"

"I like watching you move."

Jonah squinted at him like he'd grown horns. "That's creepy."

Billy followed him to the door. "No, it's not. You like watching me play basketball."

"If I looked at you like that, they'd arrest me for indecent expression."

"There's no such thing."

"They would make it up on the spot."

Jonah opened the door. Rascal peered in cautiously. "Your mom sent me to get you guys. There's breakfast in Aida's place, and presents to open. Zhara's going to explode if we make her wait any longer."

Jonah stuck out a chocolate-covered tongue. "We got chocolate."

"I see that."

Billy wrapped his arms around Jonah's middle. "I'll get him dressed."

"Thank you." A notably bland expression smoothed Rascal's saturnine features, but when he turned to leave, Billy saw the tips of his ears were red.

At Aida's place, Zhara had sorted all the presents into piles for each recipient. Billy was embarrassed to discover a sizable mound waited for him under the haphazardly decorated tree. He was relieved, later, when Zhara put on the gaudy medieval princess hat he'd found in a costume store and refused to take it off even to let anyone else examine it. Jonah seemed to appreciate the basketball jersey on which Billy had collected the signatures of the entire 2013-14 Hoosier State basketball team. Jonah pulled Billy aside and asked him if he'd worn it.

Billy shook his head, not understanding.

"I want it to smell like you," Jonah explained, glaring as though it should have been obvious. "Put it on," he demanded.

Later, after the presents were opened and they'd stuffed themselves with butter and maple syrup-slathered waffles, sausage and scrambled eggs, bagels and lox, and more stuff Billy's stated brain couldn't be bothered to recall, Billy slipped off to an empty bedroom and called his mom's cell.

"Hello?"

"Merry Christmas, Mom! Did you like the scarf?"

"It was lovely." His mom sounded like she was going to cry.

"How's Grandma?"

"Tell Billy what I told you," he heard Grandma Miller yell at his mom, "I don't know what mixed-up tomfoolery you people are up to over there, but Christmas is for family, and you should be together, not calling each other on the darn telephone."

"Tell her I couldn't agree more."

"Did you talk to your dad?"

"No."

"He didn't call?"

Billy couldn't keep the bitterness from his voice. "Did you expect him to?"

His mom sighed. "He'll come around, Billy. I know he will." She sounded like she was trying to convince herself as much as him.

"You think? I gotta go. I'm helping Jonah make mashed potatoes for dinner."

"Jonah's cooking? I thought you were having dinner with the Avakians."

"I am. But everyone cooks something. It's like a family potluck."

"I see." His mom sounded impressed. "That sounds fun."

"Tell Grandma 'Merry Christmas.'"

"I love you."

"Love you too, Mom. Bye."

When he rejoined everyone in the living room, Jonah looked up from the sofa. "How's your mom?"

"How'd you know I called?"

Jonah slid over to make room for him. "You've been checking your phone every five minutes since breakfast. You were fondling the thing again when you stepped out of the living room."

Billy hadn't realized he'd been so obvious.

"Your dad call?" asked Paul.

"No."

Paul shook his head, clearly disgusted. Davoud's hand crept over to rest on Paul's thigh.

Billy's own feelings were all over the place. Being with Jonah was amazing. Talking with his mom had hurt more than he'd expected. His dad was a closed box he refused to open. *Let the stubborn bastard eat sugar cookies by himself.*

"Mom's okay. With Grandma."

Jonah leaned his head against Billy's chest. "You should call him."

Billy shook his head mutely. *He's not like your dad. He'll call when he's good and ready.*

CHAPTER 9

<u>Stats</u>

~~Girls I'm pretty sure wanted to kiss me. 5 12 10,012~~
Girls I've kissed: 3
Boys I've kissed: 1

If Dad ever finds this, I'm dead—like broken spine, belly slit, and guts slithering out all over the floor dead.

Boys who've dumped me: 1
Boys I would kneel on the floor and worship as a basketball god: 1
Stupid nicknames: 2
Public boners: ~~1~~ 2
Teammates I'd like to knock some sense into: 2
Different kinds of underwear worn by guys on my floor: 5
~~Basketball players on the down low: 1~~

Points Scored this season: ~~12 61 206 260 421~~ 446
Assists: ~~7 31 60 87 149~~ 181
Turnovers: ~~2~~ 5 ~~11 14~~ 38
Games Won: ~~1 3 6 8~~ 15

Games Lost: ~~1~~ ~~2~~ 4

Blow jobs received: 1
Blow jobs given: ~~1~~ 2
Sexting sessions: ~~1~~ ~~7~~ 8 (Phone sex is better)
Assholes I'd like to kill: 1
Parents who aren't talking to me: ~~2~~ 1
Crazy boyfriends: 1
Families: 2
Boys I love: 1
People who know I'm gay: Ask Nielsen

THE VIDEO of Jamal and Tully's fight in the gym appeared on a video sharing site after the holidays. The clip had no sound, apart from a couple of snide remarks from the asshole who posted it. The arguing players were distant, but Jamal's punch was all too visible. With Jamal blocking the view, Tully's reaction was hard to make out. He might have leaned in to say something to Jamal's face. In any case, Jamal's combativeness and repeated attempts to attack Tully were crystal. Maybe because Hoosier State was ranked high enough to have a chance at winning the conference, or maybe because it was a slow news day in the sports world, the video went viral by evening. By the next day, University Media Relations were forced to release a statement. The university's official position was that Jamal had lost his temper in practice and been penalized appropriately for his actions. End of story, or so they hoped.

Except that wasn't the end of it, because other people had been in the gym when the video was taken. One of them saw fit to describe just what Tully had done when he leaned close. That comment generated a firestorm of others supporting Jamal, applauding Tully, or voicing random opinions on Tully's current hair color, gay sports figures, or rarely, the team's chances in March Madness. The website finally closed the video to new comments, but by then the debate had passed irretrievably into the realm of talk radio and national sports commentary.

Billy tried hard to remember if he'd seen anyone besides the team standing on the sidelines, or if anyone had been on the collapsible bleachers, but he couldn't remember for certain. The idea that one of his teammates might have pissed gasoline on the fire sickened him, and for the first time since August, he thought about transferring to another school.

He called Jonah that night, lying on his back in the warm room, nude apart from his briefs.

"People I don't even know sent me the link" were Jonah's first words.

"Goddammit."

"Is it true? Did Tully really kiss Jamal? After Jamal punched him?"

"Is this line secure?" Billy tried to sound like Obama on a call to Vladimir Putin, but the joke fell flat.

"He did, didn't he?"

Billy kneaded the bedspread with his toes. "I've never seen anyone react that way to a punch."

"Jamal totally lost it."

"I guess that was the point."

"How's the team taking it?"

"Rocker's got everyone on lockdown. He's threatened to suspend anyone who talks to the press without a representative from media relations."

"He can do that?" Jonah sounded surprised.

"Probably not, but that hasn't stopped him from threatening."

"You know the press are gonna ask about it at the next game."

"Rocker sent us a script from public relations. Boiled down, it says 'No comment.'"

Jonah laughed. "Like that's gonna make this go away."

"It's not funny. I'm thinking about quitting the team."

"Billy!" There was shock and something like disappointment in Jonah's tone. "Do I have to come up there and kick your ass?"

"I thought you would like the idea. We could find a place where I could be more open, where there'd be less pressure."

Jonah was silent for a moment. "What's keeping you from being open at Hoosier State?"

Billy opened his mouth to answer, but nothing came out.

Jonah's voice sounded distant. "I love you, Billy. I'll always love you, no matter what you do."

"I have to go." Billy was off the bed before the words were out. "I have to think. I'll talk to you tomorrow." He disconnected the call and dropped his phone like a hot brick. He shoved his legs into an old pair of jeans and threw on a sweatshirt and fleece jacket. When he opened the door to his room, Mike and Sunflower cuddled on one end of the couch. Mike's arm wrapped around her shoulders, but they weren't making out. Sunflower whispered into Mike's ear.

"Sorry, I didn't mean to…." Billy tried to tiptoe past.

Sunflower looked up. "Hey, Billy, how's Jonah tonight?"

"He's good." *Perfect.* So why had Billy hung up on him? "I need air."

"You want to walk me home? Mike has a paper to write."

"Sure, I guess."

"I'll grab my stuff." She kissed Mike on the cheek and shoved a stack of books and papers into her pack.

"You okay?" Mike twisted around to examine him over the back of the couch. "You look kind of pale."

"Fine. I just need some air." It occurred to him he hadn't thought to ask about Mike's parents since the video came out. "You heard anything from your mom?"

"She sent me a prayer card. The kind our church uses to let you know they're praying for you. Seems kind of a mixed message, under the circumstances."

"Shit. I'm sorry, Mike. I should have asked before. I've been, you know…." He mimed his head exploding.

"It's not your problem."

"Still, I should—"

"I'm ready," said Sunflower, brightly. "You. Paper." She kissed the top of Mike's head. "Call if you get stuck."

Mike grabbed her hand to kiss it.

Sunflower laughed softly. "Come on, Long John."

"Huh?"

"Would you prefer Grandpa?"

"Actually, I'm not feeling old or wise right now."

"Uh-huh."

Billy followed Sunflower from the dorm and into the darkened quad. It was cold, a few of the brighter stars visible above the orange glow of the sodium lights that lined the concrete walks. He shoved his hands into his pockets and jerked them out again when they touched bare skin. "What the…!"

Sunflower turned to look at him. "Forget something?"

Billy hooked his thumbs on the pockets. "No, just something Jonah did."

"You going to see him sometime soon? Not that I want to be around when you do," she added hastily. "Just let us know, so Mike can stay in my room."

Apparently Billy and Jonah hadn't exactly been quiet last time. He forgot and shoved his hands into his pockets, then pulled them out again just as fast.

"Something wrong with your pants?"

Billy felt his face heat. "Um… tore out a pocket."

Sunflower examined him skeptically. "Whatever. Mike says you promised to talk to Jamal."

Billy opened his mouth to say that he couldn't comment.

"Don't worry, I'm not asking you to break any confidences, but Mike, he's having a hard time dealing with this thing with his mother. All the publicity about the team isn't helping. Any chance Tully and Jamal will chill anytime soon? I wanna know what I'm dealing with, you know, for Mike."

"You and Mike are serious."

Sunflower shrugged. "Until we aren't."

Billy surprised himself and pulled Sunflower into a bear hug.

"Whoa there, big guy, you know Mike's a bit possessive, right?"

Billy let go. "I'm glad for him."

"That's sweet. What about Hatfield and McCoy?"

Billy pointed in the direction of the student union. "You wanna get some coffee?"

"Sure."

At the student union, they stood in line for coffees behind a gaggle of male and female students who all seemed to know one another better than they knew their drink preferences. After the last, a brunette wearing a cream-colored knit cap, finally ordered a half-caff caramel macchiato, she glanced at Billy.

"Aren't you Billy Preston? Like from the basketball team?"

Since getting off the bench, Billy'd been getting recognized more often. While he usually got a kick out of the attention, he could have done without it tonight.

"Actually this is Sammy, Billy's twin brother," said Sunflower, deadpan. "Terrible at sports. Couldn't make a basket with a cherry picker." She took Billy's arm possessively. "I love him anyway."

"No, I know him," said a thin guy in skintight jeans that revealed all—and nothing. Why did people insist on wearing stuff that didn't look good on them just because it was fashionable? Billy didn't get it. "You're Preston all right," the guy continued. "Is it true White called Sampson a fag and punched him when Sampson called him on it? And that Tully Sam kissed him?"

"I... uh... no comment."

"What I can't figure out is whether Tully Sam is gay or bi or just likes cross-dressing," said the girl in the cap.

You and me both.

"Whatever he is, it's none of our business," said Sunflower.

"I'm just asking. People say Tully Sam engineered the whole thing for publicity."

"I mean he's kind of sucked the whole clothes and hair thing dry, hasn't he?" said the guy in the skintight jeans.

"Come on, Billy. You don't need to answer that." Sunflower tugged his arm.

"No, you're wrong. Tully wouldn't do that," said Billy. "He's not like that."

"What about White? He really a homophobe?" The guy in the skintight jeans handed his latte to the girl next to him.

"No, Jamal is…." Billy stopped. Sunflower's grip on his arm had become painful.

"Is he a bigot?" the guy persisted.

"He's just confused," said Billy finally. He didn't notice until afterward that the brunette held a phone pointed in his direction at waist level. He felt his stomach knot.

"Come on," Sunflower whispered. "We can't stay here. You're only making it worse." She dragged him to the door.

Billy glanced over his shoulder as Sunflower slammed the safety bar on the exit door. The girl in the knit cap held her phone at eye level. "Hell and flying monkeys."

Outside, Sunflower hustled him across the quad. "Holy moly, you really need a publicist—or a keeper."

"I fucked up, didn't I?" First Jonah, and now getting caught at the student union. Billy's stomach, always first to complain, announced his dinner was no longer welcome. "I think I'm…." Looking around wildly, he dragged Sunflower to a halt. "I'm gonna be sick." He bent over against the cramp.

"This way, puppy dog." Sunflower changed direction and guided him to a trash can chained to a lamppost at the side of the path. "There."

Billy grabbed the rim of the trash barrel just in time. His stomach convulsed. Sunflower rubbed his back while he spewed a bitter fountain of masticated lasagna and salad greens into the plastic liner. After his stomach settled, he spat bile and bits of partially digested food.

"Here, drink some of this." Sunflower handed him a plastic water bottle.

"Where in hell…?"

"I always carry water in my pack."

Somehow Billy wasn't surprised. He swished water around in his mouth and spat.

"Feel better?"

"Kind of."

"Who knew basketball players were such high maintenance."

Billy groaned.

"Don't apologize to me. Jamal's the one who's gonna be gunning for you."

"Crap." His stomach convulsed again and he bent over the rim, but nothing came up.

"Sorry, puppy dog, didn't mean to make it worse."

Billy straightened. "No, you're right. I really fucked up. First Jonah and now Jamal. I don't know what I'm doing here."

"What about Jonah, or shouldn't I ask?"

"He told me he loved me, and I hung up on him."

"You *what*!" Sunflower twisted him around to stare into his face. "You did what?"

"Well, not like right then, but I didn't know what to say. He's so good to me, and I'm not treating him right. He's really, really talented and he should be going to the best damn music school in the country, but I'm holding him back. I can't help it. I can't let him go."

Sunflower clutched his arm. He was going to have *serious* bruises tomorrow. "We are going to my room this instant, and you are calling that boy to tell him you love him. Do you hear me? This instant!"

Billy followed Sunflower to her dorm meekly, sniffling as the combination of tears and stomach acid made his nose run.

Sunflower unlocked the door to her room. "God, you're a mess."

"Don't you have a roommate?"

"She's with her boyfriend."

"Do her parents know she's sleeping…?"

Sunflower turned to stare, eyes narrowed.

"Sorry. None of my business."

"Call him."

Billy searched the tiny room for a hole to crawl into.

Sunflower's hands landed on her hips. "What are you waiting for?"

"Um... could I borrow your phone?"

"Oh Holy Mother of God! Are you telling me you've probably been getting texts from him for the last hour and *ignoring them?*"

Maybe I can fit under the bed?

Sunflower slapped her phone into his hand. "You do actually have his number memorized?"

Billy punched the number in silence, afraid to make any sound that might set off the enraged dragon glaring at him.

After an extended set of rings that had him fearing for his life, the line connected.

"Whaaa?" Jonah sounded like a child woken from his nap.

"It's Billy."

"Billy? What's wrong?"

"Nothing's wrong."

"Oh." Jonah's voice faded, and Billy heard rustling. "It's late and I've got school tomorrow. Could we skip—"

"I love you."

The rustling stopped. "You do?"

"Yes. I love you. I don't deserve you, but I love you, and I want to find a way for us to be together—even if it means giving up basketball."

"You must be feeling *really* guilty."

"Please don't...." Billy collapsed onto the bed behind him. "I love you. I'll do anything to be with you."

Jonah was silent for what must have been a few seconds, but it seemed like an eternity. His voice, when he answered, was almost inaudible. "Okay, but I don't want you to give up basketball."

"Why not?"

"Because you love it."

"I do?"

"Yeah. Your dad almost made you forget. And Tully and Jamal aren't helping either, but you do. I could never make you give it up."

"What about music school?"

"We'll work something out."

"How can you be sure?"

"We love each other," said Jonah, as if that was all the answer Billy should need. "Go to bed, Billy. Don't you have a game tomorrow?"

"Arkansas."

"Good night, Billy."

"I love you."

Sunflower grinned at him. "How hard was that?"

Billy fell backward on the bed until his head hit the soft squares of the quilt.

THE NEXT day, Billy tapped on Jamal's door. "Jamal, it's Billy. Can I talk to you?" He'd followed Jamal home after practice.

"What do you want, cocksucker?" The door remained shut.

"I want you to stop calling me that, for starters."

"Yeah, well, tough titty."

"Have you any idea how juvenile you sound?"

The door flew inward to bang the inside wall of Jamal's suite. "Who are you calling juvenile, asshole? Say that to my face."

Billy pitched his voice at barely audible. "Come on, Jamal. You sound like a ten-year-old on the school playground." Billy was pretty sure he'd gone too far when Jamal grabbed the front of his shirt and yanked him into the room. It occurred to Billy belatedly that he could have brought backup.

Jamal shoved him into the room and let go. "You condescending shit. You don't know fuck-all about me."

Billy let himself fall backward onto the couch. "I know you grew up in South Side Chicago." He stared up at Jamal's angry face. "I know you got out."

Jamal stared like he couldn't believe they were having this conversation. "Yeah, I got out."

"So you can't be stupid or unmotivated." Billy paused. "I know it's got to be hard to be gay in that kind of place."

Jamal leaned down and hissed in Billy's face. "You *ever* call me that again, I'll beat that pretty white face of yours until it looks like the inside of a pumpkin the day after Halloween."

"Nice image. Okay, so you're not gay." Billy closed his eyes and braced for a blow. "You just like sucking cock."

A loud bang made Billy flinch and open his eyes. A new dent decorated the drywall next to the TV.

"Trying to study in here!" came a half-hearted yell from the other side of the wall.

Jamal wrung out his hand. Billy let out a shaky breath. "Feel better?"

"It don't mean shit."

"That hole in the wall says it does."

Jamal's eyes narrowed. "I suppose your parents are all like 'Oh goody! Little Billy's light in the loafers, let's all go to the PFLAG convention.'"

Like my dad would ever show his face at PFLAG. Billy was amazed Jamal even knew about the LGBT support organization. It was another sign that Jamal wasn't nearly as resigned to staying on the down-low as he appeared. Billy had only heard of the organization himself from Paul after he'd gotten to know Jonah. The notion that he was the privileged brat of PC parents made him want to laugh. He fought for control of his voice and went to get some ice from the little kitchenette. He found a plastic sandwich bag in a drawer, filled it with ice, and sealed it up. Jamal watched in silence.

When he was done, Billy returned to the living area and handed Jamal the bag. "Put that on your knuckles."

Jamal shook his head. "I can't believe you, man."

"My dad isn't speaking to me."

"Yeah? You looking for sympathy?"

"Yeah. So you're not the only one who's got shit to deal with."

"*I'm* good with my family. You're the fairy with the *boyfriend* and the dad who won't talk to you. What did you expect?"

"So when you sucked my cock that was just youthful experimentation?"

"I'd known you were a fag, I never woulda—"

"If I wasn't gay, you'd never have gotten near my cock."

"Listen to the fairy talk."

"I think you knew exactly what you were doing—and with whom."

"Your *boyfriend* know you're out getting your knob polished?"

Billy's heart pounded, and he dug fingernails into his palms. "If you tell anyone about that, I'll tell the next reporter who asks who's the real cocksucker on the team."

For long seconds, Billy thought Jamal was going to either hit him or hyperventilate. He figured it was only the fact that Jamal was already on probation for violence that saved him from a black eye or worse.

"You wouldn't dare. You got as much to lose as me."

"Maybe not. You gonna risk it?"

Jamal glared, sucking short choppy breaths, until Billy looked away, afraid his own stomach would come up through his mouth. Then Jamal seemed to deflate. He slid to the floor with his back to the wall. "I got two kid brothers and one sister, and I promised Mama I would get them out. I promised if I made it, I'd pay for their college. How the fuck am I gonna do that if word gets out I'm... that I like...."

"What about your dad?"

Jamal's eyelids slid open to expose a flat stare. "What about him? He's doing time for popping some Korean dude in an armed robbery. I haven't seen him since I was six. He finds out, he'll probably break out just to beat the crap outta me."

"You ever tell any of this to Tully? Maybe he'd tone it down a little, if he knew what you're up against."

Jamal closed his eyes. "Fuck! I can't even *look* at the guy. How am I gonna talk to him?"

Billy sighed. "Would it help if I went with you?"

"Keep that motherfucker away from me."

"I'll set it up."

"You ain't gonna give up, are you?"

Billy shrugged. "Not so long as you and Tully keep messing with each other."

Jamal shook his head. "Son of a bitch."

"You got any antacid pills around here?"

Jamal's mouth opened.

TWO IN the morning. The athletic center closed at midnight, but there was a rusty hoop mounted on the side of the dorm next to Billy's. There wasn't room between the buildings for a full-size court, but guys sometimes played one-on-one in the paved gap. Unable to sleep, Billy had come down to shoot a few, but he'd failed to account for the weather. Great wet snowflakes the size of dandelion pods floated down to accumulate on the blacktop. He hugged his arms around the ball he'd brought with him and tried to remember what he'd expected college life to be like before he'd arrived on campus, but the memory eluded him.

A muscular figure in a hooded fleece trotted around the corner of the building and slid to a halt on the slushy blacktop.

"Goddammit, Grandpa."

Billy peered into the shadow under the hood. "Jamal?"

"Two in the morning and I still can't fucking get away from you people." Jamal sounded like he'd been drinking.

You people? "Sorry."

"Why you always have to be so damn polite?"

Was he polite? Billy had never thought of himself as polite. "I don't know."

"Your daddy beat you?"

"I don't under—"

Jamal raised fists to a boxer's stance. "I asked if he beat you. To make you polite."

"No."

"Then why you always so polite?"

"Do I need a reason?"

"Don't you ever tell someone to go fuck himself." Jamal leaned close, his breath an acrid cloud. "To fuck off."

Billy stepped backward involuntarily until his back hit the brick wall behind him. "I get mad."

"Mad? I wanted to kill Tully. Woulda done it too, if you and Whirlpool hadn't grabbed me. Maybe I'm like my daddy after all. Maybe I didn't get out. Maybe the bastard came with me."

"You wanna go inside, Jamal? It's cold out here. I've got hot chocolate if—"

"There you go again like the fucking welcome wagon. Like you don't know what I am."

"Do you love your brothers and sister?"

"The fuck you talking 'bout?"

"Do you love your brothers and sister?" Billy repeated.

Jamal shoved his hood back and raised his face to the swirling dark, snowflakes melting on his skin.

"Jordan, he okay. Kinda dumb, but he'll fight for you. Jump right in without askin' why. Malik, he's funny. Talks a mile a minute. Ooh, yeah. You lucky you walk away with your wallet." He smiled, teeth white in the gloom. "Alyssa, she smarter than anyone. Half the time I can't hardly read the shit she brings home from the public library. But she never makes you feel it." He lowered his head. "That what you wanna know? I wouldn't be here, weren't for them."

Billy nodded, half-melted snow falling from his watch cap. "Come inside, there's no point staying out in this."

Jamal shook his head in wonder. "Like we never met." But he followed when Billy slipped and slid around to the side door and swiped his ID to open it. He stepped into the stairwell with Jamal close behind.

"Grandpa, why you tell those folks I'm confused?"

Billy had been hoping the girl hadn't caught that part. Or that Jamal hadn't seen it. Or that the Earth was about to be hit by a giant eruption from the sun. He slipped on the wet stairs, his foot slamming down a step. He flinched when Jamal put a hand on his back to steady him, and heard a chuckle.

"That's the thing 'bout you, Grandpa. You're so fucking scared you're fallen' all over yourself, but here you are, takin' me to your room anyhow."

"I didn't mean anything by it. The girl who recorded it was asking all these questions, saying stuff I didn't—"

"She asked if I was an asshole. You answered."

Billy stopped at the next landing. "I'm sorry. I should have just said—"

"No, I *am* an asshole."

Billy started moving again. "I don't—"

"You think I should tell Tully… I don't even know what the fuck you figure I should do."

Billy turned at the landing for his floor. "You and Tully, you're like Yin and Yang."

Jamal laughed, a crooked grin stretching his mouth. "Guess that makes me the White half."

"Ha!" The laugh burst out of Billy. "All I know is I'd rather see you and Tully talking than fighting."

Jamal's grin faded. "What do you figure we're gonna talk about?"

"Whatever, man. Anything at all."

In the tiny kitchen, Billy made hot chocolate for Jamal. They both seemed to have talked themselves out. Their silence seemed, if not wholly comfortable, then at least civil. When he finished his drink, Jamal got up and washed the mug, then set it in the drying rack carefully like it was fine china instead of dollar store special.

"I better go." Jamal glanced over his shoulder. "The confused thing don't matter."

Billy nodded.

Jamal shook his head as he opened the door. "Chocolate. Holy fuck, he gives me chocolate."

When Jamal was gone, Billy dropped onto the couch with his head in his hands. *He's right. You* are *scared of him.* Every time Billy talked with Jamal, he ended more confused than before. Was Jamal a good guy or not? What about Tully? So much of what they were seemed a reaction to the people around them. What would they be like if they lived in a world where a guy's sexuality was as inconsequential as the shape of his ears? What would he be like?

JAMAL AND Tully agreed to talk on Saturday in Billy and Mike's room at the hotel where the team was quartered after their game with UNC Wilmington. They'd lost 92 to 107. After the game, a former NBA player now reporting for ESPN asked Coach Rocker about the game.

"This loss has got to hit you hard with the conference finals coming up so soon. Preston looked like he could use a break out there. Why'd you keep White on the bench?"

Rocker frowned. "White is sitting out a couple of games."

"Why, Coach?" The reporter turned to the camera and raised his eyebrows with false concern. "Is he injured?"

Rocker ignored the camera and stared at the reporter, a muscle in his cheek twitching visibly. "White has been suspended for three games due to a rule violation."

"What rule, Coach?"

"That's all I have to say about it." Rocker pushed his way past the reporter, the camera following.

"Wait, Coach. Coach Rocker!"

The reporter tried to follow, but Digger stepped casually into his path. When the reporter sidestepped to go around, Digger stepped in the same direction. "Sorry!" The reporter stepped in the other direction, but

Digger moved at the same time. "Whoops, sorry." Digger backed out of the reporter's path, but by then, Rocker had left the press room.

In the hotel afterward, Mike got on the same elevator as Billy. "Tully agreed?"

"Yup."

"You need anything?"

Billy shrugged. "I don't know what the fuck I'm doing."

"Better you than me, man."

On their floor, Mike stopped at the door to Jamal and Otter's room. "Five minutes, Grandpa." He slipped into the room.

"Thanks." Billy trod the carpeted corridor to Tully's room and tapped on the door.

Tully opened the door. He wore skintight black leather pants, a bloodred silk shirt, and lime green converse sneakers to match the streak in his hair. For him, it was a pretty tame outfit, but Billy knew Jamal wouldn't see it that way. *Fuck it. Jamal is just gonna have to cope.* That was what this was all about, right?

"You ready?"

Tully shrugged, his expression uncharacteristically serious.

Billy ushered Tully into his room. "Have a seat. You want something to drink?"

Tully raised his eyebrows and chuckled. "You've got this all planned out."

"You know what's riding on this."

"Do you?"

"You got more to lose than anyone, we keep blowing games."

Something dark flashed in Tully's expression, then his face smoothed into its usual humor. "Bring it on, Grandpa."

Before Billy could reply, someone knocked on the door. Billy pointed to a set of matching plaid armchairs he'd shoved around until they faced each other. "Sit."

Tully shrugged again and dropped into the chair. Billy gave him a last look before opening the door.

Otter stepped back, ushering Jamal before him. Billy caught Otter's eye and nodded his thanks. "Hi, Jamal. Thanks for coming."

Jamal's eyes were on Tully. He was dressed in black jeans and a black hoodie.

"Have a seat. Something to drink?"

Jamal glanced at Billy, a smile flirting with the corners of his mouth. "Hot chocolate?"

"Beer or water."

"I'll have a beer," said Tully.

Jamal's face lost all expression. "Whatever."

Billy went to the mini refrigerator by the TV and retrieved a couple of Corona Lights.

"The fuck?" said Tully, when Billy handed him the bottle.

Billy shrugged. In fact, he and Mike had decided to stock only light beer. They figured a little social lubrication might help, but too much might be dangerous.

"Okay, so here are the ground rules." In fact, both Tully and Jamal had agreed to the rules in advance, but Billy thought a reminder warranted. "You each get three minutes. You can talk about anything, but no name calling, and no labeling. While you talk, the other party will be silent. Completely silent. No comments, no sounds, no nothing. Nothing you say will leave this room. After each round, you each get a minute for follow-ups. We'll do as many rounds as you can take. Either party can call a halt at any time. I am the referee. My word is law. We'll toss a coin to see who starts."

Jamal laughed. "Just like a fucking presidential debate. And you're that old dude from PBS."

"What if I don't want to start?" said Tully.

"Sorry, heads he starts, tails you start," said Billy firmly, looking back and forth.

Tully took a swig of beer. "Whatever you say, *Grandpa.*"

Billy took a quarter from his pocket and tossed it into the air, the faces of the coin catching the light from the lamps on either side of the bed when it spun. He caught the coin in his palm and flipped it to the back of his hand. "Heads. Jamal, you've got three minutes." He dropped the quarter in his pocket and picked up his smartphone from the bed. He held it up so they could see the stopwatch function and pressed Start.

"Who says I got fuck-all to say to him?"

Tully laughed, the sound harsh.

"Tully, shut up. No sounds."

"Please, Jamal. This is your chance," said Billy, trying to keep the exasperation from his voice.

"Maybe I just want him to leave me the fuck alone."

Tully crossed his legs and examined the sole of one shoe, but the muscles tightened around his mouth.

"What—"

"I mean what the fuck does he want from me?" Jamal interrupted Billy. "I can't *be* like him."

Tully took a breath like he was going to speak, his eyes dark. Billy clapped his hands, wishing he had a judge's mallet. When Tully and Jamal's heads turned, he glared at Tully and ran a finger along his pursed lips. *Zip it.*

When Jamal stayed silent, Billy opened his mouth to speak.

"I can't be a fag like him," said Jamal.

"We agreed there would be no name calling," said Billy.

Tully laughed. "Let him speak, Grandpa. I can take it."

"No, we agreed," said Billy. "You may not care if he calls you that, but I do."

"So much for the impartial referee," said Jamal.

Billy waved the smartphone. "You've got another minute, Jamal. Talk to him, not me."

"Like you ain't part of this."

It took everything Billy had not to answer.

"Look at him," said Jamal pointing at Tully. "What do *you* call that?"

Tully opened his mouth.

"Wait your turn," said Billy sharply.

"It's not fair," said Jamal. "People see you play, and it's like they don't even see the hair and the nails—" He pointed at Tully's fingernails, which were red to match his shirt. "—and the...." He stopped, eyes on the leather-covered bulge at Tully's crotch. He tore his gaze away. "Nah, it's like they see you play and they don't fucking *care*. It isn't fair. Where I come from, they care, all right. You dress like that, you get your ass reamed."

Billy watched the last few seconds run out on his smartphone. "Okay, Tully. Your turn. Three minutes."

"The clothes make the man, Jamal? That what Mama taught you?"

"Leave my mama out of this or I'll—"

Billy clapped his hands. "Stop it! Both of you."

"What did I say?" asked Tully, the picture innocence.

"You were baiting him, and you know it, Tully. Jamal, please. It's Tully's turn now."

"What am I supposed to say?" Tully lifted a lime green sneaker. "I like it when people look at me. I'm supposed to be something else just for him?"

Maybe Tully saw something in Jamal's expression, because he rolled his eyes. "Okay, so maybe I like it when *you* look at me. Why do you gotta make me try so hard? Half the time it's like I'm not even in the room. Why you gotta act like I'm not there?"

Billy glanced at Jamal to see his reaction. Jamal took that as license to speak.

"I don't know how the hell to act around you."

"Jamal—"

Tully glanced at Billy. "No, let him talk. I said enough."

"Why you gotta act so crazy all the time?" Jamal continued. "If you didn't act so crazy, maybe we—"

"Maybe we what? We could be friends? Teammates? After what you did to me?" Tully's eyes shifted to Billy, and he stopped.

"All we did was kiss." Jamal glanced at Billy, his ears red. "I didn't even—"

A harsh sound tore from Tully's chest, and Jamal stared at him, surprise on his face. Tully examined his shoes.

Billy glanced from one to the other, fascinated. So Jamal hadn't sucked Tully off like he'd done for Billy—and for others, from what Billy had heard. But Jamal had never kissed Billy, and he apparently *had* kissed Tully.

Jamal frowned. "You're jealous because I didn't give you a BJ?"

"No." The word broke from Tully. "You kissed me, and then you pretended I didn't exist. I wouldn't have given a shit if you'd blown me like—" Tully laughed, the sound like an organ with a pipe out of tune. "—blown me like everyone else, but you had to fucking kiss me. If you hadn't kissed me, it would only have been sex. I could have handled that."

"I kissed you," said Jamal incredulously. "That's what this is all about? Well, how do. The great Tully Sam thought 'cause I kissed him...'cause I kissed him...."

Amazingly, the expression contorting Jamal's face was shame.

"Kissing isn't—"

"Shut the fuck up, Billy," said Tully quietly.

Jamal sucked a long pull from his beer and glanced from one to the other. "You wanna know what my mama told me? When I was in high school, she came home from work one day and caught me with another boy. Kissing. On the couch with our clothes on. We didn't even... I didn't even know what it meant. I just—" He shrugged. "I liked him, wanted to know how he would taste. She dragged him outta the house by his ear, screaming she ever saw him again she'd cut off his balls with a kitchen knife. She told me I better learn how the world worked and fast. I wanted outta the hood—I wanted to play basketball and to help my brothers and sister with college, I wasn't gonna kiss another boy again, ever."

"Then you met me," said Tully.

"I screwed up, and you won't let me fix it."

"By pretending I don't exist," said Tully.

"You didn't fuck up," said Billy.

"You gonna tell me it don't count? That the world has changed and gay athletes are popping outta the closet all over the place." Jamal gestured at Tully. "Maybe that's true for people like you and him, but not for folk like me. Not for me."

"You're wrong," said Billy. "You're wrong."

"Wanting makes it so, right Tully?" said Jamal.

"I am who I am, Jamal," said Tully.

"Well goody for you, twinkletoes. We're done here." Jamal put down his beer and got to his feet. "It's been real, Grandpa. Next time, you leave me off your guest list."

TRANSCRIPT

"Mom?"

"Billy! It's late, dear. Is everything all right?"

"How am I supposed to answer that? Dad comes to games, but he won't even say hello afterward. That all right in your book?"

"He's embarrassed. He's never been forced to question himself before. It's really thrown him for a loop."

"So now I'm supposed to feel sorry for him?"

"You're asking him to rethink a lot of stuff."

"The only thing I'm asking is that he talk to me. Maybe tell me I played a good game. That would be rad."

"He watches every game—even the ones when he can't get up there."

"Good for him. Speaking of games, can you give Jonah a ride up this weekend? It's for the conference title, and he wants to see it."

"I don't know if that's a good idea."

"I've got to go. I've got reading to do."

"I'm sorry, Billy. Your dad isn't talking to me either right now. I don't want to antagonize—"

"Forget it, Mom. Sorry I asked."

"Billy, wait!"

JONAH WAITED in the lobby of a theater at the Jacobs School for his name to be called. Davoud, Paul, and Aida sat with him.

Paul rolled his eyes after he jerked to his feet for the third time in as many minutes. "Will you please sit down? You're making *me* nervous."

Jonah couldn't sit for more than ten seconds without bouncing his knees or tapping his thighs. He glanced at the empty folding chair. "I can't."

Davoud put his arm around Paul's shoulders. "Leave him alone, Paul. Let him pace if he wants to."

Jonah sent a grateful look in Davoud's direction.

Aida touched her chest above her heart. "Musicality, Jonah. That's what will get you in. Not technique. That you can learn."

When a middle-aged woman with graying hair and a floor-length skirt pushed open the double doors and called his name, he spun around in panic.

"Just pretend you're jamming at the Music Box," said Paul.

Unable to speak, he grabbed his music and followed the woman down the aisle. The theater where the piano auditions were held had acoustic panels on the walls and laminated wood seats. Aida had explained it was used for student recitals and small group performances. Jonah didn't ask how she knew that. A Yamaha grand held pride of place on the low stage. A table for the judges had been set up before the first row of seats. Technically, they were an admissions jury, but the term judges seemed more appropriate to Jonah, since they were anything but a jury of peers. The woman stopped at the judge's table and waved him toward the piano. He climbed stiffly to the stage and took his place at the piano, trying not to squint at the faces behind the bright lights.

A disembodied male voice addressed him from the direction of the judges table. "You are Jonah Winfield?"

"That's right."

"Good. Take your time. When you're ready, start with the Bach."

Jonah nodded and found the knob to adjust the height of the bench. He cranked it until his arms were perpendicular to the keys. He rolled his shoulders, took a breath, and began to play.

The acoustics in the little theater were different from the Music Box—harder. The sound disconcerted him at first. He hesitated and adjusted his volume. Someone coughed, and he knew he'd already blown it. *Fuck it. Might as well enjoy the Bach. You may never play it for anyone again.* He closed his eyes and imagined himself in the airy space of a medieval cathedral. The harder-edged sound suddenly felt more appropriate.

When he finished, no one clapped. The silence was cut by the scratchy sound of someone writing with an old-fashioned pen on paper. Jonah's heart pounded. He drew long breaths through his nose, fearful he was having a panic attack.

"Thank you, Jonah. The Beethoven now, if you please."

He'd originally heard the Beethoven sonata on radio and taught himself to play it from memory. Only later, he'd found the sheet music in the files at Avakian music and memorized the piece as Beethoven wrote it. His memory for music was remarkably good; he'd only injected his own notes in a couple of spots. Unfortunately, his unorthodox method of learning the piece proved his downfall. Reaching a spot where he'd improvised, he was horrified to hear himself play his own notes instead of Beethoven's. It took every ounce of self-control he had to continue stiffly to the end. Two mistakes in two pieces. They would laugh him out of the theater.

Later, he would not remember playing the remaining pieces. What he would remember was running through the lobby of the theater, past the concerned faces of his family to the men's room, where he vomited his breakfast into the cold embrace of a piss-stained toilet.

HOOSIER STATE was favored in the final game of the conference tournament. It was a home game, which would help, but their opponents from Arkansas were tough this year, with a new crop of young players who'd proved eager to show what they could do. Jamal was back on the active list for Hoosier State, and Rocker decided to start his more experienced point guard.

The tip-off went in State's favor, and Tully passed the ball to Jamal. He and Otter passed the ball back and forth as they pounded down the court to the Arkansas end. At the basket, Tully faked his way from behind the covering Arkansas player. Jamal passed him the ball. Tully caught the pass and hesitated for a beat, as if surprised, before lofting the ball into the basket almost as an afterthought.

The Hoosier State fans roared in approval. For the day, Tully's hair was streaked in State's colors of blue and white. His fingernails alternated blue and white as well.

Some Arkansas fan yelled, "Tully Sam is a freak!" and Billy scanned the crowd behind the opposing bench. As his gaze passed over the writhing mass of students, he caught the distinctive scarlet of his father's jacket. More surprising, his mom and Jonah jammed in next to him. Had his mom negotiated a détente between his dad and boyfriend? Billy's belly settled for the first time in weeks.

On the court, Jamal and Tully reached a new accommodation as well. Jamal's change of heart was so extreme, in fact, he seemed determined to pass the ball to Tully at every opening. Rocker rolled his eyes more than once when Jamal ignored a teammate with a better play. Lucky for the team, Tully wasted no chance to loft, tip, dunk, slam, or dance his way to a basket.

Whatever the coach thought, the crowd clearly didn't care whether anyone else got a chance to play. Air horns, coordinated cheers, chants of "Tully Sam, Tully Sam" or "Defense, Defense"—

from the Arkansas side—and random screaming reached a painful intensity. By the end of the first half, Hoosier State was up 48 to 42. The hapless Arkansas team looked like the stooges hired to play the Harlem Globetrotters.

Partway through the second half, Rocker nodded at Billy. "You're up, Preston. Let's give the rest of the team a chance, huh?"

"Sure, Coach."

On the court, Billy's relief transformed into a degree of focus that had eluded him in recent weeks. His usual partnership with Mike gave way to a three-way with Tully and Mike, one on the inside and the other on the outside. At the final buzzer, Hoosier State had routed Arkansas 108 to 96.

In the press room, after the game, Billy allowed himself to gloat. Arkansas should've stayed home with the flu. A crowd of reporters led by Mark Murray, the same former NBA player who'd questioned Rocker about Jamal's suspension, requested interviews with Billy, Mike, Tully Sam, and Jamal. To his surprise, Billy got the first slot.

"Great game, Billy. You shut down the Arkansas defense."

"Thanks, Mark. The team was really strong today."

"You've won a slot in the NCAA semifinals in your freshman year. That's got to feel pretty good. What do you think of your chances of making it to the sweet sixteen?"

"Pretty good if we keep working together."

"I think it fair to say State's fans were pleasantly surprised to see the cooperation between Sampson and White, given the, ah… tension we saw in that practice video." Murray apparently didn't feel it necessary to explain what video he was talking about.

Fuck. Billy resisted rolling his eyes. Why couldn't they stick to questions about the game for once? Why did they always have to bring up other crap? "Yeah, well, we all like to win."

Maybe the reporter sensed blood in the water, or maybe Billy's expression gave him away, but instead of moving on, he pushed his mic into Billy's face.

"The video made it pretty clear Sampson and White don't get along. Is that because Sampson is gay?"

All the anger and disappointment of the past month flooded like acid into Billy's stomach. He tasted bile. Past the reporter's shoulder, he saw the warning in Mike's expression, but it wasn't enough. The press's constant focus on the inflammatory, his father's bigotry, Tully and Jamal's pain and confusion, even Mike's conflict with his mother—it all shoved him past the point of reckless abandon.

"What makes you think I'm the kind of guy who would out a teammate, even if he were gay? You want to ask about someone's sexuality, how 'bout you do it to their face? Ask me if I'm gay, why don't you?"

The most well-meaning reporter wouldn't have let that invitation pass—not if he wanted to retain his job. Murray's mouth dropped open, perhaps more in surprise at being handed a blank check than surprise at Billy's anger, but he didn't hesitate to cash in.

"Are you saying that you're gay?"

Billy stared at the impersonal gleam of the camera lens. What had he done? How had he gotten trapped? At least Jonah wouldn't have to choose between music school and proximity to Hoosier State now. Billy could quit the team and follow Jonah wherever he needed to go.

"Yep. I'm the gay boy. Mystery solved." Billy pushed past the reporter and the line of waiting players, ignoring Mike's frantic attempt to get his attention, barely noticing when Coach Rocker and Assistant Coach Paulson moved in tandem to block the reporters who tried to follow. Before he escaped the crowded press room, he saw Mike whisper urgently into Tully's ear and the odd smile that transformed Tully's face.

The arena had a VIP lounge in the locker room complex that was sometimes used by the players' families or by visiting alumni. Billy shoved past the security guard at the door, ignoring every attempt to get his attention. Slamming the door behind him, he dropped into an armchair and covered his face with his hands. The post-game TV coverage continued, Murray's excited voice blaring from a widescreen mounted on the wall of the room.

"I have with me Mike Brooks, shooting guard from Hoosier State. Mike, what do you think of Preston's admission that he's gay?"

"Billy Preston has done more than anybody to pull this team together. You saw how he played today. What do I think of his *admission* that he's gay?" Mike's emphasis on the word made Billy look up at the TV. Mike stared directly into the camera. "I'm gay too. You got any questions about basketball?"

When it was his turn, Tully didn't even wait for the reporter, he pushed up to the camera and grabbed the mic. "Don't even bother to ask, man." Tully's laughter boomed from the TV. "Gay as a goose."

By this time, the reporter had undoubtedly figured out what was going on, but it was a train he had no desire to stop. "That was Tulane Sampson, announcing that he's gay too. What about you, Jamal White? Are you gay too?"

Jamal turned to the camera, his features slack.

Billy dropped his head, unable to watch, the burning in his belly reaching five-alarm intensity. What would Jamal do? Would he stand with them, or would he bring the whole ridiculous charade to a screeching halt?

Jamal made a low sound like a moan, and Billy looked up to see his shoulders twitch. Then Jamal's face came to life in a grin to break his mother's heart. "Yeah, I'm gay too. That's who I am."

"There you have it. Billy Preston, Mike Brooks, Tulane Sampson, and Jamal White have all announced they're gay. I have the feeling there's more to this story than we're hearing, but for now, this is Mark Murray, reporting from McPherson Arena, where Hoosier State has just defeated Arkansas for the Missouri Valley Conference title."

Every nerve in Billy's body howled for release. He let go and bawled.

CHAPTER 10

Stats

~~Girls I'm pretty sure wanted to kiss me. 5 12 10,012~~
Girls I've kissed: 3
Boys I've kissed: 1

If Dad ever finds this, I'm dead—like broken spine, belly slit, and guts slithering out all over the floor dead.

Boys who've dumped me: 1
Boys I would kneel on the floor and worship as a basketball god: 1
Stupid nicknames: 2
Public boners: ~~1~~ 2
~~Teammates I'd like to knock some sense into. 2~~
Different kinds of underwear worn by guys on my floor: 5
~~Basketball players on the down-low. 1~~

Points Scored this season: ~~12 61 206 260 421 446~~ 473
Assists: ~~7 31 60 87 149 181~~ 190
Turnovers: ~~2 5 11 14 38~~ 43
Games Won: ~~1 3 6 8 15~~ 16 In the post-season:

Games Lost: ~~1~~ ~~2~~ ~~4~~ ~~5~~

Blow jobs received: 1
Blow jobs given: ~~1~~ 2
Sexting sessions: ~~1~~ ~~7~~ 8 (Phone sex is better)
Assholes I'd like to kill: 1
~~Parents who aren't talking to me: 2 1~~
Crazy boyfriends: 1
Families: 2
Boys I love: 1
People who know I'm gay: Ask Nielsen

Billy stayed in the VIP lounge until the sweat dried to a salty crust on his forehead and his tears left gritty tracks on his cheeks. The sound outside the lounge had died down, so he figured most reporters had given up. He hadn't exactly forgotten that his parents and boyfriend were probably waiting outside, but he wasn't ready to speak to anyone. His skin felt stretched and dry. Slipping from the lounge, he made his way to the showers, where he scrubbed until his face was raw.

When he returned to his locker with a towel wrapped around his waist, Mike, fully dressed in jeans and a Hoosier State sweatshirt, slouched on the bench.

Billy reached for the latch. "I thought you'd be gone by now."

Mike got to his feet. "ESPN on in the lounge?"

"You knew I was there?"

"We figured you could use a break."

Unable to voice a suitable thank-you for what Mike had done for him and for the team, Billy pulled Mike into a bear hug.

Mike tolerated him for a few seconds before pulling away. "You do know I'm not really—"

"Sorry." Billy let go and opened his locker. "Tully and Jamal okay?"

Mike shrugged. "I don't think it's hit them yet. They're like a couple of ten-year-olds who've pulled off the best prank ever."

Billy shook his head in amazement. "The rest of the guys?"

Mike grinned. "They're more focused on the conference title."

"There is that." To his amazement, Billy found himself grinning back. He began to dress. "What about you?"

Mike was silent so long Billy had zipped his fly and was rooting around his locker for a clean shirt before he answered. "I think I just chose a new family."

Billy dropped the shirt. "God, Mike. I'm so sorry. I didn't even think—"

Mike smiled tiredly. "I'm not. I don't have anything in common with them anymore."

"Speaking of family, mine is probably wondering if I've been kidnapped by posse from Media Relations—Sheriff Rocker in the lead." He picked up the T-shirt and dragged it over his head. "You talked to Sunflower yet? She'll be looking for you."

"You think?" Mike's smile looked brittle. "I did just announce I'm gay on national television."

"Give her some credit, man. She knows the score. And she's got plenty of evidence you're not gay." He paused dramatically. "At least not exclusively so."

Mike glared. "You're a bastard, you know that?"

Billy finished tying his sneakers and grabbed his duffle. He found his phone in the side pocket and turned it on, by habit. It started to ring instantly. He stared at the unfamiliar number for a second, then turned the phone off again. This time, when he slung an arm around Mike's shoulder, Mike didn't resist. "Go find her. Don't make me drag you."

"Whatever, *Grandpa*."

Giving Mike's shoulder a last squeeze before letting go, Billy spoke quietly, his voice cracking. "Thank you. What you guys did was amazing."

"I couldn't watch you throw yourself to the wolves."

"Yeah, you could have, but I'm glad you didn't. I hope you don't regret it."

They split up outside, Mike already texting furiously. Billy scanned for a tall man in a scarlet jacket. He found him just outside the crowd barrier. He caught his dad's eye and nodded. His dad's face tightened, but he raised a hand in an abortive wave. His mom looked tired but happy. Next to her, Jonah vibrated gleefully. *So they know.* It was something of a relief. He hadn't been sure they'd see the TV coverage before he found them. As if he could read Billy's mind, Jonah held up his smartphone.

"Hi, guys. Sorry to keep you waiting. Kind of a zoo in there."

"Whose idea was that clusterfuck, anyway?" asked his dad.

Billy glanced at Jonah before responding. The answering grin on Jonah's face said he knew exactly how it had gone down.

"We're a team, Dad—a real team."

"Damn pack of fools, if you ask—"

"David Preston." His mom cut off his father like a scythe. "You promised."

Billy looked at his dad. "So what about them Bulls?"

When his dad didn't reply, he did what he'd wanted to do ever since he'd seen Jonah in the stands. Ignoring his parents—they seemed locked in some kind of silent argument—Billy looked into Jonah's bright eyes and leaned down to kiss him on the mouth. Jonah tilted his head up and pressed his compact frame into Billy's. His mouth tasted weirdly of hotdog and spearmint, but Billy didn't care.

"Uh, guys?" said his mom after a moment. "There are people looking. Are you sure you're ready for this?"

"I don't care." Billy turned his head, scraping stubble against Jonah's cheek.

Jonah moaned.

"Do you want to end up on the Internet again?" said his dad.

"I want to kiss my boyfriend," said Billy. "Is that too much to ask?"

But Jonah was already pulling back. "There are places and there are places," he murmured.

"We're not done with this," said Billy, thinking about the conversation they were going to have about PDAs.

"I hope not," Jonah said fervently.

"That's not what I—"

"Who's up for ice cream?" said his mom brightly.

"Jesus Christ!" his dad growled.

"David! You promised you'd keep a civil tongue."

"It's okay, Mom." Billy turned to face his dad. "Right now, it's enough he's here. We don't want bits of him all over the parking lot."

His dad's expression softened, an involuntary smile twitching at the corner of his mouth. "Smartass."

"Bigot." His mom's eyes widened in shock. His dad lost his smile. For a second Billy thought he'd gone too far. Jonah's arm tightened around his waist. But he held his dad's gaze until his dad shook his head.

"I don't know what I did to deserve—"

"Yes, you do," said Billy's mother curtly.

"Holy mother of God, will you cut me some slack! I'm here, aren't I?" A measure of bitter flavored his dad's response.

"I know who I married."

"I don't know about you guys, but I would love some ice cream," said Jonah.

THE NEXT morning, Billy, Mike, Tully, and Jamal received a summons to attend a meeting with Coach Rocker and a representative from the Hoosier State Office of Media Relations. Billy nibbled a piece of toast in the dining hall with his economics textbook balanced on his knee when the e-mail popped up on his phone. Rocker made it crystal clear the meeting was mandatory. Before he could acknowledge the e-mail, he got a succinct text from Mike showing Tully and Jamal as recipients as well.

"Our room at 10."

Billy and Jamal arrived at the Brookhouse Lobby simultaneously. Billy pressed the Up button on the elevator.

"I got three hundred sixty-one text messages and e-mails last night." Jamal started in when the doors *thunked* shut. "I'm going to Hell, 'cause all faggots go to Hell. I'm a hero for coming out. I'm an irresponsible prankster—who the fuck talks like that? Oh, and I'll pay with my basketball career."

Billy thought they were probably right, but he tried to reassure Jamal anyway. "They can't know that. Everything's changing. Jason Collins is playing for the Nets. College and professional athletes are coming out all over the place."

"Did I come out? I thought I stood up for a teammate who's too dumb to—"

"Come off it, Jamal." The doors opened on Billy's floor. It being prime time for classes, the hallway was deserted. "I saw your face when you said it. So did the rest of the world. What did your mom say?"

Jamal's mouth tightened, but he didn't speak until Billy opened the door to the suite. He pushed past. "Apparently, nobody can take a joke."

Mike leaned against the door to his room, arms folded.

"Where's Tully?" Billy asked.

"He went out partying last night with the rest of the guys," said Mike. "I had to drag his sorry ass out of bed. He's in the shower." He looked at Jamal. "I thought you left with him after the game."

"Yeah, well, I had to listen to my mama ream my ass for an hour on the telephone."

"The meeting's in an hour," Billy said to no one in particular.

"What did you tell her?" Mike asked.

"Said it was team thing. Had to do it." Jamal dropped onto the couch. "She called me a damned fool—just like my father."

Mike grimaced. "Ouch."

"Thing was, she never asked me if it was true."

Billy caught Mike's eye. *She already knows it is.*

Someone pounded on the door. Billy went over to let Tully in. Tully strolled in on a cloud of musk-scented bodywash.

Billy fanned his nose. "Phew. What is that stuff?"

"Whassup, Grandpa. Whirlpool." Tully nodded at Jamal. "He okay?"

"Yo, over here!" said Mike. "I'm the guy who just announced on national TV he's gay—and isn't. How am I doing?"

Tully and Jamal growled simultaneously. "Who the fuck you calling gay?"

"Enough! What are we gonna tell the coach?"

"Not to mention the rest of the world," said Mike.

Someone knocked on the door. Mike got it this time. "Sunflower! I thought you were in class. What are you—"

"I'm here because my boyfriend is an idiot. Sorta brave, but an idiot."

"I told you I could handle this."

"Uh-huh? You figured out what you're going to say to the coach yet?"

"The guys just got here."

"I thought not."

Billy sighed. "Okay, so I figure I just own up and tell them I have a boyfriend. They'll find out soon enough, and I'm tired of—"

Everyone in the room spoke at once.

"No!" said Mike.

"You'll tank your career," said Jamal.

"It's not like they don't already think I'm—"

"Fabulous," Tully minced.

"You can't pretend you're gay, boyo," said Sunflower to Mike. "For one thing, you'll never—"

"My mama wants me to take it back," said Jamal.

"Take what back?" said Jason, the door to his room swinging open. He scratched his belly absently, nothing but a low-slung pair of boxers hiding his tackle.

Sunflower shuddered. "Put on some pants, dude."

Tully flopped onto the couch and leaned against Jamal. "You can't."

Jamal turned his head. "Get the fuck off me, fag!"

Tully didn't move.

Jason hooked his thumbs in the waistband of his boxers, exposing a band of pubic hair. "Take *what* back?"

"Didn't you watch the game?" asked Billy.

"You're not a fag, Jamal, you're gay," said Tully.

Jason squinted. "Cherrie and me holed up last night. What happened?"

"Grandpa got cranky and came out to a reporter," said Sunflower listing facts as calmly as entries in a seed catalog. "Mike decided to be a hero and come out too—to confuse the press or something."

Jason's eyebrows flew up. Mike whirled a finger by the side of his own head.

"Then Tully and Jamal came out, too, because... well... they *are* gay. Or Jamal is. I'm not sure *Tully* even knows what he is."

Somewhere in that recital Jason's thumbs slipped from his waistband and he raised his hands to his face. "I missed all that? On TV? I am never gonna forgive myself. What did Rocker say?"

Tully laughed. "We won the conference. Some folks actually care 'bout that."

"We're meeting to decide what to tell Rocker," said Billy.

"Can I come?" Jason asked. "I want to see his face. Before he dies of apoplexy, I mean."

"No!" Billy reached the point of overload and actually stamped on the floor, but the thinly padded concrete floor made the gesture painful and nearly silent. "Everybody. Shut. Up! We gotta think this out."

"What's to think out?" said Sunflower. "Tell 'em the truth. You and Jamal are gay. Mike was protecting his teammates. Tully says whatever he wants. Done and done."

Jamal wouldn't meet Tully's look. "I can't do it."

Tully closed his eyes.

"Fuck 'em," said Jason. "If my uncle can marry his old fishing buddy, I guess you can be gay in NCAA basketball."

Billy clutched his belly. "I think I'm gonna hurl."

THE CONFERENCE room to which they were summoned was in the administration building near the president's office. It had oak wainscoting, blue walls, and white crown moldings decorated with the state flower. A set of flags hung at either end, one embroidered with the state seal, the other with the stars and stripes.

When they were ushered in by the receptionist, coaches Rocker and Paulson already sat at one side of the polished table, which had seats for twenty.

Digger waved. Rocker appeared to be counting the stars on the flag.

"Please be seated. May I get anyone coffee or tea?" the receptionist, a pretty young woman with burnished red hair and freckles, asked brightly.

Billy didn't think his stomach could take any caffeine. "No, thanks."

"Mighty kind of you, miss," said Tully. "Perhaps a cup of coffee?"

"Cream and sugar?"

Tully grinned at the receptionist. "Yes, please, if it's not too much trouble."

"Anyone else?"

Mike and Jamal shook their heads mutely.

The coaches already had identical china cups of black coffee in front of them. It occurred to Billy that they had probably met with media relations prior to the arrival of the players. He wondered what they'd talked about. After an awkward moment while the guys found seats, eventually sorting themselves out into a cluster on the same side of the table with the coaches, but separated from them by an empty seat, the receptionist returned with a cup and saucer for Tully.

"Thank you, kindly." Tully poured on the Big Easy charm. Billy half expected him to write his number on a napkin and pass it to the woman on the way out. Maybe by then he wouldn't feel like it.

The door swung open and an older man and woman in business attire filed in. The woman wore a textured maroon tailored suit over a cream-colored silk blouse. The man wore a gray pin-striped suit that would not have been out of place in a bank or a court room—a lawyer, then. They chose seats across from Billy and his teammates. The man sat down and looked deliberately around the room, open interest on his face. The woman clicked open a briefcase and placed a pen and notebook before her on the table before clearing her throat.

"Good morning, gentlemen. My name is Lacy Pasternik. I'm Director of Media Relations at Hoosier State University. This is Robert

Rutherford from legal affairs. Incidentally, Bob is also our Title IX administrator."

Title IX? Isn't that for women? What did it have to do with men's basketball? Maybe they thought all minorities were alike.

As if in answer to Billy's thoughts, Pasternik continued, "Bob has long experience with our athletic programs."

From the sour look on Rocker's face, Rutherford's experience hadn't necessarily made him friends at the athletic center.

"Our meeting today has two purposes. The first is fact finding. If we are to chart a course for the university in dealing with the attention we're receiving as a result of yesterday's... incident... we need to know what we're dealing with. The second purpose is to assist you—" Her gaze swept from Jamal, slouched in the chair nearest the door, to Mike, rigid in the seat nearest Digger Paulson. "—in navigating this difficult time in your lives."

She sounded like a grief counselor after a school shooting.

"In the course of our discussion, Bob's job is to ensure nothing we do or say infringes your rights in any way. In short, he will be your advocate."

If Billy knew anything about legal processes, it was that if you wanted a lawyer to protect your interests, you'd better be the one paying him. Ol' pin-stripe Bob worked for the university.

"Any questions so far?"

"Yeah," Tully drawled. "Whatever happened to don't ask, don't tell?"

"It didn't work," said Mike flatly.

"That was military policy, asshole." Jamal reclined in his chair.

Rutherford nodded, his eyes on Tully. "Nevertheless, your point is well-taken. While we believe we can better help if we understand who is gay and who is not, we cannot compel you to disclose your sexuality."

Pasternik frowned. "On the other hand, if we don't know who is gay, I don't know that we'll be able to control our message."

The phrase *divide and conquer* popped into Billy's head. He tried to catch Mike's attention, but Mike's eyes had slammed down on the word control.

After a second, Mike visibly took a breath and opened his eyes. "I'm not sure how it would be to our advantage to tell you anything."

Pasternik glanced at Rocker. "From what I understand, you might have as much to lose as anyone, if you keep up this pretense, Mr. Brooks."

Mike produced a closed-mouth smile. "Maybe I've already lost whatever it is I have to lose."

"What about you, Mr. White? Are you prepared for the attention from the press, from the public, from your family, that you're going to receive if you persist in this?"

So the coaches had no clue about Jamal. Or maybe Pasternik thought Jamal had a good chance of staying on the down-low. He wasn't exactly obvious. Billy wondered if she would even bother asking him or Tully the same question.

Pasternik looked down her nose as if to demonstrate her point. "There are people who will condemn you. People whose religious beliefs—"

"You mean like the boneheads been texting me?" Jamal held up his phone. "Too late. They already having their say."

"Do you have something to add, Coach Rocker? Perhaps you can outline the kind of response your players are likely to receive in the NBA should they continue down this path."

Billy sat up, curious what Rocker had said about them. Who did he think had a chance at a slot in the NBA? Pasternik focused on Jamal and Tully. That made sense. They were seniors. Tully was widely acknowledged in the press to have a shot at a career in the NBA. If the rumors were true, he'd started to receive offers last year.

Rocker examined her sourly. "You think that's necessary, Ms. Pasternik? They know how real men feel about fags."

Rutherford half rose from his seat as though he were making an objection in court. "Whoa there, Coach! Out of bounds."

Billy sighed. There it was, out in the open. Rocker was a homophobe. More illuminating was the distasteful expression on Paulson's face as he regarded his boss.

"You know"—Rocker ignored Rutherford as if he hadn't spoken—"I thought White, here, knew the score. In my day, the last thing a straight guy was gonna do was joke about being gay. Shit like that sticks."

Pasternik returned her attention to Jamal. "However distastefully, Coach Rocker has made my point for me."

Jamal's face was a study in conflicting emotions. His dislike for Rocker was plain, but he struggled for words.

Mike spoke up before Jamal could get it together. "It seems to me, you and Rocker make a great argument for none of us"—Mike's gaze swept from Jamal to Billy—"telling you people anything. Maybe we just leave things as they are and tell the press we've already said all we have to say about our personal lives—at least until after March Madness." Mike shot a look at Billy when he added that last bit.

Tully laughed. "Maybe we should play the game for a while."

Jamal's head snapped around. "Is that what this is for you, a game?"

Tully's smile faded. "Basketball is a game, Jamal. This?" Tully glanced around the room. "This is something else entirely."

Billy's stomach burned, and he thought about asking the receptionist where he could get an antacid pill. "Guys, can we just—"

"It's okay, Grandpa." Jamal shook his head, eyes on Tully. "We got this."

Tully's grin returned with full force. "We *got* this."

"Am I to understand none of you wish to make any further statement regarding your sexuality?" Pasternik looked at each player in turn.

"Nope," said Jamal tiredly.

When her gaze reached him, Tully just laughed.

Mike nodded, his face showing equal parts pride and anxiety.

By the time she reached him, Billy's pride in his teammates had affected his breathing, but he looked her in the eye. "I said what I needed to. I've got nothing to add."

"Well, I do." Rutherford leaned forward. "This university's nondiscrimination policy includes sexual preference. Among other things, Coach Rocker, that means you will keep a lid on your language. Is that clear? Moreover, I expect to see every one of these men on the court next game and every game thereafter until the season is over."

Rocker shrugged. "You've got me wrong, Rutherford. I always put winning ahead of my personal feelings toward my players—no matter what I might think of their personal habits."

Rutherford smiled unexpectedly. "It may interest you to know that my office is obsessed with March Madness, Coach Rocker. I believe we even have a little pool going."

Rocker returned to his examination of the flag.

Pasternik whispered into Rutherford's ear.

Rutherford broke into a full-throated laugh, his answer clearly audible. "I wouldn't worry about it. The president is a basketball fan." He got to his feet. "Good luck, gentlemen. We'll be rooting for you."

Pasternik rose from her seat as well. "Some advice to you. Practice the phrase, 'I have no comment on that.'" She placed her notepad and pen back into her briefcase. "In front of a mirror."

Apparently, the meeting was over.

NCAA MARCH Madness: a month of office pools, online betting, favorites, rivals, and upsets. If the team's prospects in post-season play weren't enough to keep Billy occupied, it was also a time of year students received thick or thin envelopes from college admissions departments. And while Jonah continued to put Billy off or change the subject every time Billy asked about his plans, Billy knew from his spy at the Music Box—Paul—that Jonah had applied and auditioned at least three music schools, not including Vanderbilt. It irritated Billy that Jonah wouldn't tell him where he'd applied or even when he was auditioning. After all, *he* couldn't have a bad day without watching it on television afterward, enduring not only the criticism of his coaches, teammates, and sportscasters, but the frequently ridiculous or insulting comments of the chronically ill-informed. Why should Jonah get to keep his applications private? It wasn't like he'd be able to keep his successes or failures private for long.

The night before State's first game in the series with Wichita State, he asked Jonah about music school again.

"Can't we talk about it after March Madness?"

"Why are you so secretive? Aren't we a couple now? I practically announced it on television. Don't I have a right to know what's happening with you?" Billy knew he sounded like a nagging wife, but he couldn't help it. He worried that Jonah had attached a giant fucking wrecking ball of significance to the whole business, and that if something didn't swing the way he wanted, he'd fall apart like he had after his dad's suicide.

Jonah's reply sounded suddenly more intimate, as if he'd switched from speakerphone to a headset. "I don't want to distract you during March Madness. You've got to play your best."

Billy dug his toes into his bedspread and tried to keep the irritation from his voice. "I know you're hiding something from me."

Jonah was silent.

"If you don't want me to worry, this isn't the way to go."

"Do you tell me every time you talk to a recruiter?" Jonah's reply sounded like he knew he held a losing hand.

"That isn't the same, and you know it. Anyway, I'm years away from that. I'll probably blow a knee or something like my dad and never make it through my senior year."

"Jesus, Billy. Way to keep it positive."

"I just want to know what's going on with you. Is that so bad?"

"No."

"At least tell me where you've applied."

"I've applied to three music schools. I haven't heard from any yet."

You'd have thought Billy was a special prosecutor asking Jonah if he'd inhaled. He knew better than to push. "Will you at least tell me when you do?"

Jonah was silent so long Billy checked his phone to see if the connection had dropped.

"I think I blew it."

This was progress, even if Billy didn't like how lost and small Jonah sounded. "I bet everyone thinks that."

"No, really, I didn't play well. I made mistakes."

"I'm sure it's not as bad as you think."

"Please stop. I know what I did. I didn't want to tell you until after the games."

"I'm coming to visit you. I can get a flight from Saint Louis tomorrow night."

"You can't!" Jonah sounded close to panic. "You're gonna win, and you'll have another game to train for. Promise me, you won't mess that up. Promise me. I'm okay, really. I'll tell you everything after March Madness. I couldn't bear it if you—"

"Okay, okay, I promise. Just don't... I love you."

"I love you too. You've got no idea."

THERE WAS no question in Billy's mind that Hoosier State was better than Kentucky. Hoosier State had more seniors, a center who was certain to go on to the NBA, and they had spent the season compiling a solid, if not exactly spectacular, 14-4 win loss record in regular conference play. Had it not been for the conflict between Jamal and Tully they would have done even better. They'd beat Wichita in a hard-fought game to survive the first round elimination and trounced Cal Poly to capture one of the thirty-two remaining slots. Now they had to beat Kentucky to reach the sweet sixteen. Kentucky had a better record: 18-0 in regular conference play. But despite their wins, their defense had been lackluster against Kansas State in the last round, and they'd barely scraped by due to a series of really spectacular three pointers from their senior shooting guard, Matt Taylor.

Billy's stomach seemed unconvinced. The burning he experienced in moments of high stress was now nearly constant. At breakfast in the Saint Louis hotel near the neutral arena where they would play, he chose a bland meal of oatmeal and told himself he'd tell the team doctor after they finished the season. There was no way he was doing anything that might get him benched now. Not after what his teammates had done for him.

"If you don't eat faster, you're gonna have to ask for a doggie bag. Coach wants to talk to us before the game."

"I'm not hungry." Billy caught Mike's skeptical look.

"You haven't been hungry a lot lately."

Billy glanced around at the linen-covered tables and well-stocked breakfast bar piled with fresh fruit and trays of bacon, sausage, scrambled eggs, and grits. None of it appealed. At least Jamal and Tully were enjoying it, judging from the loud laughter coming from the table they shared with Otter and Liam.

"I guess I'm a little stressed."

"Hey, win or lose, we've had a better season than I predicted."

"Yeah, that's not really...."

Mike pushed a hand through his buzz cut. "Everything okay with Jonah?"

"I don't know." Billy poured milk into his oatmeal and rotated his spoon like he was mixing a dollop of color into a can of paint. "He's really secretive about college."

"I thought he was going to music school in the fall."

"That's what he wants—what he deserves—but he won't tell me where he's applied."

Mike's eyes narrowed. "You thinking Juilliard or someplace far away?"

"I don't think… I don't know. He thinks he screwed up his auditions. That much I know."

Mike frowned. "I thought you said he was really good."

"He is. But he's mostly self-taught and kind of insecure about it. How's Sunflower? She coming to the game?"

Mike smiled, his eyes lighting up. "She's wonderful. Do you know she got credited in a journal—along with her professor, of course. I think she's gonna—"

"Grandpa! Time to get a move on!" Billy looked over. The rest of the guys had gotten up and were waiting by the hostess stand. Tully waved vigorously. "Snap Whirlpool out of his love trance, huh?"

Billy took out his wallet and dropped a twenty on the table. "Come on, Whirlpool. You can tell me all about it after we hear what Coach has to say."

IF COACH Rocker had one rule about talking to the press, it was that you never badmouthed another member of your team. The rule was a tad more flexible where players on opposing teams were concerned, but the idea was to keep it positive. If the Cal Poly players they'd beaten in Dayton had received any instruction regarding their comments to the press, it wasn't obvious. Some had expressed opinions on the sexuality of their opponents, and the usual extremists pronounced religious beliefs regarding the future Southern residences of "the gays." One guy said he thought Billy was "a brave role model" for LGBTQ youth and suggested he make a video for a youth group. Listening to the interview on the radio, Billy had wondered if he wasn't hearing a future member of the boys club. But most of the team had apparently decided that Billy and his teammates were perpetrating a prank designed to garner press attention and distract their opponents. Generally, the issue proved of greatest interest to the press.

Coach Rocker's reaction was more interesting. At Dayton, he'd been awkward with the team, starting sentences and stopping them with whole clauses missing, like the only white guy at an African-American family reunion. His talk before the game in Dayton focused on zone defense and Cal Poly's weakness outside the three point line. Whatever he thought about his team's comments to the press, he'd said nothing beyond a half-hearted "Go get 'em," accompanied by a flip of his fingers in the direction of the opposing locker room. If he found any joy in their continued success on the court that day, it was not expressed in the sagging lines of his jowls.

No matter how ambivalent their coach, the atmosphere in Saint Louis's Chaifetz Arena was charged. The training room seemed cramped, packed as it was, with a group of guys averaging well over six and a half feet. As they waited for the coach, Liam caught Billy's attention.

"Think we got a chance, Grandpa? That Taylor dude's been racking up the points all season."

"Sure we do."

Liam peered at him out of the corner of his eye. "They're not giving you a hard time?"

"They who?"

"You know, like… people, the press."

"I turned off my phone after Arkansas."

"Seriously? I'd die without mine. My girlfriend would kill me."

Billy laughed. "Jonah and I have an arrangement. I turn it on every night at 10:00 p.m."

"Shit, man. You got a boyfriend? I thought you guys were just fucking with that reporter."

Billy froze. He'd assumed everyone knew about him at this point. He took a breath and tried to ignore the burn in his stomach. "Yup. Jonah's my boyfriend."

Liam's eyes widened. "Shit, gay I get, but I never pictured a boyfriend. That's like… wow."

Billy stared at Liam in confusion. *Gay is okay, but a boyfriend is a surprise?* What did the guy *think* it meant to be gay?

"Doesn't it like… hurt? With a guy? Doesn't your… does he get sore?"

In a less crowded venue, Billy would have been more patient fielding Liam's questions. Despite their carefully averted gazes, some of the guys around them had assumed the still postures of active listeners. Some of the acid in his stomach made it into his reply.

"Jesus, man. Do I ask you if your girlfriend's tits get chafed?"

Liam shrugged. "She likes 'em pinched."

Billy cringed. "TMI."

The double doors swung open. Coach Rocker stalked in, followed closely by Digger Paulson. Rocker took up position before the whiteboard mounted on one wall and looked around the room.

"Well." Rocker raised his eyebrows and bobbed his head up and down twice. "So you're here, the NCAA national championship semifinals. March Madness. Nearly the end of the road. You think you got what it takes to win?"

The sprinkle of affirmatives that erupted around the room didn't seem to impress the coach. Rocker's gaze dropped to his polished loafers and he shook his head. "You know, maybe I should retire." He glanced up at the shocked silence. "I could stand here and tell you that—on a good day—you're the best damn team I've ever coached, that you've got what it takes to win. But the truth is, I've never in my career had a team less interested in what I had to say. You guys go your own way. Maybe you'll decide to win this thing and go on to the sweet sixteen. That would be fine with me. Maybe you got other things on your minds." Rocker pursed his lips and shrugged. "I do know this." His gaze swept the room until it found Billy. "You wanna win this thing, you got the skills to do it."

Rocker turned and motioned at Digger. "Digger, here, is going to remind you about some things we know about Kentucky." He walked out, the click of the door latch loud in the silent room.

"Holy shit!" Liam whispered loudly.

IT WAS the kind of game basketball fans love, with little in the way of defense, the teams' scores leapfrogging until the last play. It wasn't their heads that defeated the losing team; it was merely an unfortunate sequence of events from which they didn't have time to recover. Kentucky's shooting guard, Favorite Taylor, a guy who'd been missing all day, finally dropped one from outside the three point line. Jamal, who'd taken over from Billy for the second half, hustled the ball down court and passed to Tully. Tully, who'd already amassed more points that season than any player on either team, lofted what should have been a perfect swisher from the left-hand corner. Then Tiny Martinez, the seven foot center from Kentucky who'd matched Tully point for point all evening, leapt up from the far side of the basket and stretched an arm farther over the basket than Billy would have thought possible unless the guy spent his summer vacations strapped into a medieval rack, and tipped the ball away. It was a spectacular move that had fans and players alike hooting and screaming.

Kentucky recovered the ball and hustled down court past the stunned Hoosier State players for a quick slam dunk by their power forward. Liam recovered the ball and sent it down court to Jamal and Jamal drilled it over to Mike, but Mike's three pointer dropped through the rim a fraction of a second after the buzzer.

Hoosier State lost by a point. March Madness was over—at least for them.

Soaping up in the shower while Martinez held court with the press, Billy took inventory. While the loss hurt, the rush of acid he'd come to expect in stressful moments didn't come. He wouldn't admit it to the other players, but a part of him was glad the season was over. They'd done well. There would be other seasons for basketball. It was time to have a talk with his secretive boyfriend about what it meant for them to be a couple. Whatever the future held, they should plan for it together. If there was one thing the season had taught him, it was that he was resilient. He would find a way to stay with Jonah, however near or far they were from each other.

Billy ran into Mike on the way back to his locker.

"Your dad come?" Mike asked, snapping a spare towel at Billy.

Billy leapt out of the way. "Hell yeah. No way he was missing this."

Mike grinned and slung the towel over his shoulder.

"You want to join us for dinner? Jonah's here, and Paul and Davoud came down."

"Nah, I appreciate the offer, but Sunflower's here."

Billy hesitated. "And your parents?"

Mike shook his head. "They sent another prayer card."

"They pray for the win or for your soul?"

"What do you think?"

"Shit, man. You sure you don't want to join us? I'd love to introduce Sunflower to Paul and Davoud."

"No thanks, I plan to let Sunflower lick my wounds."

"Listen to you, choir boy." Billy punched Mike in the shoulder and lit off for their lockers.

Mike gave chase. "Like you won't be doing the same with Jonah."

THE HOTEL room was bland, with beige walls, brown carpet, and abstract prints on the walls vaguely reminiscent of flowers, or possibly, female genitalia. Billy cringed and lay back on the tan bedspread, noticing the faint lines of old water stains in the ceiling. None of it mattered. The young man currently singing in the shower mattered. The thought of Jonah naked in the shower sent Billy's rapidly hardening cock sliding past his belly button. He reached automatically for the sheet to cover himself and then stopped. Why shouldn't his boyfriend see how much he turned Billy on? They'd had so little time together in the past seven months. Let Jonah enjoy the sight of him, just as Billy reveled in the sight of Jonah's messy blond spikes, bright gray eyes, creamy skin, and compact frame. Billy spread his legs and ran a finger along the underside of his cock, which twitched in response, a bead of liquid forming at the tip.

The sound of running water stopped with a squeak. Jonah's singing faded to a contented hum. Billy closed his eyes and grinned. Just the little sounds Jonah made were enough to make him want to bust from sheer joy.

"Holy fuck."

Billy opened his eyes. Jonah stood at the base of the bed, a towel wrapped around his middle. The towel dropped to the carpet and Billy watched Jonah's dick go from zero to sixty.

"Happy to see me?"

"I was happy to see you before. This?" Jonah touched his straining cock. "This is something different."

"Come here, I want to explore the phenomenon."

Jonah crawled onto the bed, straddling Billy, giving Billy a close-up of his throbbing cock.

"Get up here and I'll lick that into submission."

Jonah's eyes danced. "No way. I want to kiss you first." He leaned down and pressed his lips to Billy's. His aggressive tongue pushed into Billy's mouth, tasting of toothpaste. Billy let him explore a little before shoving back with his own.

Jonah flexed his hips, the friction along Billy's cock delicious.

"Keep that up, and this'll be a short round."

"So?"

Billy erupted from the bed and flipped Jonah over onto his back. Holding Jonah's shoulders, he scooted down and took Jonah's cock into his mouth, tasting bitter at the tip and the salty sea of Jonah's warm skin. He swallowed the shaft as far as he could without choking and hummed.

Jonah moaned.

Billy let Jonah slide halfway out and then flicked his tongue around his shaft while he rubbed the head against his soft palate.

Jonah moaned again, louder, and tried to escape. Billy straddled his legs and redoubled his efforts.

"God, Billy. Where did you learn to do that?"

Billy had to pull back to answer, which was probably what his squirming boyfriend intended. "Some of us are naturally talented."

"Some of us would like to be fucked before we come."

"Really?"

"It was all I could think about during dinner. Your parents probably thought I was on crack."

"Maybe I'd like to try it, sometime."

"Crack?"

"Getting fucked."

"Seriously? I've always thought of you as a top."

"A top? Listen to you, gay boy. How am I supposed to know *what* I am if we never try it?" There was a message in there, if Jonah wanted to hear it.

Jonah's eyelids clamped down, his long lashes pale against tan cheeks. Billy was horrified to see liquid collecting in the corners of his eyes. "What's wrong?"

Jonah broke into a shaky smile. "I'm okay, just happy."

"The wet stuff makes me nervous."

"Get used to it." Jonah lost his smile. "Ever since my dad, everything's just under the surface—good and bad."

"I'll cope." Even as he said it, Billy knew it was true. Tully and Jamal, Mike's family, their ambivalent coach, losing to Kentucky in the last second, he could deal with it all if he could come home to this: Jonah's heat against his own and the smell of Jonah's skin spreading through his brain like drops of dye in water.

Jonah moved beneath him. "Get off. There's something I gotta get."

Billy reached for his pillow. "I've got supplies right here."

Jonah laughed. "No, something else."

Billy rolled onto his back.

Jonah went to the luggage stand and pulled something from his pack. "I've been saving this. I was gonna wait until after, but...." He returned to the bed and pulled Billy's arm around him, before handing an envelope to Billy. "I can't bear to look at it."

Billy examined the envelope. "Bloomington, Indiana. The Jacobs School of Music. Wait, Bloomington? You applied to Bloomington? That's only an hour from Hoosier State."

"Don't get your hopes up." Jonah shrank against Billy's side. "I'm pretty sure I fucked it up."

"If we're gonna be together, you can't do this anymore. You have to promise me."

"Do what?"

"Keep stuff from me."

"I didn't want you to—"

"It's not your job to keep me from worrying. We're better, stronger, when we're together, right?"

"Yeah."

"I did worry. I worried about what you weren't telling me."

Jonah stared. "You thought I was planning to break up with you."

Billy shrugged. Maybe a part of him had thought that. Jonah had done it before, after all.

"I would never.... God, I'm so sorry. I fucked up again, didn't I?"

Billy touched the skin above Jonah's jutting hipbone. "It's okay. I figured it out. Just... promise me you'll talk to me when you need to, okay? Let me help."

"Okay."

"Is it any good? The school, I mean. I've never heard of it."

"Jock." Jonah's whisper was almost inaudible.

"You're sure you want me to open this?"

"Open it. I've waited too long as it is."

Billy flipped the wrinkled and stained envelope and ran a finger under the flap. The letter he removed was printed on cream-colored, textured paper. He read the first few lines and stopped breathing.

Jonah moaned. "I knew it."

Billy read on. He started to breathe again.

"Tell me."

"Okay. You didn't get in to the piano program."

Jonah took a ragged breath.

"Wait! There's more. They want you for the music composition program. You sent them a concerto?"

Jonah began to tremble. At first, Billy thought Jonah had lost it completely. Then he realized Jonah was laughing and crying at the same time. Billy tossed the letter aside and began to stroke Jonah's torso.

"Aida made me send them. My pieces. She said it was insurance."

"They really liked the concerto. How come I haven't heard it?"

Jonah rolled toward Billy. "I wrote it for you last fall. When we weren't… when I didn't know what was happening with us."

"You've played me other stuff."

Jonah wiped his eyes. "It's kind of… sensual."

Jonah's ears and cheeks had taken on a distinct flush. "Am I going to be able to look those people in the eye when I visit you?"

Jonah shrugged.

"God, why does my entire life have to be public?"

"Karma. For pretending you were straight when we first met."

"I got over it, didn't I?"

"Yeah, you did." Jonah bounced up and straddled Billy's torso, wiggling his butt. "I think I want to do it this way, this time."

Billy's cock liked the idea. A lot. He reached back under the pillow for the lube.

STATS

~~Girls I'm pretty sure wanted to kiss me: 5 12 10.012~~
Girls I've kissed: 3
Boys I've kissed: 1

If Dad ever finds this, I'm dead—like broken spine, belly slit, and guts slithering out all over the floor dead.

Boys who've dumped me: 1

Boys I would kneel on the floor and worship as a basketball god: 1
Stupid nicknames: 2
Public boners: 1
~~Teammates I'd like to knock some sense into: 2~~
Different kinds of underwear worn by guys on my floor: 5
~~Basketball players on the down-low: 1~~

Points Scored this season: ~~12~~ ~~61~~ ~~206~~ ~~260~~ ~~421~~ ~~446~~ 473
Assists: ~~7~~ ~~31~~ ~~60~~ ~~87~~ ~~149~~ ~~181~~ 190
Turnovers: ~~2~~ ~~5~~ ~~11~~ ~~14~~ ~~38~~ 43
Games Won: ~~1~~ ~~3~~ ~~6~~ ~~8~~ ~~15~~ 16 In the post-season: 3
Games Lost: ~~1~~ ~~2~~ ~~4~~ 5

Blow jobs received: 1
Blow jobs given: 1
Sexting sessions: ~~1~~ ~~7~~ 14 (Phone sex is better)
Assholes I'd like to kill: 1
Parents who aren't talking to me: ~~2~~ ~~1~~ 0
Crazy boyfriends: 1
Families: 2
Boys I love: 1
People who know I'm gay: Ask Nielsen
Conference championships: 1
Boyfriends I get to live with next year: 1

TRANSCRIPT

"Billy?"

"Yeah?"

"What's a turnover?"

"That's when a player loses possession of the ball to the other team. Why do you—"

"How do you know how many kinds of underwear the guys on your floor wear?"

"Oh Jesus. Give me that back."

"Tell me about the public boners."

"Stop reading that, right now!"

"Make me."

JOHN C. HOUSER's father, stepmother, and mother were all psychotherapists. When old enough, he escaped to Grinnell College, which was exactly halfway between his mother's and father's homes—and half a continent away from each. After graduation, he taught English for a year in Greece, attended graduate school, and eventually began a career of creating computer systems for libraries. Now he works in a strange old building that boasts a historic collection of mantelpieces—but no fireplaces. John loves to hear from his readers. His contact information, stray thoughts, and links to his publications are available at his website.

Website: http://johnchouser.com

The Door Behind Us

By John C. Houser

It's 1919, and Frank Huddleston has survived the battlefields of the Great War. A serious head injury has left him with amnesia so profound he must re-learn his name every morning from a note posted on the privy door.

Gerald "Jersey" Rohn, joined the Army because he wanted to feel like a man, but he returned from the trenches minus a leg and with no goal for his life. He's plagued by the nightmare of his best friend's death and has nervous fits, but refuses to associate those things with battle fatigue. He can't work his father's farm, so he takes a job supervising Frank, who is working his grandparents' farm despite his head injury.

When Frank recovers enough to ask about his past, he discovers his grandparents know almost nothing about him, and they're lying about what they do know. The men set out to discover Frank's past and get Jersey a prosthesis. They soon begin to care for each other, but they'll need to trust their hearts and put their pasts to rest if they are to turn attraction into a loving future.

http://www.dreamspinnerpress.com

KRISTIAN F. POWER

FIRST LOVE

CURRENTS OF LOVE

http://www.dreamspinnerpress.com

INNOCENCE
Suki Fleet

http://www.dreamspinnerpress.com

FOR **MORE** OF THE **BEST GAY ROMANCE**

DREAMSPINNER
PRESS

dreamspinnerpress.com